PRICE OF JUSTICE

A Mara Brent Legal Thriller

ROBIN JAMES

Robin James Books

The Blitz. That phrase conjures something far different for most people than it does for those of us here in Waynetown, Ohio. Here, it's what everyone calls Belitzer Quarry. Abandoned fifty years ago, this place once formed part of the backbone of the local economy.

Now, a diamond-shaped crystal blue lake shimmers at the bottom of high limestone walls marred only by layers of moss and dirt. Dense woods filled with white pine and maple trees frame it, making it the perfect landscape for the Waynetown postcards still sold at the nearest rest stop on I-75.

For two generations, the place has become our town's favorite swimming hole. Daredevil teens ignore all the warning signs and jump from the tallest heights of those stone walls like urban cliff divers. Miraculously, no one has ever drowned at the Blitz. Not in fifty years. Still, the place carries the haunted chill of death, anyway.

"You ready for this?" Kenya Spaulding asked. Maumee County's newly appointed prosecuting attorney stood at the head of the conference room table. Beside her, she'd set up a large easel and covered it with a blue tarp.

I turned to the girl sitting at my left shoulder and wondered if I'd ever been that young. The start of the school year came with a fresh crop of law school interns. This one weighed maybe a hundred pounds dripping wet and had a name that didn't help people take her seriously either. Melody Chance.

I locked eyes with Kenya. She stood with her arms crossed in front of her. In the two months since she'd accepted this job, I hadn't seen her smile once. There had been little reason. Her tenure started under the specter of her predecessor's misdeeds. Most days, I knew she felt like she was just treading water.

"I'm fine," Melody said.

Kenya lifted the corner of the tarp and flipped it back with a quick snap of her wrist. She'd asked Melody if she was ready. It hadn't occurred to me to tell her I might not be.

"Take a good look," Kenya said. "Get used to it. If you can."

Melody shuddered and looked away. I didn't. Hot tears sprang to my eyes, and I forced them back.

I'd read about what happened at the Blitz before I took the job as assistant prosecutor almost nine years ago now. It made national news. The trial ended in a double murder conviction the year before I came in. My first few months here, I'd heard the war stories of everyone who worked on it. That victory had been my old boss, Phil Halsey's crowning achievement. It took him from assistant to head prosecutor that summer, building the platform he planned to use for higher office.

Now, it all might come crashing down.

I rose from my seat and angled my head to match the view of the bodies I saw before me. You could barely recognize them as such.

"They think Krista Nadler died first," Kenya explained. She pointed to the body lying prone at the top of the 16 x 20 photograph. I could make out Krista's blonde hair, but little else because of the extent of the burns. Arms and legs at wrong angles and no face.

"Cause of death was blunt force trauma to the head," Kenya said. "Before that, we believe they flogged her with a bike chain."

Melody sucked in a breath.

"Charlie was alive during it," she said. "That's the theory, anyway."

They found Charlie Brinkman on his knees, hands tied in front of him in a prayer pose. He was charred and frozen in place like some ghostly figure from the ruins of Pompeii.

"They made him watch," Melody whispered.

Kenya let her words hang in the air. The horror of it settled over all of us.

"How could anyone do anything like that?" Melody asked.

I gave Kenya a silent nod, telling her "that's enough." Kenya hesitated. Then she dragged the tarp back over the crime scene photos.

That's when Melody fell apart. Gasping, she covered her mouth with her hand and ran out, heading for the restroom. Her violent retching echoed down the hall.

I got up and closed the door, then retook my seat. "Was that necessary?" I asked.

Kenya pulled up a chair opposite me. "Might as well get it out of her system now. Yours too. You weren't here the first time around," she said.

"Ah," I nodded. "It's been a while since anyone held that against me."

Kenya's words were sharp, but her eyes were soft. We'd been through a lot together since I came to this office. Maumee County was a small, but politically important part of Northwest Ohio. It had been a bellwether for the rest of the state in the last four presidential elections.

"Mara," she said, her tone becoming more serious. "That wasn't for show. Not for Melody or for you."

My heart dropped to the floor. I knew there had to be more to this than Kenya just trying to haze the new kid.

"Kenya..."

She held up a hand. "I got the word a little while ago. The King brothers are gonna get a new trial. Judge Ivey's office gave me a courtesy heads up, but the order will come down by tomorrow morning."

I'd never dove off the cliffs at Belitzer Quarry. I didn't grow up here. My husband did. He took me out there once, right after we first got married. Kenya's words hit my stomach with the pull of a thirty-foot drop and the icy splash down that might have followed.

"On what grounds?" I asked.

Kenya folded her hands in front of her. "Our former boss left us with a mess, Mara," she said.

I knew that better than anyone. Phil Halsey had covered up evidence in a different high-profile murder case that had nearly let a serial rapist walk free. Since then, the state attorney general's office had opened an investigation into several of his most notable, successful prosecutions.

Kenya had a file opened up on the table. The grim faces of Damon and Lyle King stared up at me from their original mugshots.

I picked up Damon's. He'd been handsome. Devastatingly so with thick, dark hair and blazing blue eyes. His younger brother Lyle had the same features, but somehow, where Damon was rakishly good-looking, Lyle looked soulless.

I flipped the page. The state prison took new inmate identification photographs every year. It was like looking at time lapse photography on each of them. Damon's face remained mostly unchanged. A few new lines here and there. A bit of peppered gray as he matured over the last decade. He got leaner, with harder muscles. But still he had rugged good looks and penetrating eyes.

Prison seemed to change Lyle much more. It was almost as if each year drained more hope from his eyes. Hardened him. The ink on his arms, his neck, his chest became more intricate. They documented each new tattoo with a different photograph.

"It could be an art exhibit," Kenya said as she looked over my shoulder.

I knew what she meant. Whoever did Lyle's tattoos had a creative eye. Spider webs. His mother's birthdate. A skull on his right bicep with ruby-red eyes. By year ten, Lyle had hardly a bare patch of skin on his back.

"Lyle was more hands-on in the murders," Kenya said. "But we proved it was all at Damon's direction."

"I remember," I said. "Lyle's lawyer wanted to argue he wasn't mentally competent to stand trial."

"He found himself out of a job right after that," Kenya said. "It baffled Phil. In a lot of ways, he thought it made his case for him. The jury saw Damon as the mastermind after that. Lyle wasn't even capable of standing up for himself when aligning with Damon went against sound legal advice and his own self-interests."

"The Demon King," I whispered. "That's what the press called Damon."

"Clever of them," Kenya said. "Though I'll tell you a secret. I'm sure that was Phil's doing."

"I'm not surprised. So smart."

She pressed a hand to her forehead. Kenya had always had one of those ageless faces. A granite jawline and deep-set eyes along with flawless skin that made her glow. Today, though, I saw fresh lines beneath her eyes.

"An alibi witness has come forward," she said. "She claims Phil interviewed her ten years ago during trial prep. She says she knows where Lyle King was during the time frame we established when Krista Nadler and Charlie Brinkman were murdered."

Again, I felt the drop in my stomach.

"She's lying," I said.

"Maybe," Kenya said. "But there's an email that showed up on our servers. Phil definitely talked to her when she says he did."

Kenya took another stack of papers out of the file and slid it across the table to me. She had one page tabbed. I flipped to it.

"Sierra Joy," I said. "This is from Caroline, confirming an appointment with Phil." On the next page was an email from this Sierra Joy to Phil asking for the meeting three days prior.

Kenya nodded.

"Don't tell me," I said, dropping the stack of papers back to the table.

"He never disclosed the meeting to the defense," Kenya said.

"But that doesn't mean..."

"We're screwed, Mara," Kenya said. "Even if Phil's actions were entirely appropriate, the stink of what he did in the Shumway case is all over this. Damon and Lyle King have a major player backing them. Their case has been taken up by a non-profit called the Servants of Divine Justice. They have very deep pockets. Damon was a self-styled preacher man before all of this. They think he's a noble cause."

I bit my lip past the four-letter word I wanted to shout. Kenya knew my mind.

"Exactly," she said. "Mara, Phil wasn't wrong about the King brothers. They tortured and murdered those two kids. They were seventeen years old. Seventeen. And they died for the grave sin of getting caught parking at the Blitz. Heck, half the town lost their virginity out there."

I squeezed my eyes shut, feeling that drop in my stomach once more. Cliff-diving.

"They're going for bail," she said. "Both of them."

My eyes snapped open. "There's no way..."

"We're bleeding," Kenya said. "Badly. And there's no one I trust to keep those psychopaths where they belong more than you."

It was as if the icy waters at the bottom of the Blitz hit me all at once. I struggled to come up for air. The charred images of Krista Nadler and Charlie Brinkman would haunt my dreams. Now, it would be up to me to slay the Demon King all over again.

"Is that all of it?" I asked. Melody stood in the doorway to my office holding a hand cart. There were three cardboard boxes stacked on top of it.

"This plus those other two boxes in the corner," she said. "You sure you want all this set up in here?"

"For now," I said, sliding out from behind my desk. Overnight, the King brothers' murder case had taken over my office. I'd start moving things piece by piece into the adjoining conference room as I sifted through it.

"Isn't all of this digitized?" Melody asked.

I smiled at her. "Well, actually."

She rolled her eyes. "That'll teach me to open my big mouth," she said.

"Phil was old school," I said. "He liked to roll up his literal sleeves and get elbow deep in a case when he prepped for trial."

"Where do you want me to start?" she asked.

I grabbed a box off the top stack and set it on my desk. I had a box cutter already waiting and sliced through the packing tape. It was filled with notepads. At least a dozen of them.

Melody came to my side and pulled one out. She thumbed through it.

"Can you read this?" she asked.

I took it from her. I felt the same twin emotions I always did whenever I laid hands on something that reminded me of Phil Halsey. He'd been my mentor. The man who hired me when I had very little experience as a lawyer and virtually none in criminal law.

Phil's notebooks were filled with his slanted cursive. He pressed his pen so tightly to the page, he often punctured the paper.

"I don't know how much of this I will even need," I said.

The intercom flashed on my landline. I reached over to unmute it.

"You got a few minutes for Kenya?" Caroline Flowers, our office manager, called out with her bright voice.

"Be right there."

Melody looked frightened. I put a reassuring hand on her arm. "Just ... I don't know ... find the trial transcripts. Start reading. The more familiar you are with what happened, the better."

She nodded. I shut the door behind me as I headed down the hall to Kenya's corner office. Phil's former office.

In the first few weeks since Phil's death, I'd avoided the room altogether. The county hired a crime scene clean-up crew. They scrubbed the walls, removing any trace of the horror I'd witnessed in here. Phil had shot himself right in front of me. For a moment, he'd pointed the gun at me.

Fresh paint coated the walls. Kenya had chosen a soft gray. My heels sank into the new, plush carpeting she picked out. Not a single thing about this room was the same. Kenya had moved her desk to the far corner of the room, not centered like Phil had his. You couldn't even see the wall that suffered the worst ... damage. Kenya had installed bookshelves and filled them with gleaming, gold-embossed volumes of the *Ohio Revised Code*.

Still, when the office fell silent, and I closed my eyes, I could see the scene play out all over again. I moved in slow motion as Phil raised his gun and blew out the back of his head. Then, red and blue streaks pulsed over the blood-stained walls as the waiting police surrounded the building and called my name.

"You okay?" Kenya said. "Oh crap. I'm sorry. I could have met you down in your office."

"It's okay." I raised a hand. Though it wasn't. Maybe it never would be again. "What's up? Melody and I are just starting to sort through the State versus King trial files."

"Good," she said. "I just wanted to check in with you to make sure you had the support you needed. I mean ... is Melody ... I can assign someone else. I think I can even swing a request for another intern."

"Not yet," I said. "Plus, I feel like we're just starting to break Melody in. I don't feel like starting over with someone new. She's green, but she's curious. I'll let you know by the end of next week whether she's a good match for this one."

"Got it," Kenya said. "What about you though? Do you think you'll have any issues ... uh ... focusing over the next couple of weeks?"

I raised a brow and pulled up a chair in front of Kenya's desk. "Just do me a favor and say what you mean."

Kenya sat back in her chair. She gave me a wry smile. One thing I liked most about her was her aversion to BS. I could always count on Kenya Spaulding to hit me right between the eyes with whatever was on her mind.

"Okay," she said. "The new bail hearing is tomorrow. I know you can handle it. It's better if I'm not even there. I want it out there that this is your case all the way. The county trusts you. I trust you. And we have to win."

I let Kenya go quiet before I answered. When I did, I

leaned forward and folded my hands on her desk. "You're worried about the same thing Phil was when he assigned the Shumway case to me instead of you. So, I'll tell you the same thing I told him. You have nothing to worry about. My personal life isn't a factor when I walk in this building."

It was Kenya's turn to let my words sink in before she responded. Her face split into a wide grin.

"Who are you trying to kid? I *let* you have the Shumway case."

Then we both laughed. Hard. It felt good. I realized it was the first time I really had since Phil's suicide. Since a lot of things. "Well, thanks," I said.

"So," she said. "Five weeks, huh? Until the election?"

"Five weeks," I answered.

"Then what?" she asked.

I stared at the wall for a moment. "Are you asking me that as my boss or my friend?"

Kenya pursed her lips. "A little of both, maybe. But mostly as your friend."

"I don't know," I said. "That's the truth."

"Do you still love the bastard?" she asked.

That one took me aback. I hadn't really talked to anyone about how I felt about my husband Jason. Barely even Jason. Almost a year ago, I'd gotten a text from a random woman that split my world apart. She followed it up with explicit photographs she'd taken of the two of them together making love.

"Are you still going to vote for him?" I asked her.

Kenya flapped her hands in defeat. "I already did. Sent in my absentee ballot three days ago. Hated doing it. But ... he's a lesser evil than the other guy."

"He makes a lousy husband," I said. "He'll make an excellent U.S. congressman."

"Am I going to lose you then?" she asked. "Mr. and Mrs. Brent go to Washington?"

"Kenya, I'm just trying to put one foot in front of the other as far as Jason's concerned. It's complicated. Besides being a good congressman, he's also a pretty good dad. And Will ... well ... he doesn't handle change all that great. I'm just trying to figure out what's best for him."

"Mara," she said. "You also have to do what's best for you. Don't give me a line of bull about staying together for the kid. And he's a great kid. His mother deserves to be happy too, though. I just don't want to see you lose sight of that in all this."

"Thanks," I said. "I appreciate it. To be honest, you're one of the few people who's actually said anything like that to me. Jason wants, um, everything. My mother's worried about our future as a political couple and her ambitions for Jason. Will's just trying to understand."

I can't believe I'd said that much. I practically gushed. This was new to me. Especially with Kenya.

"Anyway," I said, straightening my back. "This isn't something that you need to add to your list of worries. I've got everything under control."

"Good," she said. "And you know I've got your back." She lowered her eyes. "On all of it."

Her words caught me off guard. All of this had. I blinked fast, then quickly recovered. "Please don't tell me we're gonna hug now," I said.

Kenya burst out laughing. It was good to hear. As much stress as I'd been under dealing with my personal life, stepping into Phil Halsey's shoes had been no simple task for Kenya. She'd inherited a giant steaming pile of manure in his wake. Now it would be up to me to make sure Phil's biggest triumph didn't turn into our biggest failure.

I had more to say to her, but my phone buzzed. I pulled it out of my suit pocket. It was a number I didn't recognize.

"Go ahead and take that," she said. "I've got a few other fires to put out. Let me know if you need anything from me before tomorrow's hearing."

"Thanks," I said. I ignored the call, assuming it was car warranty spam or something like it. I left Kenya's office and made it halfway to my own before the tone went off, alerting me that the caller had left a voicemail.

Kenya moved past me down the hall. Something made me stop. I pulled up the voicemail and pressed the phone to my ear.

Within thirty seconds, every assurance I'd just given Kenya about my personal life melted away.

"Mara ... this is ... Abby Morgan. I know you know who I am. We need to meet. Today. Now."

I clicked out of my mailbox, heart thundering in my chest. Abby Morgan. Jason's ... lord, I couldn't even bring myself to say it in my own head. Mistress? Girlfriend?

My phone lit up as she called back. I went down the short hallway leading to the service entrance. I stood in the stairwell before I answered the call. I didn't even say hello.

"Mara," Abby said.

"I told you never to call me."

"That's convenient for you," she said. She sounded out of breath, scared even.

"I'm hanging up and I'm blocking this number."

"You shouldn't," she said. "There are some things you need to know. I don't care if you hate my guts. I don't really care what you think of me, honestly. But I know you still care about Jason. And you care about your family. So we need to meet. I'll be at Bailey's Pub on the docks in an hour."

"Are you threatening me?" I asked.

"I need fifteen minutes of your time," she said. "Then you'll never have to hear from me again. It's your choice. I know you like to think you're the victim in all of this. You're not the only one. Jason's ruined my life too. Meet me once. Then I swear you'll never hear from me again."

She hung up. Sweat trickled down my back. I nearly dropped the phone; my hands were shaking so badly. Then the walls started to close in.

※ 3 ※

I had to be out of my mind. Certifiable. It didn't even feel like me walking into that dark pub in the middle of a Tuesday afternoon. I was locked inside somewhere, a body snatcher having invaded, making the drive, parking the car, then walking through the alley entrance and past the bar.

She was sitting in a booth along the wall. I spotted her blonde hair first. Tanned skin. Perfectly applied make-up. I wanted to pretend I didn't know her. That I hadn't trolled her a hundred times on social media. That I was above all of this and she couldn't really touch me.

But she had. As much as I knew it had taken two people to destroy my marriage and Jason was a willing participant, some primal instinct kicked in. I envisioned myself wrapping Abigail Morgan's perfect blonde hair around my fist and dragging her out into the street.

She sensed my approach in her peripheral vision and turned. Abigail's painted face froze. She looked terrified. Of me. Good.

I thought about just flipping her off, turning on my heel and leaving. It's what I should have done. Second best to never coming at all. But I needed this. I needed to look this bitch in the eye and let her see I was stronger than she was. I was better. I didn't like what that said about me but couldn't find the moral high ground to care at that moment.

I lifted my chin, straightened my shoulders, then sat down opposite her. Though I'd imagined this moment a million times, now that I was here, I found there was nothing I wanted to say.

"I'm glad you came," she said. That voice. Light. High. She almost sounded like a little kid. The words she'd spoken to me in that random phone call all those months ago had turned my life upside down.

"You sure about that?" I said. The waitress came by and asked for my drink order.

"Nothing, thank you," I said. "I'm not going to stay."

Did she recognize me? The waitress's face went a little white. She found an uneasy smile and excused herself, likely wishing we'd sat in someone else's section.

"Listen," Abigail said. I couldn't even bring myself to think of her the way Jason referred to her. Abby.

"You said fifteen minutes of my time," I said. "You have five. Then I never want to see or hear from you again."

"Fair enough," she said. "You can hate me all you want. I get it. I hate you too."

My face felt hot.

"You want to think of me as some slut. Jason probably told you some story about how I was just a fling. A lapse in judgment. He's ruined my life."

My brow went up. "Your life? Are you kidding me?"

"Who do you think I am?" she asked. "I'm not some dumb blonde who threw herself at your husband. Whatever he's told you is a lie. Remember that. Jason lies about everything. I think he's lied to everyone he's ever loved."

"What. Do. You. Want?" I said. "You're down to four minutes."

"I said he's ruined my life. He has. I lost my internship at the attorney general's office. He's had me blackballed. No one will hire me in the legal field. I can't even get into law school now. Did you know that? My references have all withdrawn their recommendations. You think that's a coincidence? I graduated from Case with almost a four point. I earned that internship on my own merits."

I felt nothing. I felt cold. I hated it. "You want me to write you a letter of recommendation?" I quipped, suddenly wishing I'd ordered a whiskey.

She looked behind her. Her eyelashes fluttered. Those were fake too. She was pretty. Stunning, even. I tried not to imagine what she looked like in the pictures she sent me of her and Jason together. I failed.

"I've got no other options," she said. "I will not let Jason Brent ruin me. I'm fighting back. Hard. The only reason I'm here is as a courtesy to you. Regardless of what you think of me, I am sorry that you got hurt. Jason ... he swore to me that your marriage was over. He said ... well, he said a lot of things. I'm sure you can relate."

"Okay," I said. "We're done here. I don't know what you thought you'd gain out of this conversation. Believe it or not, I don't wish you ill. I try not to think about you at all. But we've all made our own choices, haven't we? And we all have to live with them."

I started to get up. "I'm writing a book," she blurted out.

Heat crawled down my spine.

"A publisher approached me. He made me a decent offer."

"You're being used," I said.

"I'll turn it down," she said. "If ... if I get a better offer."

I felt as if Medusa just stared me in the face. My body turned to stone. Slowly, I sank back down into the booth.

"If you get a better offer?" I said.

"I don't have a job. I'm unhirable right now because your

husband is having me blackballed. He's getting away with every-thing. He dodged an ethics inquiry when he tried to pay me off. He's leading in the polls. My God. He's going to win, Mara. Everyone knows it. He thinks he's untouchable. It doesn't matter what he does. Not to me. Not to you. So I have to look out for myself. You should too."

I folded my hands in front of me and rested them on the table. "So hire a lawyer. Go to the EEOC."

"And you know exactly what'll happen if I do that," she said. "It'll go nowhere. Jason Brent gets what he wants. He's surrounded by powerful people. You think they don't have the ability to quash any complaint I tried to file? I know you're not that naïve."

"We're done here," I said. "So you haven't made it very far in your legal career, but what you're laying out for me is called extortion, Abby." I couldn't hold back the contempt with which I uttered her name.

"It'll ruin you too," she said. "He's good. Jason. Really good. Did he tell you it was a one-time thing? A momentary lapse in judgment? He's lying to you. He told me he was going to divorce you. He told me he was in love with me. He even bought me a ring."

She slapped a red velvet ring box on the table. I couldn't breathe. I could hardly see straight. She opened the box. Inside, a teardrop diamond glittered in a gold setting.

"Recognize it?" she asked. "It was his mother's. He told me you wanted something of your own when he proposed to you."

My thumb went to my ring finger on my left hand. There was no ring there now. I'd stopped wearing my wedding and engagement rings months ago.

I couldn't help the slow smile that spread across my face. "Well," I said. "You're right about one thing. He was lying to you."

Abby opened her mouth to say something, then clamped it

shut. I left her wondering just which thing Jason was lying about.

He had no mother. Not one who ever had the means to own a ring like that, if it was real. If he'd given it to her at all. It could all be one more lie meant to hurt me.

I hated her. I really didn't want to. But I did.

"Keep it," I said. "It's the only thing you'll ever get from me or my family. And if you try anything like this again, I'll press charges. I won't be bullied. Not by you. Not by Jason."

I slid my purse over my shoulder and turned my back on her. Once again, I felt as though someone else had taken over my body. I wanted to scream. I wanted to cry. I did none of those things. Instead, I kept my head held high as I walked out the back of the bar the way I came.

4

It was dusk by the time I made it back to my house. I avoided the office, texting Kenya that I wanted to do some research from home to get ready for tomorrow's bail hearing on the King case. She didn't question me. She trusted me.

The lights were on in the kitchen when I pulled up the wooded, winding drive to the house I used to share with Jason. I didn't bother pulling the car in the garage. His Mercedes was still parked there. He'd been gone for weeks campaigning.

I shut off my engine and went through the front door. I heard my sister-in-law Kat's lilting laughter. My heart warmed as I found her leaning over the dining room table, her head pressed against my nine-year-old son Will's forehead. "One thousand pieces!" Will declared when he saw me.

"Wow," I said. Will and Kat sat back in unison, revealing their completed puzzle. They'd put together a colorful painting of the *Titanic* as it sailed across the Atlantic.

"Nice job," I said. I went to Will. He stiffened, as he always did. Hugs were hard to come by for him. Leaning near Jason's sister, his Aunt Kat was about as close as he'd come most days. He let me tousle his hair.

"Looks great," I said. "Sorry I missed dinner." I mouthed a thank-you to Kat. For all the wreckage Jason had left in his wake, I thanked God every day Kat wasn't one of them. She didn't take sides. No. That wasn't true. She took Will's side. I would love her forever for that.

"How was school?" I asked. It was a loaded question. Will had just started fourth grade at Grantham Elementary. It cost a fortune, but the smaller class sizes made a world of difference for him.

"We're learning about the branches of government," he said. "My teacher didn't like my answer."

"To what?" I asked.

"She asked me which branch of government makes laws. I said all of them. She told me that was wrong."

I raised a brow. Kat hid a smile behind her hand.

"Oh boy," I said. "Am I gonna have to volunteer to give a guest lecture again?"

"Not yet," Will said. "We'll give her another chance."

It was my turn to hide a smile. It felt good. In my son's presence, the events of the day melted away. None of it mattered. There was only him.

"I'll let you two catch up," Kat said, grabbing her purse from the other end of the table.

"I'll walk you out," I said, smoothing a hand over Will's head. He was already busy pounding a few loose puzzle pieces back in near the *Titanic*'s fourth funnel. I'd get a lecture on which one was fake in a minute.

"You okay?" Kat asked as we made our way out the front door.

I hesitated. Part of me wanted to confide in her. Unload. But it wasn't fair of me. I made a pact with myself never to badmouth Jason in front of her. I would stick to it.

"Big day tomorrow?" she asked. "Your bail hearing?"

"Yeah," I said.

"I mean, they won't really let those two monsters out of jail, will they? Mara, you and Will hadn't moved out here yet when that nightmare went down. I was here. The King brothers ... we were all terrified. I ... Mara, I babysat Krista Nadler."

My heart skipped. "I ... wow. I didn't know that."

Kat wrapped her arms around herself as if she could ward off the memory of what happened to those poor kids out at the Blitz.

"You have to make sure they never see the light of day again," Kat said. "I mean ... you have to." I knew what she meant. The weight of it settled over me and I gave my sister-in-law a reassuring hug.

I found a smile for her. "I know."

The worry lines didn't leave her face as I let her go, but her eyes softened. "There's leftover lasagna in the fridge," she said. "Eat. Get some sleep. Then kick some ass tomorrow. We need you."

We. The town. And every kid who'd ever swum out at the Blitz.

5

Judge Donald Ivey had been a controversial pick for the
Maumee County Court of Common Pleas. He'd spent ten
years as an Ohio State trooper before heading to law
school. After that, he worked his way up through the ranks in
one of the most prestigious criminal defense firms in Columbus
before settling in Waynetown with his second wife Joan, also a
cop. As jurists went, I found him erratic. He liked to showboat
and landing the King brothers' retrial would be the feather in
his cap as he laid the groundwork to move on to the Court of
Appeals in two years. I had absolutely no idea how to read him
today.

I made my way past a row of reporters and in through the
lawyers' entrance to the courthouse. Out on the street, a few
picketers had gathered from the Servants of Divine Justice. So
far, the general flavor of their signs seemed to think Damon
King was the Second Coming. I ignored the barked questions
from the reporters. I'd give no statement today, no matter the
outcome. Kenya could have that job. I had enough on my plate.

A lonely figure waited for me outside of courtroom number
four. Melody sat beside her, peering into the thin woman's

haggard face. She wore an ill-fitting green suit in a size too big. It wasn't hers. Someone had loaned or donated it. Melody handed her a tissue to wipe her face. When they saw me approach, the woman rose.

"Mrs. Brent," she said.

"I am, yes," I answered, putting my hand out to shake hers.

"Mara," Melody said. "This is Stephanie Nadler, Krista's mother."

I could see it. I'd only known Krista through the awful school photos the press had used after her murder. She'd been a pretty girl with dark-blonde hair and deeply dimpled cheeks. Her mother had that too. But the years and horrors she'd faced made her look thirty years older than her true age. She was forty-four. I'd read it in the file. She'd been a teen mother when she had Krista twenty-seven years ago.

"I had to be here," she said. "I have to make sure. People forget Krista was a genuine person. All they know is the awful way she died."

"I understand," I said. "Are you here alone?"

Stephanie nodded. "Krista's dad was never really in the picture. My own parents are gone. They weren't really part of her life either."

"There are some members of the Silver Angels victims' group waiting in the courtroom," Melody said. "And if it's okay, I'll stay with Ms. Nadler until the hearing is over."

"Okay," I said. "Is that all right with you?"

Stephanie Nadler nodded. "Krista was the only family I had. They can't set those boys free."

"I will do my best," I said. "It's good that you're here. Because you're right. People need to remember."

I put a light hand on Stephanie's arm, met Melody's eyes, and mouthed a thank-you. Then I headed into the courtroom.

Trevor Page stood at the defense table rifling through paperwork. He'd come up from Columbus. A top-tier litigator,

Trevor had political aspirations of his own. I'd heard from Jason he was being groomed to make a run for governor in four years.

A young kid from Trevor's team nudged him as I walked in. Trevor looked my way. He was surfer blond, handsome, and wearing an Armani suit that likely cost more than most of the citizens of Waynetown made in a year. Good. A jury would notice that, and not in a positive way.

"Ms. Brent," Trevor smiled. He walked over and shook my hand. "Good to meet you. I wanted to thank you for the cooperation your office has extended. I know how difficult things must have been since losing Phil Halsey. I knew him. I'm so sorry for your loss."

His words took me aback. His sentiment seemed genuine. It was a classy thing to say, and I appreciated it for what it was.

"Thanks," I said.

"Good luck," Trevor said. Then, his attention left me as the doors to the back of the courtroom opened and Damon King strode in.

My eyes immediately shot to Stephanie Nadler. Tears streamed down her face, but she sat straight and silent.

Damon King had aged ten years since his most famous mugshot. Even in prison orange and shackles, he held himself with a regal air. His thick, black hair had a clean cut and just the hint of gray throughout. He was handsome. There was no doubt about it. His eyes went straight to me.

Cold. The palest blue, almost like ice.

Damon King had the physique of a bodybuilder now. He had muscled forearms covered in tattoos. Crosses. Praying hands and what I assumed were lines of scripture. I could make out one reference along his right arm. Luke 3:16. I wrote it on my legal pad.

The sheriffs led him to a bench behind Trevor Page. The doors opened again, and they led Lyle King in.

Lyle was the younger brother by four years. Only now, he

seemed to have aged beyond Damon. Lyle's hair had gone silver. Lyle was almost obese now, cutting a huge, hulking figure as he took his place on the opposite end of the bench from his brother. He had his own lawyer, a skinny kid named Noel Stamford. But it soon became clear Page would call all the shots.

"All rise!"

The King brothers' shackles rattled as Judge Ivey took the bench. Ivey shaved his dome-shaped head bald and wore his reading glasses on a chain around his neck. He didn't so much as spare a glance toward the King brothers, or the lawyers in the room. Instead, Ivey sorted through papers, making us wait.

"All right," he finally said. "We're here on People of the State of Ohio versus Damian and Lyle King."

"Damon, Your Honor," Trevor said. "Damon King."

Unbelievable. Ivey knew the defendants' names well. What was he doing?

"Motion for new trial was granted in the Court of Appeals and we're on remand to set bail," Ivey said. "I'll hear from the State first."

"Yes, Your Honor." I stepped up to the lectern. "The State is requesting bail be denied pending new trial. I cannot overstate the brutality of this crime. Krista Nadler and Charlie Brinkman weren't just murdered in cold blood. They were systematically beaten and tortured for as long as an hour. Charlie Brinkman was burned alive. Frankly, we would argue there is no crime more brutal than what happened to this young couple. In addition, we believe Damon and Lyle King pose significant flight risks. They no longer have family here in Waynetown, or even Ohio, for that matter. The families of Krista Nadler and Charlie Brinkman still live in this community. We believe the interests of justice are best served by having Damon and Lyle King remain behind bars pending the outcome."

Judge Ivey furrowed his brow and rifled through his file. "Defense?"

"Your Honor, Trevor Page appearing on behalf of the defendants."

Ivey looked up. "Both defendants?"

"Sorry. No. I represent Damon King."

Stamford leaned forward. The kid didn't even stand to address the judge. Oh boy. "Your Honor, I'm Noel Stamford on behalf of Lyle King."

Ivey finally put his paperwork down and looked at the King brothers. "So glad you could join us," Ivey sneered. "Go ahead, Mr. Page."

"Thank you," Page said. "The King brothers have maintained their innocence throughout this ordeal. New trial was granted due to prosecutorial misconduct by the State. Though I don't think that's even a suitable phrase for what happened. Ms. Brent's predecessor, the late Mr. Halsey, withheld crucial, exculpatory evidence that would have proven my client's innocence. No one denies that these crimes were brutal. I assure you, both the Kings pray for the souls of Krista Nadler and Charlie Brinkman every single day. But they are innocent. And even as they sit in prison paying the price not for murders they never committed, but for the criminal actions of an unscrupulous prosecutor, they have used that time to better themselves. Damon King is an ordained minister. He has counseled hundreds of inmates and directly assisted in their reform and re-entry into the world as productive, God-fearing members of society. Lyle King has learned a skilled trade. He's a welder. Ms. Brent is correct, the King brothers no longer have immediate family in Waynetown. But they still have strong ties to this community. Damon King wants nothing more than to return to the new family he has made within the community. I've provided letters of recommendation from members of Mr. King's former congregation. If released on bail, both brothers will be welcomed into the homes of Reverend Daryl Lewis and Doctor Gayle Gerard, respectively. In consideration of all of those things, we respectfully request that reasonable bail be set."

"Mr. Stamford?" Judge Ivey said.

Stamford dropped his papers all over the floor. Awkwardly clearing his throat, he finally made it up to the lectern. When he did, he said merely, "Um ... Judge, I think Mr. Page has said all that needs to be said. I second it on behalf of Lyle King."

He started to sit down, then popped back up. "Oh wait. Judge...actually one thing. Bail was actually set in the original trial wasn't it?"

"You're asking me?" Judge Ivey said.

Noel shook his head. "No. Sorry. I meant that rhetorically. Bail was set in the original trial at a hundred thousand dollars. There's no reason it shouldn't be set now."

"Fine," the judge said. "You actually raise a fair point, Mr. Stamford. I'm setting bail at two-hundred and fifty thousand dollars each. I'll release Damon King to Reverend Lewis's residence and Lyle King with Dr. Gerard. Standard bond conditions apply."

"Your Honor!" I jumped up. "The State would like the opportunity to rebut Mr. Page's claims. The fact remains ..."

"I've ruled, Ms. Brent," Judge Ivey shouted. "You'll have your chance to prosecute. In the meantime, I don't find your arguments compelling. So ordered."

He banged his gavel. The sound of it went straight down my spine.

He didn't. He couldn't. Behind me, Stephanie Nadler broke as Melody quietly explained to her what just happened.

I stood there slack-jawed, wishing someone could explain it to me.

6

Kenya had assembled the troops in the war room by the time I got back to the office. She paced at the end of the conference table. Howard, the only other litigator in the office, sat sipping coffee from a plastic cup. At the moment, I wanted something stronger.

"What the hell happened?" he asked as I walked in. Melody stayed behind with Stephanie Nadler. I'd only had about ten seconds to reassure her before reporters and the growing number of Divine Justice picketers swarmed.

"You tell me," I said. "Ivey had his mind made up before he took the bench."

"He caved," Kenya said. "That son of a ... somebody got to him. He's worried about his own path to the Court of Appeals."

"So he lets two psychopaths out of their cages?" Howard asked, his voice cracking.

"I need to know more about the special interest group backing the King brothers," I said. "Something doesn't smell right about any of this. Page pitched it as though Damon is the Second Coming and that's pretty much the messaging those picketers are trying to convey."

"This is about Phil," Kenya said. "Ivey figures he scores points and distances himself from the mess Phil left."

"Risky move," I said. "Because Hojo's right. Those men are psychopaths."

Melody walked in, breathless.

"Thank you for handling that," I said. Melody had a calming effect on Stephanie. I was grateful for it. She was still pretty new to the office. It remained to be seen what kind of asset she'd be during trial, but she might have a calling in victim advocacy.

"I put her in a cab," Melody said. "A couple of reporters figured out which car was hers. And there were some people milling around it. They said they were from the Church of the Living Flame."

"Damon's former congregation," Howard said. "I didn't realize there were any of them left."

"He has his own church?" Melody asked.

"That was his deal," Kenya said. "King started preaching out of a pole barn on his property a couple of years before the murders. He had a place out on Millbury Road. The house is gone now, but you can still see three enormous crosses he built on a hill during autumn, when the leaves fall."

Melody wrapped her arms around herself. I could see her goosebumps from here.

"He's been preaching from prison," I said.

"He's got an even bigger following now," Hojo said. He had a laptop in front of him. He turned it so I could see the screen. Sure enough, Damon King's Church of the Living Flame had a web presence. I leaned in closer. Howard had pulled up a message board connected to it. There were already thousands of posters. "We will need to monitor that," I said. "Kenya, we're gonna need more help."

"I'm way ahead of you," she said. "I'm pulling more interns."

"That's good," I said. "But we need to make sure they're

fully vetted. I wouldn't put it past Trevor Page to plant someone."

"We'll work with the sheriff's office," she said. "Their computer crime guys live for this stuff and they know what they're looking for. I can't imagine Damon or Lyle have been dumb enough to admit to anything online, but you never know."

"And I need to talk to this so-called alibi witness. Like, yesterday."

"Sierra Joy," Kenya answered. "She's dodged my calls so far."

"Can't we subpoena her?" Melody asked.

"Sure," I said. "I'll want to depose her. But right now I'd just like to have a conversation."

"I'll see what I can find out about her background," Hojo said.

"She came out of nowhere," Kenya said.

I looked at the mountain of boxes in the corner. "Not nowhere," I said. "If Phil really had talked to her, he'd have noted it somewhere."

"The cops never did?" Hojo asked.

"They don't have a record of it," Kenya said. "That's her entire story. She said she called Phil when she saw his name in the paper as the lead prosecutor. She claims he told her he'd relay her information to the police. That never happened."

"She's lying," I said.

"You sure about that?" Hojo asked.

I sank into the chair beside him. I rubbed my forehead with my hand. "Phil was using at the time. We know that now. He was willing to cover up evidence in the Shumway trial to hide that fact."

"Shumway almost got away with everything," Hojo said. "Phil was going to let that happen. It's not that much of a stretch to think he'd doctor evidence to secure a conviction."

"I just don't see how it would have made a difference?"

Melody asked. "Don't you think even with this mystery witness, the King brothers would have been convicted? Lyle confessed to the crime, didn't he?"

"A prison confession, yes," Kenya said.

"I need to talk to that guy too," I said.

I couldn't shake the ever-growing sick pit in my stomach. As we sat there spinning our wheels, Damon and Lyle King were being processed out of jail. Stephanie Nadler's haunted eyes burned into my brain.

"We'll get you everything you need," Kenya said, putting a hand on my shoulder. "I'm not going to let you be outmaneuvered by Trevor Page. I don't care who Damon King is connected to now. No matter what Phil's problems were, he was right on this case. Those two are guilty. And I will not let them walk on my watch."

"I need some air," I said.

"Let me see if I can get Sierra Joy on the phone," Melody said. She left the room. Howard followed her.

"She's good, maybe," Kenya said. "I was kinda worried when we started pulling the file."

"I need good," I said.

"You're gonna win this," Kenya said.

"I have to win this," I answered. I had more to say, but my phone rang. I had it face down on the table. I flipped it and Kenya stiffened beside me when she saw the caller ID.

Jason.

"I'll give you some privacy," she said. I thanked her. She shut the door behind her. I knew Howard kept a bottle of rum in his desk drawer for emergencies. This was feeling like one.

My head pounded as I picked up the phone.

"Mara," he said. "I'm sorry."

I couldn't help it. I laughed. "For which thing, Jason? I'm losing track."

He let out a hard sigh on the other end of the phone. "I'm sorry for the day you're having."

"Again, which thing, Jason?"

"Your bail hearing," he said. "Mara, what's going on?"

I debated even getting into it with him. It occurred to me Jason might already know about my meeting with Abigail Morris. She could have told him. The idea that they were still in contact made my blood turn to ice. Would he lie to me again if I asked him point blank? I decided not to give him the opportunity.

"Your girlfriend wanted to meet with me yesterday," I said.

The phone went silent. Then the background noises changed. Wind. Jason had stepped outside from wherever he was.

"What did she want?" he asked. "And she isn't my girlfriend. No. Wait. Don't even say it. Not like this. Not on the phone."

"Is someone listening?" I asked. "Christ, Jason. Did you have my phone bugged?"

"No," he said. "Just ... Mara, I'm three weeks out from an election that will define our future. I don't want to do this over the phone. I'm coming over. I want to see Will, anyway. I'll bring his favorite Thai takeout. Will you be home by seven?"

"No," I said. "No way. I can't do this with you right now."

"Mara, I have some things to say. I'm sorry is the least of it. But this isn't just about you. We're in the home stretch. I need to know what happened. What you said. What she said. And I need to make sure my son understands why I'm not going to be around a lot for the next few weeks."

"He understands," I said. "He knows about the election, Jason."

"I'm coming," he said.

"Fine," I said, tight-lipped. "But plan on taking a suitcase with you when you leave."

I hung up on him. Even with all the turmoil, that was one

thing I'd never done before. I'd railed, screamed, thrown things, called him every name in the book, but somehow, I'd never hung up on him.

I crashed my head to the table and tried to stop the world from spinning. I had half a mind to just stay here tonight and blow Jason off completely. If it weren't for Will, I might have.

A soft knock on the door pulled me back out of my head. Melody stepped in.

"Mara," she said. "Er ... Ms. Brent."

I smiled. "Mara's perfect."

"I have Sierra Joy on line one," she said.

I perked up. "Thank you."

I grabbed a notepad from the center of the table and a pen from the holder we kept there. I motioned for Melody to come all the way in. It wouldn't hurt to have a second set of ears.

I pushed the speaker button. "Ms. Joy?" I said. "This is Mara Brent."

"I know who you are," said a thin, female voice. "And I don't want to talk to you."

"But you are," I said. "And I appreciate it. Also, I'm sorry for whatever may have happened with you in the past with this office."

"You have no idea about that," she said.

"Ms. Joy," I said. "I don't know if you've seen the news today, but Damon and Lyle King have been released on bail. I wanted to make sure you heard that from me."

"They're free?" she asked. I couldn't place the emotion in her voice without seeing her facial expression. Was that fear? Relief?

"They'll be out on bail. There will be stiff restrictions on where they can go and what they can do. If you're afraid ..."

"Why should I be afraid?" she asked. "I've just been trying to tell the truth."

"Will you meet with me?" I asked. "I'd like to discuss your

statement in more detail. You understand you'll be called as a witness in the upcoming trial."

"But why?" she asked. "I told the truth. Lyle wasn't at the Blitz. He didn't kill those people."

"Ms. Joy, they're still charged with double murder and conspiracy to commit murder. There will be a new trial. I really would like to talk to you."

"I'm not meeting with you alone," she said. "I learned my lesson."

"That's fine," I said. "And we can talk whenever you feel comfortable. I can come to you."

"No!" she snapped. "I don't trust you. How do I know you won't do something to … to make me disappear?"

"I can assure you, that's not my intention at all. I want the truth to come out as much as you do. I swear."

"I'll come to you," she said. "But not alone. Can I bring my own lawyer?"

"Of course you can," I said.

"Monday," she said. "I'll be there in the morning."

Then Sierra Joy gave me a taste of my own medicine and hung up on me.

7

The back door felt like walking through a portal to a different time, as if I were seeing a museum exhibit or time capsule of life from my past. This wasn't my life anymore. Jason sitting at the dinner table next to Will. They slurped up their Thai noodles with gusto, leaning over their plates with identical postures.

Jason leaned over and smoothed a wayward cowlick down at the back of Will's head. He let him. That alone told me how much fun my son was having.

I stood frozen, watching them. In some back corner of my mind, I played a child's game. Or a fool's. If I held my breath, didn't blink, maybe the last year would melt away and things could be like they used to be. We were happy, weren't we?

Then I exhaled. No. We weren't happy. We were a lie.

"Hey, guys," I said, putting on a smile. It had to be good. Though Will had trouble expressing his own emotions, he could zero in on others' with remarkable accuracy. He always knew when I was lying.

Jason sat back. "Sorry," he said. "We tried to wait for you. Will's stomach growled so loud it shook the walls."

"It's fine," I said. "I'm actually not that hungry. Someone ordered from Papa Leoni's and brought it into work around two o'clock. I'll have leftovers later."

"We put yours in the fridge," Will said. "Dad's gonna look over some blueprints with me."

"After you get ready for bed," Jason said. "And only twenty minutes. You've got school in the morning. Mom's pretty tired."

"She's always tired the days she goes to court." It wasn't an accusation, just a factual observation. Will met my eyes for the briefest of seconds. He was brilliant. An eighty-year-old's wisdom in the mind of a nine-year-old. The past year had blown his security apart. Piece by piece he'd rebuilt it like the intricate Lego worlds he built in the spare bedroom above our heads.

"Yeah," I said, taking my seat at the table. I reached over and took a forkful of Will's discarded noodles. Even lukewarm now, they were delicious.

"How'd it go at school today?" I asked.

Will stared at a point on the wall. "Brown vs. Board of Education," he said. "I want to read the full opinion. Our books only have three-paragraph summaries."

"You're studying Brown?" Jason asked.

"No," Will said. "Separation of powers. The Constitution. They have case law highlights in the chapters. I don't like to read those."

"Sure," I said. "I'll show you a website where you can pull up the full opinions. You can even listen to the oral argument the parties presented to the court."

"I'll get my laptop," he said.

"Tomorrow." Jason and I said it together. We both knew how this went. Will could easily spend the next twelve hours, well into morning, reading and listening if it caught his interest.

Our son frowned at us. Lord, he looked more and more like his dad. They had the same gray eyes, clefts in their chin, and ability to look at me like I was crazy with just a small flicker of their mouth.

"Fine," he said. "But I get extra credit if I do a case brief."

"A case brief?" I said. "In the fourth grade?"

Will already had about a hundred and fifty percent in each of his classes for doing projects like this.

"Bath," Jason said, smiling. "Then twenty minutes on the glacier blueprint."

My heart jumped a little when Jason said it. Will's latest Lego project involved sculpting glaciers, representative of those the *Titanic* iceberg might have chipped off from. This spring, I'd promised to take him on a cruise of the Prince William Sound where he could see some of them up close and personal. It would be just the two of us. My first vacation as a single parent.

Finally, Will disappeared up the stairs, leaving me alone with Jason and their Thai food leftovers. I started clearing the table and walked into the kitchen. Jason followed. I waited until I heard the water running in my bathtub. Rinsing off the plates, I stacked them in the dishwasher.

Jason came to me. He put a hand on my arm, stopping me before I could load the soap into the receptacle and start a wash cycle.

"Tell me what happened."

I jerked my hand away. I didn't mean to. It was just ... I couldn't bear to have him touch me. Not now. Maybe never.

"Ivey let those psychopaths out on bail," I said.

Jason dropped his head. "I heard. Tough break. He's trying to give himself political cover. Halsey really screwed you over on this one."

"I don't want to talk about that," I said. It was true and not true. Regardless of his other flaws, my husband had always been my greatest strategy sounding board. He could see a problem from every angle without becoming emotionally attached to any one of them. Will's particular brand of analytical mind came from Jason. No question.

Above us, I could hear music playing. Will had turned on my Bluetooth speakers in the bathroom. He did it often, but I knew he also did it when he thought Jason and I would argue. That was a new thing.

"We need to talk about your girlfriend," I said.

I took a seat at one of the stools I kept around the kitchen island. Jason didn't. He stayed standing but leaned against the kitchen counter, gripping it with his hands behind him.

"I know you know she's not my girlfriend," he said.

I was tired. Bone tired. Will was right. Court drained me. Losing ... drained me.

"She's peddling a tell-all," I said. "I think it's clear Evan Sampson's people have gotten to her."

Evan Sampson was Jason's competitor in his upcoming congressional race. They'd been the ones who tried to break the story of Jason's affair. Ever the shrewd politician, Jason got out ahead of it. His smooth talking might just be enough to save his ambitions, but not what was happening between us.

Jason's posture didn't change. I let that sink in for a moment, then mine did. "You know," I said. "Jason. You already know all about it? When were you going to tell me?"

"We're talking right now," he said. "And I wasn't completely sure. I'd heard some rumblings. I'll take care of this. Abigail won't be a problem. It's not anything you need to worry about."

"Really?" I said. "I'd love to hear how you're gonna spin that."

"This will all be over, one way or the other, in three weeks. I know you hate me. You also know I hate myself for what I've done to you and Will. If there was some way I could put everything on hold and ... fix things ... I would."

"Fix things?"

Jason put a hand up, realizing the idiocy of what he'd just

said. I really was too damn tired to have the same fight we'd had a hundred times before.

"You asked me to be patient," I said. "Hold on until after the election. I've done that. I'm doing that. But I will not sit quietly by while this woman drags me and your son through the press again. You know how this goes. We'll have reporters camped out at the end of the street again. Rifling through my garbage. Circling Will's school."

"I'll handle it," Jason said, his voice rising.

I shook my head. "I don't think I want to know what that even means. Jason, this woman is a victim too. I hate that I hate her. I hate what that says about me. But I can't separate my need to protect Will from any of this. He's all that matters. But...my God, Jason. She was your *intern*! You had power over her. As much as I want to protect my son, I'm not so heartless that I don't realize this girl needs someone protecting her too."

"I did a stupid thing," he shouted, cutting me off. "An unforgivable thing when it comes to you and Will. I own that. I know what it might cost me. But I will not let Abby destroy what I'm building for this country. My work is too important. The people who trust me to lead them are too important. So just ... for now ... don't respond. I'll make sure you won't have to deal with reporters or anything like that. I promise."

I smoothed my hair behind my ears. "Well, as long as you promise." I hated this side of me. This bitter, sarcastic person. I could feel the negativity eating away at my soul. I knew full well that's what forgiveness meant. But I wasn't there yet. I couldn't fully let go.

I met my husband's eyes. Even after everything, the pain in his expression called to something inside of me. I still loved him. And I knew that was entirely beside the point.

"We're going to trial again on the Kings," I said. "Me. I'm going to trial. It's happening. And it's happening fast. They're not waiving speedy trial. We'll probably have a date as early as January. Maybe late December."

"Damn," Jason said. He came forward and finally took a seat.

"Exactly," I said.

"I wish I could help you," he said. "My office ... Mara, the AG's office's hands are tied."

"Oh, I know they're waiting to see which way the wind blows too. I'm on my own. Believe me, we all know that."

"This will ruin Kenya Spaulding," he said. "If they walk. You were smart to turn that job down. She will forever be tainted after this."

"You mean if I lose," I said. "Thanks for the vote of confidence."

Jason let out a sigh. "Sorry. I didn't mean that. I was just thinking about the politics of it."

"Well, I'm thinking about Krista Nadler and Charlie Brinkman. The Brinkman family. Stephanie Nadler. She was in the courtroom. Krista was her whole life. I've never seen anything as brutal as that murder scene, Jason. I know in my heart that there would have been more if Damon King hadn't been convicted of these killings."

"Yeah," Jason said. "Wasn't there a kill file? A hit list or something?"

"Yes," I said. I didn't want to discuss too much of the case with him. But they had already reported the most gruesome details in the press during the first trial.

"Damon King," Jason said. "New Age savior. He would cleanse Waynetown of all sins. Wasn't Phil on his hit list? That's what I remember. Some headline where Phil slayed the dragon who'd vowed to kill him next."

"Yes," I said. "Phil was on Damon's kill list."

"Then he shouldn't have even been allowed to try that case in the first place. How the hell did that even happen?"

"Before my time," I said. "And what does it matter now? It just matters that I figure out a way to put those two monsters away for good."

"I used to love the Blitz," he said. "You know I took my very first date there after a junior high dance. We all did. It was a rite of passage."

"I know," I said.

"Mara," he said. Jason reached across the table and put his hand over mine. A chill went through me. That familiar, heated pull started in my core. My brain short-circuited. Jason froze. I pulled my hand away.

"I'll take care of you," Jason said, and I knew we were no longer talking about the King case. I wanted to believe him. I couldn't.

"You'd better hurry," I said, sliding off my stool. "Will's done with his bath. He'll be waiting for you."

With that, I turned my back on Jason and headed up the stairs.

🐾 8 🐾

Sierra Joy came to my office at eight a.m. the following Monday morning. She wasn't alone. She'd brought a disheveled attorney I knew from neighboring Toledo named Hollis Woodburn. He was ancient and trailing an oxygen tank behind him. I learned within a few seconds he was Sierra's grandfather's best friend and a bankruptcy lawyer.

Fine. At least I got her in the office.

Melody joined me and sat poised with a pen and pad of paper.

Sierra was small, maybe four foot eleven, and she wore low heels. She had thin, straight brown hair that hung in her eyes. She wore a tight blue skirt and white silk blouse. Beneath that, her pink bra was visible.

"Thanks for coming," I said. "I know the last few months have to have been trying for you."

"Months?" she asked. "Try years, Mrs. Brent."

"You can call me Mara," I said.

"Ms. Joy is here to repeat her statement, that's all," Hollis interjected. I could smell his lunch on his breath. Onions, garlic, and if I wasn't mistaken, a trace of bourbon. Great.

"Well," I said. "Ms. Joy will have to be prepared to answer questions on the witness stand. I'd just like to give her an opportunity to ..."

"I'm not going to lie," Sierra said. "I never lie."

"No one's accused you of that."

"You understand, Ms. Joy has also been asked to appear for an interview with the Ohio attorney general's office," Hollis said. "That's actually the next stop after here."

I nodded. "I assumed as much."

"And I can assure you, she will fully cooperate with them."

"I would expect nothing less," I said. "Ms. Joy, Mr. Woodburn, I don't think we're on the same page. Let me clear something up. I'm interested in the truth. I'm interested in hearing what Ms. Joy has to say. That's all. This isn't some game of gotcha."

"I'll tell you what I told Mr. Halsey," Sierra said.

"Excellent," I said. "Can you tell me when you spoke with him? Do you remember that far back?"

"December 17th," she answered. "2008."

Melody wrote it down. "So roughly four months after the Brinkman and Nadler murders took place."

"Yes," she said. "It was after Lyle and his brother got charged. I saw the dates in the news. They said Lyle killed those people on the night of August 11th in 2008. I knew that wasn't right. I remember that night."

"Were you ever questioned by the police prior to calling Mr. Halsey?" I asked.

"No," she said. "Lyle didn't know me. I mean, not then. He probably does now because of all of this. I always felt really bad that they never used what I told Mr. Halsey. Nobody ever called me as a witness."

"You never reached out to the police at any time? You never contacted Mr. King's defense lawyer?"

Sierra slumped in her seat. "Everyone said Lyle and Damon

did this. It would have ruined my life back then if I said anything else. Mr. Halsey didn't believe me. He told me he'd have to tell everyone about ... what I did for a living."

"Which was?" I asked.

"I'm not the same person I was ten years ago. I was ... I was just trying to survive."

I gestured to Melody. She slid a thin stack of papers across the table. Sierra Joy's rap sheet.

"You've been arrested for prostitution twice," I said. "In 2005. But you had another arrest in early 2008 as part of a task force prostitution sting. And then a few minor drug possession charges."

"I'm not ashamed of any of that. I got clean. I wasn't some trust fund rich kid. I don't have Mommy and Daddy money. I've had to rely on myself."

Hollis put a light hand on her arm. It was a clear dig at my background. My mother's family was an old, influential name in New Hampshire politics. My father had made a fortune on his own. It was my family's financial backing that made Jason's congressional run even possible. With everything that had happened, my mother was still Jason's biggest political supporter. I refused to take the bait.

"Your life is your life," I said. "If you think I'm judging you for that, you're wrong. As I said, I'm interested in one thing only. The truth."

"I told Mr. Halsey I'd seen Lyle King on the night of August 12th. He wasn't in Waynetown. We were in Toledo. He came into a club where I worked part-time. Downtown. Scarlett and Lace. It's not even there anymore. Anyway, I was a waitress for a little while."

"You're saying Lyle was at that bar on the night of the 12th. You're sure?"

"I'm sure. I mean, it was the 11th when he came in. But the 12th when he left. You know. Because it was after midnight into the 12th. He came in alone and sat at the bar. It was ... Scarlett and Lace was a strip club back in those days. I remember him because it was odd. He just sat there ordering draft beer. One after the other. He never turned around and looked at the dancers. He stayed until we closed. The owner, a guy named Nicky Baldwin, finally had to ask him to cash out."

"How can you be so sure?" I asked.

"There was a boxing match that night. The bar was packed. The kid was a Toledo local. Um...Mule? Yeah. Mule McKinney. I think he ended up getting knocked out in the first round. Everybody made a big joke about it. There were billboards in town and the kid's career ended in like two seconds. Anyway, you can look it up."

Melody took notes. The name didn't ring any bells for me, but it was before my time in this area. I'd seen nothing in Phil's notes about the Mule McKinney fight. It would be easy enough to look up. Which also meant it would have been easy enough for Sierra to look up after the fact.

It was a thin story. I could see why Phil wouldn't have worried much about it. There were about a dozen things I could do to discredit Sierra Joy on the stand. The trouble was none of that was the point. As much as Kenya and I would try to make it otherwise, Phil Halsey would be on trial as much as Lyle and Damon King.

"Where did you meet with Mr. Halsey?" I asked.

"He came to my apartment," she said.

"Alone?"

"Yes," she said. "I emailed him a day or two before and told him I had something to say about Lyle King's whereabouts that he'd want to know."

"That's not what your email to him says. It just says you wanted to talk," I said.

"Well, we talked on the phone after that. I told him then it was about Lyle."

I had no way to independently verify that.

"Why didn't you just contact the police?" Melody asked.

Sierra rolled her eyes. "I didn't like talking to cops in those days. Still don't. And I thought Phil Halsey was an honest man. He sure seemed like it."

"Ms. Joy, of course, has records of what she's describing," Hollis offered. He slid his own stack of papers across the desk.

They were printouts from Sierra's email account. I'd seen them before. They formed part of Trevor Page's motion for a new trial. Alone, they weren't much. Just an email to Phil's government account asking for a meeting. There wasn't even a reply. Our office had no phone records of a returned call out of our office or on Phil's cell phone. But since her version of events took place almost ten years ago, that wasn't surprising. There was, however, the notation of her appointment with Phil in Caro's appointment book. They met. I had no doubt about that.

"Ms. Brent, your office knows all of this," Hollis said. "You've had the benefit of all of my client's information when the motion for new trial was filed. The county's appellate attorney responded. He lost. Ms. Joy is uncomfortable being here but came as a courtesy to you. You want to see her in person. See what kind of witness she's going to make. See how easily she rattles. I assure you, she doesn't."

"I appreciate that," I said. So Hollis Woodburn knew what he was doing. "I also want you to know that I'm not Phil Halsey. I'm not your enemy."

Hollis leaned forward. "Kenya Spaulding didn't take this seriously enough. She's in over her head."

I resisted the urge to get defensive. Hollis might have been at least partially right. I'd barely even been briefed on the motion for new trial in this case. As the office's principle litigator, it hadn't been my job. Appeals and post-judgment motions were handled down the hall. Kenya never dreamed in a million years they could overturn the King case. She had a full plate dealing with the broader investigation into Phil's misconduct. Now, Charlie Brinkman and Krista Nadler might pay for that all over again.

"He cut me a deal," Sierra said, her voice breaking. "I'm not proud of that. Halsey looked down on me. I mean, he actually rolled his eyes the second he saw me. He stopped just short of calling me a whore to my face."

That didn't sound like the Phil Halsey I knew. My heart tripped as that thought entered my mind. It turned out none of us really knew Phil Halsey at all.

"I'm sorry that happened to you," I said, and I meant it.

"I knew what would happen if I pushed it," she said. "He would have put me on the stand and made me feel worthless. He would have shamed me in front of the whole town. Whore would have been the kindest thing he would have said."

"We'll never know," I said.

"So," Sierra said, blowing her nose into a tissue. "I took the deal he offered. Deal. That's a pretty word for it. It felt like blackmail. He told me if I kept my mouth shut, he'd make my charges go away. And if I didn't, he'd make sure I did real time. He said he could get the word out I was talking to the cops and him. He did his homework. He knew exactly which people in town I was afraid of. And it was lies. All lies. I was a nobody. I didn't have dirt on anyone. I minded my business. I told you. I was just trying to survive."

Melody pulled out another piece of paper. It was the one other piece of Sierra Joy's story that had documentation to back it up. Two weeks after Sierra's email to Phil, he filed paperwork dropping all pending charges against her.

"He said those words exactly?" I asked. "If you keep your mouth shut, he'd make your charges go away? And if you didn't, he'd throw you to the wolves?"

"Pretty much," she said. "At the time, it seemed like an easy choice. I mean, I didn't know Lyle King from anyone. He'd come into the club a few times. He tipped well and kept to himself. Nicky said he was thinking of hiring him as a bouncer. I remember thinking he'd make a good one. And he didn't leer at the girls the way most of those guys did. That's why I remember him. He seemed like a good guy."

"I see," I said. "I really do want to thank you for your time. You've been very helpful."

"We're done here?" Hollis asked.

"For now," I said. "I may reach out in a few weeks as we get closer to the trial date."

"You're going to put her on the stand?" Hollis asked, incredulous.

"Most likely," I said, though I didn't care to discuss trial strategy with him.

"Bold move," he said. "Get her out of the way before the defense does. You know Trevor Page will eat you alive. He's the best there is."

"Thank you," I said, rising.

Sierra folded herself against Hollis Woodburn. He shook my hand and ushered her out.

Once the door closed behind them, I sank back into my chair.

"She's going to kill us," Melody said, echoing my own thoughts. "The jury will want to protect her."

"It's bad," I said. "I won't deny that. Except that Lyle King confessed to the killings. I believe Sierra Joy thinks she's telling the truth. Only Lyle wasn't in the Scarlett and Lace that night. She's got to be wrong about the dates. I just have to prove it."

"And you're going to have to kill her on the stand. Ugh. That sucks. You'll have to do to her the exact thing she was afraid of with Phil."

"Probably," I finally admitted. My other thought I kept to myself. Sometimes, I truly hated my job.

❊ 9 ❊

"Well," Kenya said. "What do we think?"

I sat in the war room with her, Melody, Howard, our newest intern, Steve, and Herc Manfield. Herc had handled the King brothers' criminal appeal and post-judgment motions for the State. He was here at my request. He knew the pleadings in this case better than anyone and had a sharp mind I respected.

"I think the jury will find her very sympathetic," I said. "Sierra's softly spoken, comes across as earnest. She's also got something to lose by coming forward."

"Did you bother to meet with her yourself?" Kenya asked Herc. I winced at her tone. Herc and Kenya had butted heads on other cases and she blamed him for losing against Trevor Page.

"Of course," Herc said, unflappable as always. "And I don't personally think she's going to make that great a witness for the defense because of her past."

"It could go either way," I said. "That's the truth of it. She doesn't have a history of lying that we've been able to find. She just kept quiet to keep herself out of jail."

"Your problem is Phil," Herc said. "Page will paint him as the villain. I think you need to be prepared that this won't even be about the murders from his perspective. The Kings will be the victims."

"Well," I said. "I've got a crime scene and two mutilated bodies the jury will have to contend with."

"I'll share what I have," Herc said. "But Sierra Joy came up clean. Her last brush with the law was ten years ago, same time frame as the King brothers' trial prep. She got scared straight by something."

"She got scared straight by Phil," Kenya said. "That's the kicker in all this. The deal he cut her was the end of her criminal activity. I've been in the room when Phil dealt with people like her. He was good at it. He probably came off like a father figure."

I looked down at my shoes. At times, Phil had been that way with me. I came to work for him not long after losing my dad. In those early days, it had been easy to transfer feelings. I could only imagine how it might have been for Sierra. She didn't appear to have much in the way of a support system.

"We need to keep digging," I said. "As much as I like the girl, I need to sew at least a kernel of doubt about her story."

Herc nodded. Kenya drummed her fingers on the table.

"Where are we on Aaron Clyde?" I asked.

"Who's Aaron Clyde?" Steve the intern asked. It earned him a withering glance from Kenya. I had a feeling the kid wouldn't last the month.

"If you're gonna be any help to us," she said, "I will need you to get up to speed before you come to work every day, Steve. Mara doesn't have time to spoon-feed you."

"Lyle King's confidant," I said. "They were cellmates at the county jail. Lyle confessed to killing Brinkman and Nadler to him, along with plans for a second and third set of murders over the rest of that summer. All part of this so-called kill list Damon had compiled."

"Clyde was paroled four years ago," Kenya said. "He skipped town a couple of weeks ago. He's been in the wind since then. There's a warrant out for him."

"We need him," I said. "I guarantee you Trevor Page already knows where he is."

"Isn't that a conflict of interest?" Melody asked. "I mean, if Page is counseling him?"

"I doubt he is," I said. "At least not directly. But there's no way he can successfully defend his client without being able to poke holes in Clyde's testimony. He's going to need him on the stand even more than we do."

"How are you gonna find him?" Herc asked.

"I will call in just about every favor I have," I said. "I'm meeting with his parole officer tomorrow. Clyde isn't considered a violent felon. He was in for check fraud and trying to pass counterfeit bills at a fast food place."

"We can offer him a deal," Kenya said. "Make it known we won't go after him on a parole violation if he voluntarily surrenders. I want him here."

"Thanks," I said. "That'll help."

"Well," Kenya said, "You're right. We need to make sure we lock Clyde down. It doesn't matter so much what he's done in the years since the trial, in my mind. It just matters that his story about Lyle King holds."

"I agree," I said.

"Anything else today?" Kenya asked.

"That's it for now," I said. My phone buzzed. I did a quick check of the screen to make sure it wasn't Will's school. I didn't recognize the number.

"Okay," I said. "Herc, if you can think of anything else on Clyde we can use, I'd appreciate it. I'll coordinate with your office and loop you in on what his parole officer has to say. Thanks for coming down."

"You got it," Herc said. He rose from his chair. My eyes went up and up. Herc was a bear of a man with dark eyes and a muscular build. He competed in MMA tournaments in his spare time. To anyone who didn't know him like I did, he could seem pretty menacing. I knew him for the gentle giant he was. He'd once intervened on Will's behalf during a courthouse field trip. He'd overheard a couple of Will's classmates teasing him behind his back. Herc stepped in and made it known Will was his "little buddy." Will didn't even know who Herc was at the time. He also wasn't aware of why the boys were picking on him. Either way, it worked. Those particular little jerks didn't bother Will again.

I thanked him and stepped out into the hall. I got a second call from the mystery number. It was a 313 area code.

"Mara Brent," I answered.

"Mrs. Brent," the caller said. "My name is Elise Dunam. I'm with the *Free Press*. I'm hoping you have a comment on Abigail Morgan's allegations this morning."

My pulse spiked. I moved down the hall and slipped into my office, shutting the door behind me.

"This is my personal cell," I said. "Would you mind telling me how you got a hold of it?"

"Mrs. Brent, your husband is ten days away from a congressional election. You've stayed largely silent and out of sight during his campaign. Were you aware of the book Abigail Morgan intended to publish?"

Intended?

"I have no comment," I said.

"Ms. Morgan's publisher dropped her last night in response to child abuse allegations from her former employer. Do you have anything to say about the matter?"

My brain spun. Child abuse?

"Again," I said. "I have no comment."

I hung up the phone. The back of my neck started to sweat. I sank into my desk chair and opened my laptop. A quick browser search answered some of my questions, while leading to about a dozen more.

I found a breaking news headline on *Mlive*.

Abigail Morgan had apparently been working as a nanny for a wealthy couple in Ann Arbor. That couple was now claiming they fired her two days ago after suspecting her of hitting their two-year-old daughter.

I clicked the video. "I didn't want to believe it," the mother said. The crawl identified her as Margo Wilson, a university professor. "Toddlers get hurt all the time. Cuts and scrapes are common. But I believe my child. This woman is a monster. We intend to make sure she's prosecuted to the fullest extent of the law. This woman is a lying, scheming, evil person. The world needs to know what she's capable of."

I clicked off the video. My throat felt thick. My phone buzzed again; this time it was Jason.

Shaking, I picked it up.

"Mara," he said, breathless. "I'm sorry to drop this on you like this. It's all happening so fast. Listen, you might get called by the press. God. I'm so sorry. Again. Always."

"You're too late," I said, my voice sounding flat to my own ears. "Is it true?"

Jason let out a bitter laugh. "I have no idea what Abigail is capable of. But this wouldn't surprise me."

I couldn't listen. I didn't want to hear. Abigail's words thundered through my brain. Jason would lie about anything to save his own skin. Jason's words echoed after hers to me.

I'll take care of this. Abigail won't be a problem.

"Jason," I said. "Was this you?"

"What?" he asked.

"Did you leak this story?"

Jason let out a sigh. "Mara, I don't want to talk about this over the phone. I can't get away to see you right now. Christ. I'm little more than a week out from the election. I need you to come out here. One or two campaign stops. I'll make sure the press stays away from you. Baby, I wouldn't ask if I didn't really need you. I know I have no right to."

"You didn't answer my question," I said. "Was this you?"

There was so much implied in my words. Did he leak the story? Were the allegations even true, or was this just a way to cancel Abigail Morgan in the eyes of the world? Would he do it? Was my husband that ruthless?

"I have to go," I said. "This is a critical time for me too. I have a murder trial to prepare for."

"Mara, you're not going to trial for weeks. Months, even. Can we just get through a few days together? Please. If you want me to beg, I'll beg."

"We'll talk later," I said, feeling my face flush. "I can't do this right now. I told you how I feel. I won't normalize what you did to that woman. To us."

The soft knock on my door gave me the respite I needed. I stepped around my desk and opened it. Kenya's kind eyes nearly undid me. She knew. She already knew.

I said goodbye to my husband and gestured for Kenya to come inside.

"Hey," she said. "Do you mind if I'm not your boss for a little while? Because right now I'd really like to go have lunch with my friend."

It took a monstrous effort not to burst into tears. Instead, I found a smile.

"I'd like that. Lately I feel like I don't have too many of those. Friends, I mean."

Laughing, Kenya put an arm around me. "Me neither, Mara. Me neither."

F
our days later, I stood at the edge of a pond, staring at my reflection in the water. I pulled the ends of my coat around me. Last week had brought temperatures in the eighties. Today, on Halloween, we'd had our first frost.

My breath misted in front of me as I turned. Stephanie Nadler made her way down the hill toward me. Our location had been her choice.

Stephanie wore a purple sweatshirt and tattered jeans. She carried a bouquet of pink roses and paused on a path circling the pond. Beckoning me with her sad smile, I slowly made my way to her side.

She sat on a limestone bench before the simple, flat headstone bearing her daughter's name.

Krista Jean Nadler, beloved daughter and friend.

"I'd been saving since the day I found out I was pregnant," she said. "I was seventeen myself. I waited tables at the Barbie. God, back then I thought I was rich."

The Barbie had been Waynetown's answer to the Outback. They went out of business two years ago, but for a while, it was one of the busiest restaurants in town.

"I'd put twenty percent of whatever I earned in a savings account for Krista. I mean, at the time we're talking forty or fifty bucks a week. It was a lot of money to me then. I guess it still kind of is. By the time Krista was sixteen, though, I had a few thousand dollars saved up. Can you believe that? It would be enough to pay for her tuition at the University of Toledo. Two years' worth. And her counselors said she would have gotten some in scholarships. She was that smart."

My heart broke for her. For Krista.

"She was such a good girl," Stephanie said. "Responsible. Heck, half the time she mothered me more than I did her. She used to pack a lunch for me when I had to work nights. She never complained about what we didn't have. Never. She had friends with more money. They could afford to go to summer camps. Krista wanted to go, but she never even asked. She'd lie and say how it didn't sound fun to her and she'd rather stay home with me."

Stephanie fingered a pendant she wore around her neck. She pulled it out and showed it to me. On its face, it had a picture of a brown and white pony.

"She loved horses. Her best friend, Mia, used to go to this horse camp, Hunter's Meadow, and Krista tried not to be jealous. A friend of mine did their bookkeeping and arranged for Krista to volunteer out there, sweeping out stalls. That kind of thing. In exchange, she got free riding lessons. She always said it was the best summer of her life. I found out later the other girls teased her. They would come for their private lessons while Krista was working. They tried to make her feel bad for it. Stupid kids. She never even told me."

"I wish I'd gotten a chance to meet her," I said.

"This was her favorite pony, Lucky Boy. I wish I could have bought that horse for her. This was Krista's pendant. I had made for her for her eleventh birthday. I took a picture of Lucky to a friend of mine who painted things like that on jewelry. Krista loved it. She never took it off. She was wearing it when ..."

Stephanie couldn't finish.

"You were a wonderful mom," I said.

"My savings paid for this, instead" she said, smoothing a few grass clippings away from Krista's headstone. "And part of the funeral."

"I'm so sorry," I said. "I wish I could spare you having to go through this all over again."

"Taking the witness stand at her trial was the second hardest thing I ever had to do," she said. "Obviously, burying Krista was worse. But to have to sit there and see those awful pictures. What they did to her. I can't do it again."

"I can protect you from that part," I said. "You don't have to be in the courtroom for that. I promise."

"I said it all before. Do you have questions that will be different? Can't you just play a video or something of the other trial?"

"No," I said. "It would be different if you weren't able to testify again. Plus, the jury needs to hear from you. They need to get to know you. You're the only person who can really help them know Krista."

Stephanie nodded. "I know. It's just ... back then, I had more people around me. My fiancé. My mom. They're all gone now, too. Even a lot of the friends I had back then just faded away. It was me. I mean, a lot of it. I pushed people away. It was them too, though. It was hard to be around me. They all wanted me to tell them I was okay. That I was moving on. The trouble is, all that's more for them than me. People don't want to feel uncomfortable anymore, so they need you to say you're fine so they can stop thinking about awful things."

"I understand," I said. I was blessed never to have lived through the nightmare Stephanie Nadler had, but I'd counseled so many violent crime victims and survivors in my career. Stephanie's story was all too familiar.

"Stephanie," I said. "Can you think back? I know it's been ten years but ..."

She turned to me. "It might have been yesterday, Ms. Brent. If you think my memory has faded, you'd be wrong. It's sharper."

"Okay," I said. "And you can tell the jury that. It will matter. But did Krista ever talk about either of the King brothers or the Church of the Living Flame?"

"No," she said. "We weren't very religious. I didn't take Krista to church. I mean, I baptized her. We were Lutheran. I did that to make my mom happy. She was a good girl though, my Krista. It was Charlie's family who were the churchgoers."

"Yes," I said. "The Brinkmans belonged to Holy Reformer. Did Krista ever attend services with him?"

"Once or twice, I think. But they didn't meet there. They met in school, like two normal teenagers. Charlie played football for River West. Krista was in the marching band. They'd picked her for drum major. She would have led them on the field her senior year if ... if the Kings hadn't done what they did."

I'd seen the heartbreaking pictures of Charlie and Krista as a young couple. The one the newspaper ran all the time was after a game during their junior year. Charlie was red-faced, sweating after just pulling off his helmet. Krista wore her marching band uniform, clutching her clarinet. Charlie had his arm around her. They were laughing. Two sweet, clueless, innocent kids with their entire lives ahead of them.

"How's your relationship with the Brinkmans?" I asked. What I didn't say was the status of mine. Charlie Sr. and his wife Sharon only lived in Waynetown part of the time. They were in Florida now and not returning my calls.

"I don't have one," Stephanie said. "You'd think we'd have

bonded after everything that happened. Sharon though, I hate to speak ill of her. She lost a child too. But even before that, I wouldn't call our relationship very warm."

"Did she not approve of Krista?" I asked.

"That's an understatement," Stephanie answered. "I don't know, Sharon was just one of those stereotypical mothers of sons who didn't think any girl would be good enough for her boy. We had a big falling out a few weeks before the kids were murdered."

"Do you mind telling me about it?" I asked.

"It didn't come out at trial," Stephanie said. "I'm glad for that. I don't want it to now, if you don't mind."

"Why don't you just tell me what happened. I'm not looking to drag those kids through the mud. But I don't know what the Kings' defense lawyers will do. It would help me to have a heads-up on everything that was going on with the kids in that time frame."

"I was trying to be a good mom. Responsible. Krista was seventeen years old. Like I said, the same age I was when I got pregnant with her. Everyone said it would ruin my life. It didn't. Krista was the best thing that ever happened to me. That doesn't mean it wasn't hard. I didn't want her to go down the same path. My mother wasn't really present. She didn't ... I mean, I knew about the birds and the bees, but she didn't help me. She ignored me. So, when Krista became ... you know ... mature ... I took her to the doctor. A woman doctor. I wanted her to have access to information and birth control. I wanted her to trust me. That doesn't mean I wanted her to start having sex. I just wanted her to be educated about it."

"Of course," I said.

"Well, Krista did eventually come to me about Charlie. She wanted to go on the pill. That was in late spring of that year. I worried, but I trusted my daughter."

"So you knew Charlie and Krista were becoming sexually active?" I asked.

"Well, I didn't ask her that point blank. I kept my door open to her. We had rules. Charlie wasn't allowed to spend the night or anything. They were never alone in my house together. I made Krista keep her bedroom door open. All those things."

"So what happened with Charlie's mom?" I asked.

Stephanie wrung her hands in her lap. "She showed up at my work one night. That summer I took a job bartending at the veteran's hall off Clinton Road. I didn't want Krista to have to take even a dime of student loans. Though I hated to see her go, I wanted her to have the option of living in the dorms. I was trying to do the right thing."

Stephanie cried. Not a sob, but slow, silent tears. My heart twisted. All I saw before me was a great mom who tried to do everything she thought was right for her kid.

"Sharon was insane," Stephanie said. "I mean, her face was purple. She was literally spitting mad. I went out behind the hall with her. Another girl covered for me. Anyway, Sharon started throwing out all these threats. Saying how my daughter might be damned, but she would not stand by and let Krista lead Charlie down a path to hell. She actually said that to me."

"Charlie was planning to enter the seminary after graduation," I said.

"That's what Sharon wanted for him," Stephanie said. "Krista told me he was having second thoughts. He was thinking about joining the military instead. I mean, Krista said he was just doing it because it was the quickest way to get as far away from his mom as possible. I defended Sharon to Krista. It's not easy being a parent. Especially not one of a teenager."

"What about the altercation?" I said.

"I kept my cool," Stephanie said. "I said over and over again, I'm sorry you feel that way. I reminded her the kids were less than a year away from graduating and they were both turning eighteen. I said I trusted my kid, even if she didn't trust hers. I guess Sharon found a condom in Charlie's room and went ballistic. She said she was going to make sure Charlie broke up with Krista. She stopped just short of calling me and my daughter whores."

"I'm sorry that happened to you," I said.

"The thing is, I don't even blame Sharon. She was just wound so tight. I got the impression she's one of those people who's always had someone to take care of her. I don't know. I just didn't want to get into it. Krista loved Charlie and I think he loved her. I didn't want to be in a war with his mom, so I just kind of played it all off. I never even told Krista about it. Charlie did. He came to the house a couple days later to apologize for Sharon."

"He sounds like a great kid too," I said.

"He was," Stephanie said, her voice catching. "I loved that boy too. I told Sharon that. I think ... I believe in my heart it would have all worked out, eventually. Once Sharon saw that Charlie wasn't going to turn into the devil or something. But then ... the kids ... I think it was less than two weeks later that we lost them."

"Did you ever get any resolution with Sharon?" I asked.

Stephanie shook her head. "They never talked to me. They didn't come to Krista's funeral. She told me not to come to Charlie's. I didn't listen though. I tried to stay in the very back. She was so angry with me. She screamed at me. Made a scene. Then later, they sat on the other side of the courtroom during the trial."

My heart twisted even more. Sharon and Charlie Brinkman were the only other people on the planet who might have shared Stephanie's pain. I knew I would make sure she had advocates with her through this whole process.

"Well," I said. "So far the Brinkmans are dodging my calls now too."

"Sorry," she said. "If you were hoping I could get them to talk to you, I'm the last person who could do that."

"Okay," I said. "I'll handle it. And who knows, maybe they've mellowed over the years."

I put a hand on Stephanie's shoulder. "Thanks for talking to me today. I can't imagine how hard this is for you. I want you to know you can call me anytime, day or night."

I handed her my card with my personal cell written on it. Stephanie thanked me and stuck it in her pocket.

She went to her knees in front of Krista's grave and I took it as my cue to go. Stuffing my hands in my coat pocket, I climbed up the hill and headed back to my car.

I cast one more glance down at Stephanie. She rocked back and forth. She was so alone. As I started the car, I saw two missed calls on my cell. I picked it up and pressed my voicemail.

The message was from Detective Sam Cruz of the Maumee County sheriff's department. We'd worked on many cases together. "Hey, Mara, sorry to bug you. I'm sure you're heading home to go trick or treating with Will. I just wanted to let you know. We picked up Aaron Clyde today on a parole violation. They want to process him out to Wood County, but I figured you'd want to talk to him first. Call me back and I'll help make the arrangements."

I threw the phone on my passenger seat. Sam was right, Will expected me back at the house by six. It was four thirty now. I had just enough time to make a quick stop at the police station.

❧ 11 ❧

Sam led me into the bullpen. Clyde was waiting in an interview room just down the hall.

"Thanks for this," I said. "How long do I have?"

Sam scratched his chin. I'd known him since I first took the job at the Maumee County prosecutor's office. In fact, he was actually the first cop I met here. He worked in the violent crimes unit. He'd been one of the youngest, promoted in at just thirty years old. They'd scooped him up from vice after he did a short stint in field ops out of the academy. None of that had earned him points with the older detectives. But Sam's work ethic and talent became abundantly clear to anyone who bothered to pay attention.

I did.

"Not long," he said. "Page has been looking pretty hard for this guy too."

"And I don't want you to think I'd ever try to withhold anything like that from him. I just want maybe a ten-minute head start."

Sam shot me a killer smile. He was good-looking with a

dark, ruddy complexion, big brown eyes, and a jawline so sharp you could break glass with it.

"Good luck," Sam said. "Guy won't talk to any of us."

"Has he asked for a lawyer?"

"Not yet," Sam answered.

"He's been Mirandized?"

Sam canted his head to the side and narrowed his eyes.

"Sorry," I said. "You know I had to ask."

Sam got a text alert. He pulled his phone off the clip on his belt. It always amazed me how those guys could walk upright after a whole shift lugging those things around. Most of them ended up with near debilitating sciatica or worse by the time they retired.

"Your ten minutes are running," Sam said, frowning as he read his text. "Page is on his way here."

"Great," I said.

"You want cameras?" he asked.

"Want? No. But better be safe than sorry. I don't want anyone accusing me of anything."

Sam and I walked to interview room two. He poked his head into the room next to it and made a circular gesture with his finger, cueing another detective to start recording.

I stepped inside. Aaron Clyde had aged a bit from the last mugshots I'd seen of him. He had disheveled gray hair and silver stubble covering his chin. Tattoos snaked up both arms, and he wore a dirty, ripped tee shirt. His mud-caked work boots made a thunderous sound as he nervously tapped his heel against the ground.

I took a seat opposite him and put my pad of paper in front of me. I clicked my pen open. "My name is Mara Brent, Mr. Clyde," I said. "I'm the prosecutor handling the case against Damon and Lyle King. You know they're being retried in the Brinkman/Nadler killings?"

Clyde chewed his thumbnail. He had angry purple sores

down his left arm. He'd been picking at them. A telltale sign of heroin use.

"I said all I gotta say about that," he said. "You gonna violate me?"

"You left town," I said. "You haven't checked in with your parole officer in what, two weeks?"

"I came back," he said. "And I tried to call. That SOB never returns my calls."

I highly doubted any of that. I'd seen a million guys like Aaron Clyde. Something triggered him and he started using again. Maybe it was something simple, like a joint here and there. He got work at a machine shop when he was first paroled. Maybe it was a few beers after work. One thing led to another. Then, before he knew it, his demons had taken full hold again. If I could get him into treatment, maybe there was still hope. For now, Charlie Brinkman and Krista Nadler had to take priority though.

"Mr. Clyde," I said. "I'd like to take your statement again. I have more questions about your time with Lyle King."

"I told you, I got nothing more to say about that. Unless you've got something to offer me."

"I don't have that authority right now," I said.

Clyde leaned back. "Then we're done. You can talk to my lawyer. I still have a right to one, don't I?"

"Of course you do," I said. "As you're processed, we'll make sure you have all the information you need."

There was a loud knock on the door. Sam came back in. Behind him, Trevor Page charged down the hall, red-faced.

"This interview needs to cease immediately," Page said.

I leaned back. "You don't represent him," I said. "Unless you're planning on explaining to your friends at the Servants of Divine Justice how you'll avoid a direct conflict of interest with your existing client."

"You don't say another word, Aaron," Page shouted. "Not a one."

Then he did a thing that shocked me. He jabbed a finger right in Sam's chest. "I want the tapes. I want to know every person who's come into contact with Clyde."

Sam took a step back. I swear, I saw literal steam coming out of his ears. He caught Trevor's finger and twisted it. Trevor's jaw dropped and his whole body contorted.

"You touch me like that again and you're the one who'll spend the night inside a cell."

I rose. "We're done here for now," I said. "Mr. Clyde, you'll be contacted by the public defender's office unless you have a lawyer of your own."

"I want that tape!" Page yelled. He'd backed off Sam.

I slipped the strap of my briefcase over my shoulder. "Then you can file a discovery request like a normal person. Until then, I suggest you get out of my way."

Sam slammed the door, leaving Clyde alone in the interview room. He put a light hand on the small of my back and we walked away from a still fuming Trevor Page.

"The hell was all that about?" Sam said under his breath.

"I have no idea," I said.

"Guy's clearly worried about what Clyde's going to say. I mean, he already told the world Lyle King confessed to those murders. What more damage does he think he'll do?"

"I don't know," I said. But my stomach churned. I didn't like it either. Anytime I had this feeling of impending doom, I was usually right.

For the next six days, everything else in my life had to be put on hold. I wouldn't campaign with Jason. I declined every request for an interview. While rumors swirled around me, I kept my focus solely on two things. Will and the King case. But on Tuesday night, November 6th, all of that came screeching to a halt.

Election Day.

Jason rented out the civic center downtown, where all of his staffers and supporters gathered to watch the returns. I had a quiet dinner with Will at home. The week before, he'd dressed up as a Secret Service agent for trick or treating. Tonight, it was my turn to put on a different costume. I had promised to be by Jason's side as the returns came in.

"Will you call me when you know?" Will asked. He was in the spare bedroom upstairs. His Lego room. He'd finished his homework early and earned himself an extra hour of play. If we let him go too long, he'd be too amped up to fall asleep.

"It'll be way past your bedtime," I said.

"I won't be able to sleep," he said. "I want Dad to win. Don't you?"

The air went out of my lungs. He'd never asked me that before. Did I?

In all of this, I really hadn't thought about it. I'd been so focused on keeping my head above water, doing my job, and making sure Will was as okay as he could be.

"I think your dad will make a very good congressman," I said.

Will tilted his entire body to one side, regarding me. It was a gesture his father made, right when he was about to call me on my BS.

"That's not an answer," he said.

"I don't know," I said. "I know how badly he wants it. And how hard he's worked for it. So, yes, for your dad, I want him to win. For me? I just worry."

"You're afraid of change. That's what Miss Holly says."

Mary Holly was Will's counselor. She'd been working with him for the past three years.

"Change can be hard," I said. "But it's not always bad."

"She says that too."

I reached over and smoothed his hair back. "Miss Holly is smart. You should listen to her."

"I try to," he said. "She doesn't always make sense to me though."

I laughed. "I think that's probably okay too."

"Are you going to be okay?" he asked. His question hit me like a blow to the chest. Here was my nine, almost ten-year-old son worrying about whether I would be okay. He didn't know about Abigail Morgan. We'd kept that ugliness from him. But he knew his parents no longer lived together, and as much as I tried to avoid it, he'd heard us fight. That was the part I hated the most.

"I'm gonna be fine," I said. "We all are."

"You better go," Will said. "Dad needs you tonight. He won't say it, but I know."

Smiling, I leaned in to kiss my son. "You're pretty special. Did you know that, buddy?"

Will's face split. It was lightning quick. He could never hold it. But my son gave me a smile.

"I love you," I said. "And if I get home before midnight, I'll come in and whisper the results in your ear."

"Deal," he said.

Then I left him alone with his Legos. I checked in with our sitter. Kat and my mother were down at the civic center with Jason. The new sitter was a godsend by the name of Lois Calhoun. She was a retired special education teacher from Grantham Elementary, Will's school. She was wonderful with him.

"I'm going to try to be home before midnight," I told Lois. "You're okay with sleeping over if I can't?"

"Of course," she said. She was new to us. I said goodbye and headed out to the garage. Jason had offered to send a car for me, but I wanted to make a getaway on my terms if it came to that.

I used a VIP pass Jason gave me as I pulled into the civic center parking garage. A valet took my car.

"Mrs. Brent!" The cheery voice of a college intern named Paul greeted me at the service entrance. He was one of Jason's. I could tell from his posture Jason might have chewed him out recently, wondering where I was.

"Hi, Paul," I said.

"Mr. Brent's waiting in the kitchen. He wants to go out with you."

"He wants me on his arm," I muttered, low enough that Paul didn't understand.

"Would you like something to drink?" he asked.

That would be Jason, too. Would I need a shot or two to put a smile on my face?

No. Not on your life. I would drive myself home when the time came.

Paul led me down a short hallway and to a sharp right turn. He opened the steel double doors. Jason stood behind them, pacing.

He cracked a smile when he saw me. My husband could take your breath away. Thick, chestnut hair, piercing gray eyes, that cavernous cleft in his chin. Tonight, he looked just like he did when I saw him all those years ago at the end of the aisle at St. Stevens Church in Pembroke, New Hampshire. Then, I'd had my father to lean on. Today, it was only me.

"Sorry I'm late," I said.

"Thank you for doing this."

"It won't matter," I said. "Polls close in an hour."

Jason gave a look to Paul. The kid disappeared back down the hall.

"It matters to me," Jason said, his voice dropping an octave. "Mara, we started this together. If it's a victory, it's yours as much as it is mine. I want to share that with you."

"I know," I said. "It matters for Will too. I want him to know that ... whatever our issues are, we can still support each other."

Jason came to me. He put a chaste kiss on my cheek. It was the closest we'd been in months. He held his hand out for me and I took it.

"Do you have your speech written?" I asked.

"Both of them," he said. "Will you give them one last look?"

We made our way past the kitchen staff. I could hear music playing behind the ballroom doors. Jason had hired a local band, eschewing one of the big name acts his team tried to book. Jason was clear. If he won tonight, he wanted Waynetown to share in it in every way. His hometown. His heart.

A cheer went up. Jason's hand went cold in mine.

The door cracked open and Len Grantham, Jason's

campaign manager, came in, flushed, beaming. Len had been the best man at our wedding in Pembroke all those years ago. He came from one of the oldest and richest founding families in Waynetown. A street and my own son's school was named after Len's second great-grandfather. Jason didn't like to talk about the fact that Len only started becoming his friend *after* Jason found career success. Growing up, Len wouldn't have given a foster kid like Jason the time of day.

"They're calling it," he said. Len's eyes shot from me to Jason.

In those few seconds, Jason's grip tightened on me. It felt like I was literally holding him up.

"They're projecting a twelve-point spread," Len said, staring at his phone. "Jason, you won!"

I turned to him. My smile was genuine. My heart flipped. "Congratulations, Congressman Brent."

Jason threw his arms around me and lifted me off the ground. I couldn't think. I couldn't breathe.

Len threw the ballroom doors opened. I drew in a breath for courage. Then I locked hands with my husband once more as he set me back down. In the wings on the other side of the stage, I saw my mother and Kat. My mom had tears in her eyes as she blew me a kiss. Jason tightened his grip on my hand. Kat and my mom came forward. Mom took my other hand.

"We did it. Darling, we did it! It's only the beginning! Now you can drop all this nonsense and go to Washington where you belong!" Laughing, she touched Jason's face and stepped into the line at my side. I felt like I'd forgotten how to breathe. My mother pulled me from one side. Jason the other.

We walked out on the stage together as red, white, and blue balloons descended from the ceiling.

❧ 13 ❧

There were parties. Receptions. A stream of well-wishers to glad-hand and donors to thank. I left most of that to Jason and my mother. Only in my life could a murder trial provide a welcome escape. Because I had no time to bask in any glow of Jason's victory. It didn't feel like mine, anyway. I had a trial to prepare for. It loomed ever closer.

If anyone had any useful insight into the minds of Damon and Lyle King, it would be Jules Smith. Ten years ago, Phil had hired Dr. Smith to evaluate Lyle ahead of his competency hearing. His original defense lawyer had claimed he lacked the mental capacity to know right from wrong.

Jules was retired now, having spent forty years as a clinical psychologist, then another ten teaching forensic psychology at university level. For the last two decades of his career, he'd been our go-to for criminal psych evaluations.

I met Jules at his condo just outside of Waynetown. He lived alone now, his wife having succumbed to ALS five years ago. His children had moved to various other parts of the country.

Jules's Schnauzer greeted me with incessant yapping at the

screen door. Jules moved in the house and scooped the dog up, cradling it under one arm. The pooch became instantly chill, slathering Jules with kisses.

"Come on in, Mara," he said, then erupted into a fit of coughing. "We'll go back out to the Davenport. I've got all my files set up there."

"Davenport," I said. "Can't say I've heard that term used since the eighties, Jules."

He waved me off and waddled his way through the house. I followed him to his screened-in porch overlooking his extensive, tree-lined backyard. He had two telescopes set up in one corner and matching floral Rutan furniture. I took a seat in an armchair.

"Help yourself," Jules said. He had a pitcher of lemonade on the table with two frosted glasses. I did as I was told.

Jules took the seat opposite me and put his dog on the ground. "This is Fritz. He's kind of a jerk until you get to know him. Sort of like me."

"Hello, Fritz," I said. Fritz sniffed my leg, then trotted off and curled up under the couch in the corner.

Jules had a banker's box on the floor by his feet, filled with dog-eared files. He pulled one out and slapped it on the table.

"I gave Phil copies of everything in here," he said.

"Thank you," I said. "I still have it. It's been very helpful. But I wanted to talk in person, get your recollections."

"Are we gonna lose you?" Jules asked. In my dealings with Jules, I'd known him to abruptly jump between topics. To the uninitiated, it could sound like riddle-speak. I was, thankfully, well initiated.

"Because of Jason's win?"

Jules nodded. "Cuz that would be a heck of a blow. My spies tell me you've been the backbone of the office for years, anyway. It's a good fit for you. And it's a good fit for Kenya too."

"I hope she can keep the job," I said. "A lot of that will

depend on what happens with the Kings."

"Yep," he said. "I don't know what the hell Phil was thinking with that one. Such a stupid mistake."

"Jules, I need your gut. I need you to tell me what I need to know about Lyle and Damon."

I took a sip of lemonade. It was a little tarter than I liked, kind of like Jules. But it was good. The real stuff.

"I met with Lyle five times," he said. "For maybe an hour at a time. His court-appointed lawyer was there too. Kid was an idiot and let me get away with far more than I should have. Nothing that would have changed my opinion on his competency, but he never had control of his client. Damon always did."

"I really think I'm seeing the same dynamic with the new trial. Trevor Page is the one calling the shots on that defense team. I think Lyle's got a lawyer on paper only. Just to keep Trevor from any ethics complaints."

Jules nodded, then dove right into the meat of the subject. "Lyle's an interesting case. Hard to form a clinical diagnosis. He tests within the low average range on all the traditional IQ tests. Though, I don't always put much stock in those. He's got what we call an executive functioning disorder. Even that is a nebulous term. It's often part of a spectrum disorder."

"I'm aware of a lot of the nomenclature," I said. *Aware* was a loose word. I'd been to so many IEP meetings for Will, I felt like I had another doctoral degree in the stuff myself. "Lyle has difficulty making decisions for himself."

"Yeah, that's a simple way to put it. He relies on Damon for just about everything. I'm going to assume that's been even more true since they have institutionalized him. Lyle is physically stronger. But he only ever got violent when he was protecting Damon, not himself. Damon makes all the decisions, Lyle acts as Damon's bodyguard. They were entirely codependent."

"Did Damon ever come to any of the sessions you had with Lyle?"

"He did, though I never allowed him in the room with us. Damon drove Lyle. The kid had a lot of trouble getting his own driver's license. He tried to take it a few times. Failed. He'd drive anyway, though, without one. Lyle doesn't do well with too many pieces of information coming at him at once. He fixates. Like he'd blow through stop signs because he was focused on staying right of the centerline."

"Did you ever see him lose his temper?" I asked.

"I saw him agitated. Once, I was running late. Our session started ten minutes past the time it was supposed to, so I was going to end ten minutes longer. Lyle started to sweat. Kept saying Damon needed him back. He didn't want to keep his brother waiting."

"Do you think Damon abused Lyle?"

Jules shrugged. "I asked him. He said Damon never hurt him. It was evasive, to say the least. My suspicion was that he had, but that in Lyle's mind, he deserved it."

"What about their parents?" I asked. "I know their father was never really around. I understand the mother passed away some years ago."

"She had a rough way," Jules said. "Stomach cancer. It was actually Lyle who took care of her during the worst of it. He was eighteen when she died. Damon was twenty. After that, it was just the two of them."

"Have they brought you up to speed on how they've coped in prison?" I asked.

Jules set his lemonade down. "I could have predicted it. Now, you need to understand that a lot of my opinions are conjecture. I'd never be able to testify about them since I've never seen Damon in a clinical setting. I'm telling you what I believe based on my experience with Lyle."

"Jules," I said. "You were a godsend during the first trial.

Phil always said he would have lost the competency hearing if it weren't for you."

"Yeah," he said. "I suppose that's true. Lyle's construct of right and wrong centers on Damon's moral compass, or lack thereof. If Damon says something's right, it doesn't matter what society says. Lyle will do whatever he has to to protect Damon. He's the perfect minion."

"He's fully emotionally dependent on Damon," I said.

"He is. He really believes it's him and Damon against the world. I couldn't break through that. Neither could his two-bit public defender. He fired him at Damon's say-so. I think if Lyle could have separated himself from Damon, he'd be in a state hospital right now, not prison. It's what he needs. But that was the double-edged sword of that competency hearing. He's a killer, I have no doubt of that. It's just the ruling to allow him to stand trial also made it so he couldn't successfully extricate himself from Damon's culpability. They're forever intertwined. Now, if you could find a way to break them apart now, if Lyle cared about protecting himself or someone else more than Damon well, that'd be something."

"That's a dead end for me," I said. "Lyle's not talking so far."

Jules snorted. "It's a shame. I'm not saying Lyle should be a free man. God, no. But he could have benefited from specialized help. Damon makes that impossible."

"He's built a new congregation inside," I said.

"Of course he has," Jules said. "He's got a literal messiah complex, Mara. Church of the Living Flame. Baptism by fire. He sold that crap to the lost souls of Waynetown. Made them think it was the only way to let the Holy Spirit into their lives. Talk to Evelyn Bishop. She was crucial in the original trial. Damon's bookkeeper. She came to the same conclusion about how dangerous Damon was becoming."

"So you don't think he believes it himself?" I asked. "That he has the power to save all these lost souls?"

"I do not," Jules answered. "I think it's the most powerful way Damon found to feed his own ego. Who knows, maybe he's even convinced himself it's true now. If you challenge him, that's when you'll see the true Damon. He's got to be smarter than everyone. I don't even think he cares whether or not he goes back to prison. As long as there are people lining up to worship him, he's content. Even if you win, he'll claim victory."

"I'm not worried about claiming victory," I said. "I'm worried he's going to start killing again."

Jules leveled a withering gaze at me. "So am I. Because I'm telling you, that's a when, not an if."

Jules's words sent a chill through my bones.

"That kill list," Jules said. "That was just the beginning. Sinners in his mind. Charlie and Krista had to burn for the sin of fornication. A few of the others were business owners Damon felt needed to check their greed."

"The mayor and a few members of city council were also on that list," I said.

"You think he stopped there?" Jules said.

"What do you mean?"

"I mean, I'd bet my reputation on the fact Damon King's been adding to that list this whole time. Maybe he's not dumb enough to commit it to paper again, but he's got one. Believe me. I'm probably on it."

"You're not even a little bit bothered by that?"

"Hell, no," Jules said. "I'd consider it a badge of honor. And I'm ready."

Before I could ask what he meant, Jules pulled out his phone and opened an app. He had feeds from security cameras all around the house. He clicked one showing my car pulling up his driveway.

"No one's getting in or out of here without me knowing about it. I send out for groceries. If those boys don't go back to prison after all this, I'll sell this house and move down to Florida with my youngest. She's been at me to for years."

"Jules, I had no idea ..."

"You haven't asked," he said.

"Asked what?"

"You haven't asked me whether I think they really did this thing."

"I thought I did," I said. "I thought that was obvious."

"I'm telling you, they did. I've never in my entire career been able to say that with one hundred percent certainty. With those two, I can. Damon was just getting warmed up. Charlie and Krista were an opening act. He would have gotten smarter."

"Jules, there's just one thing that doesn't make sense. You said Lyle's driving motivation is to protect Damon. So why would he put him at risk by confessing to killing those two to Aaron Clyde?"

Jules flapped his hands against his knees. "At the time, Lyle and Damon had been separated for a couple of weeks. That was probably the smartest thing Phil did, arranging that. Lyle got scared. Lost focus. Aaron Clyde, from what I understand, is a pretty Alpha-type personality. And smart. He knew if he could get Lyle to admit to something, he'd be able to leverage it for himself. They were alone together for what, three or four days? Then as soon as Damon got a hold of him again, Lyle clammed up. And now, they've been in the clink together for ten years. If anything, I'd say Damon's hold over Lyle is even stronger."

"I think you're right."

"Honey, I'm always right," Jules said, winking at me. But there was an ominous undertone to his words. If I lost this case. If Lyle and Damon King were free to kill again. Jules believed it so much he was willing to uproot his entire life to get as far away from the King brothers as possible. I wondered if my name would then be at the top of their kill list.

❧ 14 ❧

I tried to keep things as normal as I could for Will over the next few weeks. Jason stayed at the house on the weekends. I spent most of that time at the office working on trial prep, so we barely saw each other. Will was quietly happy for his father. So was I. But a simple, unspoken question hung between us. When Jason took a residence in Washington, would Will or I be going with him?

On Christmas Day, my mother ended up asking the question. She waited until Will and Jason left to go sledding at a park nearby. Jason planned to leave first thing in the morning and stay in D.C. indefinitely.

My mother sat in the living room, sipping a glass of red wine. The tree lights twinkled, and I had yet to clean up the carnage of wrapping paper on the floor.

"When are you going to end this nonsense?" she asked.

I brought in a garbage bag and started gathering the torn and crumpled paper. "Don't start," I said.

"You're really not coming to Jason's swearing-in next week?" she asked.

"I am not," I said. "I'm needed here."

She set her wineglass down. Natalie Montleroy was a stunning woman. Without a stitch of makeup, her skin was smooth, even without so much as a wrinkle. She attributed it to good genes and a skilled plastic surgeon, but from across the room, she could have passed for someone thirty years younger.

"You can have anything you want," she said. "You know that, right?"

I sat back on my heels. "What makes you think I don't have what I want here?" I asked.

"In Waynetown?" She made a sweeping gesture with her arms. "Mara, be serious."

"I am serious," I said.

"You came here kicking and screaming," she said. "I remember. I was the one who had to convince you to think big picture back then. Well, I'm doing that again. You have no future here."

"I have a life here," I said. "Will has a life."

"No family. Do you think Kat will stick around? Jason's already offered her a job in D.C. You can't expect her to just be your babysitter forever."

"Mom," I said. "Things have changed. I've changed. The things I thought I wanted ten years ago aren't the same anymore. I thought Jason was someone else."

She closed her eyes. When she opened them again, she fixed a killer stare at me. "They never are."

"I like what I do," I said.

"And what? You're happy working for someone else your whole life? You want to be some low-level public servant? Mara, you have so many gifts. So many other opportunities that might come your way."

"I think I'm using my gifts the best way I can, Mom. That's the thing. Believe me, it ended up coming as a shock to me too. But I love these people. My work is hard. Grueling. But it fulfills me. It feels like ... my calling."

She gritted her teeth. "You want to live your life making a sixty-thousand-dollar-a-year county salary?"

"There are more important things than money," I said.

"Only people who have it say that. All of this. Your house. This life. Will's school. You have it because of *my* money," she said. I refrained from pointing out that she had done nothing to amass my family's wealth on her own. She'd grown up relying on the Vinton Roth trust fund until my grandfather squandered most of our family's old money in a bribery scandal. He narrowly avoided federal prison. She now lived on funds my father amassed as a software developer before he died. Natalie Montleroy spent her life trying to convince people her wealth was still old, as if new money was the worst stain one could have on their reputation.

"You're not listening to me," I said. "I told you. I'm happy doing what I do for a living. It's what I'm built for."

"You sound just like your father," she said. "He was happier in that god-awful computer lab than anywhere else. If it weren't for me, we would have no power at all."

I smiled. She threw out the comparison to my dad as if I'd take it as an insult. He worked for every penny we had and became a multimillionaire by the time he was twenty-five after he sold some of the very first encryption software to the government. My smile faded as I wondered whether my mother would have even given Ford Montleroy the time of day if he hadn't already been rich.

"I'm not interested in power. And I'm not interested in staying in a lie of a marriage just because it looks good in the media."

She flounced in her seat. I remembered her doing that to my dad when he told her no. I also remembered what usually came next and my smile came back.

"Are you sure this is what you want?" she asked.

I leaned over and touched her arm. "I'm not a hundred

percent sure of anything. Except Will will always come first. And now I come second. Not Jason's career. Mine. My happiness. I love you, Mom. I know you're scared. I know you watched everything you had planned for yourself vanish when Grandpa got arrested. That won't happen to me."

"Do you think I've betrayed you?" she asked.

The question seemed to come out of nowhere. "What?"

"You think I'm taking Jason's side? Well, I'm not. I'm on your side, Mara. Always. It's just ... I can see down the road. I don't want you to be left with nothing."

"No," I said. "That's not what I think. But please, believe me when I tell you. My happiness is no longer connected to Jason. I'm building something else. For me. For Will."

Her eyes darted over my face. She touched my cheek. "Oh honey. Are you sure?"

"Yes," I said. "I don't know exactly what I'm going to decide. I just know what it is I want to fight for now."

She wrapped her arms around me. "Okay."

I felt a physical release in her as she said the word. I hadn't realized she'd been holding on so tightly.

"Okay?" I repeated.

"Okay," she said. "I am on your side. And Will's. If this life is what you want, then you can be damn sure I'll help you keep it."

There was fire in my mother's eyes. No matter her flaws, Natalie Montleroy was a tiger when it came to protecting those she loved. If I got my work ethic from my dad, I knew I got my heart from her.

❧ 15 ❧

Sunday night, January 6th, I met with my team in the office on the eve of trial in the Brinkman/Nadler murders.

Melody extended her internship for a second semester. Kenya found room in the budget to pay her. Steve the intern did not work out. We assembled in the war room. I sat at the head of the conference table as everyone else was in motion.

Kenya paced. Melody sat on the floor arranging exhibits for about the seventh time. Hojo ran in and out of the room, making last calls to witnesses at my behest. I had one more I wanted to talk to before this train started rolling. I'd spoken to Stephanie Nadler but wanted another call with the Brinkmans before morning. They were due to call at any minute.

"It's solid," Kenya said. "I mean, it's solid."

"If Clyde doesn't go south," I said. It was a huge if.

"Any sign that he might?" Hojo asked.

"None," I said. "His deposition last month was tight. He changed barely a word from his initial statement to the police ten years ago or his testimony from the first trial. And we aren't offering him any kind of deal on his parole violation. He's already been sentenced. He's doing another ninety days in county and getting five years tacked on to his probation."

"It's solid," Kenya said again. Her nerves weren't helping mine. This was uncharacteristic for her. The weight of her office was starting to strain. She faced her own election to retain her position in August. If we lost the King trial, it could be her political death.

"Lyle confessed," I said. "Clyde knows details about the murders that could only have come from him. No matter what happens with Sierra Joy, that's the deal. We've got Damon King's kill list with Charlie Brinkman and Krista Nadler's names on it. We've got an airtight search warrant. Gus Ritter did this case by the book. That list is coming in."

"It all comes down to Sierra," Kenya said. "If the jury believes her ... we're sunk."

"I still like my case better than Trevor Page's," I said. "And we're not hiding anything, no matter how much Trevor tries to paint that picture. You've gone out of your way to cooperate with the attorney general's office on the Halsey inquiry."

"We're behind you," Hojo said. "Kenya, you know that."

"Thanks," she said. "But it's Mara we need to be behind right now. I gotta be honest. I don't care about my prospects. I mean, I do. The voters might want to use me to punish Phil. I get that. But this case ... it's the one that stuck, you know? If we can't score another conviction ..."

Kenya met my eyes, and her face fell. "I'm sorry," she said. "That's not helping."

"It's okay," I said. "And I appreciate it. We're a team. I'll be relying on all of you."

Hojo popped his head in again. I hadn't even noticed him leave. "Brinkmans on the line," he said, nodding toward the phone on the table.

I pressed the speaker button.

"Charlie? Sharon?" I said.

"It's just Charlie," Charlie Brinkman answered. His voice was low, tired and haggard sounding.

"I just wanted to touch base with you both one more time," I said. Melody took a seat quietly beside me with a pen poised over a notepad, ready to write anything down I needed.

"Sharon's ... she's just too upset to talk," Charlie said. This had been a running theme. So far, Sharon had refused to meet with me other than to tell me she had nothing to add to what she said at the first trial. I felt terrible for even asking.

"I understand," I said. "But I would like to go over her testimony one more time. I don't plan on calling her first, but later in the week for sure."

"It's ... uh ... Ms. Brent ... we ran into Damon King today."

I met Kenya's eyes. Melody started writing.

"Where?" I asked.

"We were doing some shopping," Charlie said. "Sharon wanted to return some Christmas gifts. Damon was outside one store talking to a crowd. You'd think he was Jesus or something. He even had a camera crew. He tried ... he really rattled her. Told her he had forgiveness in his heart. He told her she'd had her retribution. Crazy talk."

"I'm so sorry that happened. Are you all right?" I asked.

"Just pretty shook up," Charlie said, his voice breaking. "Sharon blames herself for so much. Charlie Jr. was our life, you know? She hasn't slept a full night since this happened. She keeps going over and over what it must have been like for him. Did he call out for her? Was he scared? Is he in heaven? That's the thing that haunts her the most. Did he ask for forgiveness in the end? Was he absolved? It gets so I can't take it anymore. Ms. Brent, this trial might be the end of us. I don't know how much longer I can do this."

I dropped my head. The Brinkmans' pain was unfathomable. Almost unthinkable.

"Mr. Brinkman," I said. "Would it help if you had someone with you? I can talk to the sheriff's office and ..."

"No," he said. "We just, I don't see us going out again anytime soon. Not while those two are out there. And as soon as this thing is over, one way or the other, we're leaving for our home in Florida. At least I am. I don't know about Sharon."

"I understand," I said. "And thank you. But will you talk to Sharon about meeting with me this week? I really think it'll help."

"I'll try," he said. "I can promise you that."

"Thank you," I said. We spent the next hour going over Charlie's testimony. He would help establish part of the time-line. Later, if the Kings were convicted again, he would deliver a victim's impact statement. I fully believed him that their marriage might not survive it.

Finally, I hung up and looked at my team. They looked as drained as I felt. Kenya stood alone at the back of the room, her expression sober, but determined.

"What do you need?" Kenya asked.

I took a moment. I let the silence settle over all of us. Krista Nadler and Charlie Brinkman's senior pictures loomed large, smiling down at us from the top of the whiteboard. I closed my eyes. I don't know if I believed in ghosts. Spirits, maybe. But at that moment, I swear I could feel Charlie and Krista in the room.

I opened my eyes and looked at my team.

"I'm ready," I said, rising out of my chair. "I'll see you all tomorrow morning."

I left the room, feeling Charlie and Krista's eyes boring into my soul.

❧ 16 ❧

Judge Ivey took a casual posture, chewing on the end of his pen as I stepped up to the lectern. He waved the thing at me, almost as if bored. He'd done me no favors on voir dire, shooting down half of my challenges for cause. My strategy was to put as many parents in the jury box as I could. I got four out of twelve.

I folded my hands and rested them on the lectern and faced the jury.

"Ladies and gentlemen," I said. "Over the next two weeks, I'm going to ask you to do something that may very well be the hardest thing you've ever had to do. What happened to Charlie Brinkman and Krista Nadler represents every parent's, every *person's* worst nightmare. The evidence will show they weren't just killed, though that would be awful enough. They were brutalized. Tortured. Krista Nadler's most severe injuries happened while she was still alive. She suffered. They filled her last moments on this earth with unspeakable agony while the boy she loved had to watch. Unable to save her. Unable to protect her. Unable to comfort her. And then he drew his own last breaths while fire consumed him.

"For what? You'll ask yourselves why. You may cry out for the answers. I know I have. Charlie Brinkman was a good kid. A good son. He volunteered as a youth leader at his church. He coached community ed soccer. A straight-A student. A star football player. He had a bright future ahead of him. He was just starting to figure out what that future could hold.

"Krista Nadler had a tougher start to her life. She was raised by a single mom who loved her more than anything else in this world. Krista, too, was a leader. A drum major. She was the kid everyone in her neighborhood wanted to hire to babysit their kids. She would meet you with a smile, no matter if she knew you or not. She loved animals. She wanted to be a veterinarian. She wanted to earn enough money to support her mother, to repay her for all the sacrifices Stephanie Nadler made to secure Krista's future. What seventeen-year-old girl thinks that way?

"Krista Nadler did."

I stepped beside the lectern, holding my hands folded in front of me. "Charlie and Krista had their whole lives in front of them. They were two sweet kids who loved each other. Until one night, evil had other plans. These two men, Damon and Lyle King, played the part of the devil. They targeted Charlie and Krista for reasons we may never comprehend. They dragged these two innocent kids out of their car. They bound them. Forced them to their knees.

"Krista was beaten over every inch of her body. She was broken. Bleeding. They doused her body with kerosene. Then Lyle King lit a match and set her on fire.

"Then it was Charlie's turn," I said. In the front row, two members of the jury winced. Mothers, both of them.

"It will be hard for you to hear," I said. "We must hear them. Because only then can we do right by Charlie and Krista. Only then can we bring their killers ... their executioners to justice. By the time you hear the testimony, see the evidence, experience Charlie and Krista's last moments on earth, there will be only one just verdict. One irrefutable outcome. Damon and Lyle King must pay for their crimes. Thank you."

I turned. Stephanie Nadler sat in the back of the courtroom. She was flanked on either side by women I knew well. Betsy Silver and Collete Holmes. They were both founding members of the Silver Angels victim support and advocacy group. They would not leave Stephanie's side until they rendered the verdict. She was in excellent hands. Charlie and Sharon Brinkman did not come to court today. When the Silver Angels reached out to them, Sharon turned them away.

I walked back to the prosecution table. I took a path straight in front of Damon and Lyle King. Damon met my eyes. His face remained expressionless. He wore a tailored, designer black suit. Manicured hands. A clean shave. Lord. He could have been a movie star.

Beside him, Lyle had a completely different vibe. His suit, tailored and expensive. Still, it looked like it wore him instead of the other way around. His hair, though brushed and styled with product, stuck out in peaks at the side. He kept his eyes cast downward. When he looked up, it was toward Damon. Damon used a slight gesture, waving his hand across the table. If Lyle meant to whisper something to his brother, Damon stopped it.

He controlled him. Even now. I hoped the jury could see.

I took my seat at the table, crossed my legs and waited. Trevor Page buttoned his jacket as he rose and faced the jury.

❦

"GOOD AFTERNOON," HE STARTED. "MY NAME IS TREVOR Page. I represent Mr. Damon King. You probably already know of him and his brother. Many of you told me you read about this case in the news back when it happened. It horrified you. We were all horrified. It is horrifying. Ms. Brent is right about all of that. Krista Nadler and Charlie Brinkman deserve justice for what happened to them."

He paused. He looked over at Damon and Lyle. Trevor rested his palm on the lectern as he side-stepped it.

"But the King brothers deserve justice too. I can't equate what happened to them to the horrors Krista and Charlie faced. I won't insult your intelligence or your hearts that way. But both Damon and Lyle are victims of this crime, too.

"Because they are innocent. The only thing they are guilty of is the fact that they made easy villains for an overzealous and corrupt prosecutor who was trying to further his own career.

"Philip Halsey tried this case for the State almost ten years ago. Ten years. Lyle and Damon have sat in prison for a crime they didn't commit. You will hear how Mr. Halsey engineered evidence against the Kings. Fabricated it. Hid evidence that would have exonerated my client and his brother in violation of the oath he swore when he became a prosecutor. When he became a lawyer.

"Damon and Lyle were in the wrong place at the wrong time with the wrong names. Are they perfect men? They are not. Who among us is? Did they make mistakes? Let evil into their hearts? They did. We all do. But they did not kill Krista and Charlie. Their killers are still out there somewhere. Among us, maybe. Every second we spend trying to crucify Damon King and Lyle King does those poor kids a disservice. It heaps one tragedy after another. It's up to us, me and all of you, to make sure that doesn't happen.

"Mr. Halsey murdered those kids a second time in a way. That may sound harsh. But when a brave witness came forward and told him the truth, Mr. Halsey made sure he silenced her voice. You'll meet that witness. Her name is Sierra Joy. When you hear what she has to say, you'll understand. It will make you heartsick. And angry.

"You know what keeps me up at night? It's the knowledge

that Krista and Charlie's killers are still out there somewhere. They might have killed again. They might still kill again. Maybe it's happening now in some town not unlike Waynetown. Maybe there are other innocent kids going for a drive, thinking they have their futures ahead of them. And they don't know what evil awaits them.

"Phil Halsey is to blame for that. But you'll have a chance to save them. You'll have a chance to send a message to the Maumee County criminal justice system and make them do right by Charlie and Krista and those unsuspecting kids who might be out there right now. You're the only ones who can. Think about that. When you listen to the prosecution's witnesses in this case. When you finally understand what Phil Halsey did to those poor kids. Know that you have a chance to stop him from hurting any other kids.

"This case isn't just about what happened to Charlie and Krista. It should be. But Phil Halsey made sure that would never happen. He let the town, the country, believe he'd secured justice for them. Instead, he let the actual killers go free.

"Ms. Brent wants you to be Charlie and Krista's voice. I want more than that. I want you to be the voice for every other victim that suffered or will suffer at the hands of a monster they haven't caught yet."

Trevor pounded on the lectern. He had the jury's undivided attention. One of the two mothers in the front row had tears in her eyes. Trevor directed his gaze straight at her.

He was good. It was a smart play, making them think they could be complicit in Phil's misdeeds. It's what I would have done were I in Trevor's shoes. Still, as I stared at Damon King from across the room, I knew in my heart he was everything the press said he was. I looked into the eyes of a demon.

Page took his seat. Noel Stamford's short opening statement on Lyle's behalf amounted to little more than "what he

said." Trevor Page was the big gun on that side of the courtroom and everyone knew it, even the jury. When he finished,
Damon finally broke my gaze. Judge Ivey sat up straight now.

"Ms. Brent," he said. "If you're ready, you may call your first
witness."

❧ 17 ❧

I could have called Sierra Joy to the stand first. It's what Howard wanted me to do. It made for sound legal strategy. Get her up there first, rip the Band-Aid off. Let the jury forget about her as the trial wore on.

I didn't do any of that. I knew in my heart the jury *had* to understand what happened to Charlie and Krista above all else. I wanted the victims in the forefront of their minds for now, not the killers.

So, I called Deena Wilburn to the stand.

Deena dressed simply in a navy-blue pant suit. She had closely cropped, light-brown hair and a weathered face from too much sun. It made her look older than her thirty-four years. Her shoes squeaked as she climbed into the witness box and turned to take her oath.

"Good morning, Ms. Wilburn," I said. "I'd like to take you back to the afternoon of August 12th, 2008. Can you tell the jury what you did that day?"

Deena leaned forward and cleared her throat. "I was working in field operations for the Maumee County sheriff's department."

"You were a deputy," I said.

"Yes, ma'am. I worked the day shift. Eight a.m. to four p.m."

"How long had you worked for the department at that time?" I asked.

"I graduated from the state police academy the preceding November. So, I guess I had roughly nine months on the job."

"If you recall," I said, "did you have occasion to take a call to the Belitzer Quarry that afternoon?"

"Yes, ma'am."

"Would you mind explaining to the jury how that came about?"

Deena adjusted the microphone, bringing it closer to her face so she could sit more comfortably. "I was dispatched to the quarry at approximately 1600 hours. At roll call that morning, they advised us of a missing persons case. There was a search party forming. I patrolled the area closest to the quarry. Richmond Avenue to LaMond Street. I'd taken a few minor calls that day. There was a stalled motorist on Richmond. I helped arrange for a tow. I did a welfare check on an intoxicated individual at the hardware store on LaMond. As I was finishing up from that, they dispatched me to the quarry. There'd been an anonymous tip called in reporting suspicious activity in the woods surrounding the quarry. I was the closest unit, so I went."

"Can you explain what you did when you arrived at the quarry?"

"The quarry itself was open to the public. There were approximately a dozen swimmers enjoying the water that day. There was a lifeguard on duty. I believe his name was Fender. Jermaine Fender? I'd have to check my report to verify that ... um, to refresh my recollection. May I?"

"You may," I said. Over my shoulder, I watched Trevor Page. He was busy scribbling notes back and forth with Damon King.

Lyle picked at his thumb and looked downright bored. Noel Stamford looked ready to throw up.

"Yes," Deena answered. "Jermaine Fender is the name of the lifeguard on duty that day. I asked him if he knew about the two missing persons, Charlie Brinkman and Krista Nadler. I asked him if he knew them personally or recognized them. We had been given a flyer with their school pictures at roll call."

"Did Mr. Fender know them?"

"No," Deena answered. "He said he knew of them, but that neither of them had come out to swim that day. Fender had been on duty since the quarry opened. At that time, and today still, it closes to the public at six p.m."

"What did you do next?" I asked.

"I asked a few of the other swimmers if they saw or knew the whereabouts of Brinkman or Nadler. No one did. A few of the kids out there knew who Charlie and Krista were, but they hadn't seen them. Then I started toward the woods behind the quarry. I knew that the woods at the Blitz ... the Belitzer are a known hangout for kids after dark. They're not supposed to be out there. In those days, there was even a barbed wire fence that was meant to deter entry to the woods from the quarry. But kids used to climb over it. Now they've installed a high chain-link fence."

"Then what happened?" I asked.

"I went through the trail on the north end of the woods. There was some trash on the ground. Beer bottles. Food wrappers, that kind of thing. But none of it looked fresh. The wrappers, for example, were sun bleached and barely readable.

"I called out for Charlie and Krista. I got no response. I made my way south. The wooded area actually leads up to a fairly steep hill. There's a clearing at the top of it. And there's a sort of winding trail at the bottom. Kids sometimes drive their cars through there."

"What did you find?" I asked.

"I found an abandoned vehicle parked at an angle at the base of the hill. A Ford Ranger. It was parked in an east-west orientation. I called in the plate number and immediately verified the vehicle was registered to Charlie Brinkman Sr. I couldn't see any keys in the ignition so I assumed or hoped maybe the kids were nearby asleep or something."

"Then what did you do?"

"I called for backup. I could smell ... something smelled burned higher up the hill. I could still see a bit of smoke rising through the trees. I radioed my location and ran up the hill toward the smoke."

"Why did you do that?" I asked.

"I was worried at that point. I don't know. Something just didn't seem right. I had a reasonable belief that whoever was up there might be injured."

"What happened next?" I asked.

Deena Wilburn trembled. She took a moment and a sip of water. Then she looked me in the eye and continued.

"When I reached the top of the hill, I found two figures on the ground. The first, the one closest to me on the south portion of the hill, was lying on its side."

"Its?" I asked.

Deena's eyelids fluttered. "At first glance, I couldn't tell if I was looking at a man or a woman. It was a body. Charred black. All the hair was burned off the head. The face ... it wasn't there. Everything was just ... smashed in where there should have been a nose or eyes. The clothes were completely burned away. The skin was black and red. Then I noticed shoes. She was wearing green flip-flops. One of them hadn't been burned away. And on that foot, I noticed she had purple toenail polish. Her ankles were bound with what looked like plastic tubing. Her hands were tied behind her and looped through the bindings on her ankles. She'd been hog-tied."

A member of the jury gasped.

"What else did you observe?" I asked.

"There was a second figure a few feet to the north. At first, I mean, for a second, I thought maybe he was still alive. He was ... still kneeling upright.

"I ran over to him and asked if he was Charlie. When I got close, I could see the second individual was also dead. Also hog-tied, but like I said, kneeling upright. He was facing the body of the girl. He had a face, but his eyes, nose, lips, were all burned away."

Deena broke. Tears streamed down her face. She took a tissue from the box next to Judge Ivey.

"Ms. Wilburn," I said. "I know this is hard, but I'm going to have to ask you to look at the photographs that have been marked for identification. Can you do that for me?"

Deena set her tissue down and picked up the six crime scene photographs. She cried as she looked at them one by one.

"Do you recognize what's in those photos?" I asked.

"Yes," she said, her tone flat. "I could never, ever forget it."

"Are those pictures a true and accurate representation of the crime scene as you found it on the afternoon of August 12th?"

"It is," she said. "The crime scene tape. I put it there. That's the next thing I did after determining Charlie Brinkman was also dead. I taped off the area and immediately got back on the radio and called for a detective and the crime scene unit to come out."

"Your Honor, I'd like to now move for admission of exhibits one through six."

Trevor didn't object. I motioned to Melody. She clicked a key on my laptop. The crime scene photos popped up on the screen behind Deena's head.

I let the jury absorb the scene to the extent anyone can. One woman in the back looked like she might get sick. She recovered and raised her chin.

"Then what did you do?" I asked Deena.

"I waited," she said. "I made sure the scene stayed secure. My backup arrived just as I was taping off the area. The detective, um, Detective Ritter arrived at approximately 4:44 p.m. I turned the scene over to him."

"Thank you," I said. "I have nothing further."

"Mr. Page?"

"Thank you. Ms. Wilburn, thank you for indulging me just a few questions. I can see how difficult this is for you. To clarify. You said you'd only been with the sheriff's office for nine months when you rolled up on the Brinkman/Nadler crime scene?"

"Yes."

"And you were by yourself? You walked through that crime scene with no supervision?"

"I properly secured the crime scene," she answered. "And one-person crews are standard for that area of town. Still are, as I understand."

"As you understand," he said. "You're not with the sheriff's office anymore, are you?"

"No, sir," she said.

"Isn't it true you didn't last much longer than that day in August 2008?"

"Objection as to form," I said.

"Sustained."

"Ms. Wilburn," Trevor said. "Isn't it true you took a leave of absence from the department in February of the following year citing emotional distress? You were on disability for it."

"Yes," she said. "For a time."

"You were no longer fit for duty?"

"I needed ... I was diagnosed with post-traumatic stress disorder in the months following the Brinkman/Nadler murders. I wouldn't say I was unfit for duty. Not at all. But that day ... what I saw. Mr. Page, there's a reason I didn't need to refer to my report from ten years ago. Because I still remember every single detail of that day. It's seared into my memory forever. I don't care if we're doing this ten years later or fifty. I will never forget."

"So you left the department because you couldn't handle the job anymore, isn't that true?"

"Objection," I said. "This is irrelevant."

Deena was openly weeping now. My heart went out to her. I hope the jury's did too. Trevor risked overplaying his hand if he kept coming at her this hard. They too were still dealing with the trauma of those photographs. I wanted them to imagine what it would have been like to be inches away from those bodies the way Deena Wilburn had been.

"I'll allow it," Ivey said.

"I could handle the job fine," Deena said. "I just didn't want to anymore. After that day … I didn't want something like that to be my job anymore. So if you're asking me whether the murder of those two kids directly impacted my decision to leave the sheriff's office, yes, it did. But it wasn't because I couldn't do my job."

"Thank you," Trevor said. "I'm finished with this witness for now."

"Mr. Stamford?" Judge Ivey asked.

Noel leaned over to Lyle. Lyle shrugged in response to whatever question he'd been asked.

"Nothing from me, Your Honor."

"Ms. Brent?"

"Nothing further, Your Honor."

"You may step down," the judge said.

Deena Wilburn slowly rose. She wiped her tears as she came down from the witness stand and passed those crime scene photos, hopefully for the last time.

"The State calls Evelyn Bishop to the stand," I said. In the first trial, Mrs. Bishop had been one of the biggest nails in Lyle and Damon King's coffin. Everyone in town knew Evelyn. She'd been a lunch lady at Waynetown Junior High. When her position got eliminated because of a millage failure, she went to work at the Maumee County Public Library. She'd sung in the church choir and coordinated mobile meals for the homeless until it got too hard for her to drive anymore.

She was now eighty-three years old with a thin, frail build and advancing Parkinson's. She walked with a cane and refused any help from the bailiff when she climbed into the witness box.

She took a moment, adjusted her glasses, then planted the foot of her cane in front of her, signaling her readiness to start.

"Good morning, Mrs. Bishop," I said. "Thank you for being here."

She looked straight at me, then let her gaze veer toward Damon and Lyle King. There was disappointment in her eyes, perhaps even a tear starting to form. After everything that happened, she told me she still felt guilty for breaking a promise she'd once made regarding "the boys," as she called them.

"I'm doing what I have to," she said, more to them than to me.

"Of course," I said. "Mrs. Bishop, can you tell the jury how you know Lyle and Damon King?"

Her eyelids fluttered. She'd told this story so many times before. To the police. At the first trial. To the media.

"I've known Damon and Lyle since they were little kids. I was a friend of their mama, Patrice King. She sang in the choir with me at Holy Reformer out on Flannery Road. It's not there anymore. It got absorbed by that mega-church out on 280. I won't go there. Too showy. I need a good sermon, not laser lights."

Soft laughter worked its way through the gallery. A couple of the jurors smiled. She'd worked this same magic ten years ago when she took the stand.

"How close were you?" I asked.

"To Patrice? She was one of my best friends. And she had her hands full with those two. Their daddy wasn't around. Took off not long after Lyle was born. Patrice had to work to keep a roof over their head or food on the table. So whenever one of them got sick, I'd step in and sit with them while she went to work. It wasn't easy for her. Those boys were wild, to say the least. Wouldn't mind."

"I understand," I said. "What about after Patrice King passed away?"

"They were older by then. I think Lyle had just turned eighteen. So they were living on their own. Patrice took real bad sick. I'd bring them meals. Helped Lyle get a job at the machine shop where my Terry used to work. Sweeping floors and the like. I lost track of them for a bit through those years. I mean, I checked in from time to time, just to make sure they were making ends meet."

"Did there come a point that you became reacquainted?"

"Yeah," she said. "I'll be honest, I was worried for a time. Damon was such a smart kid. Had a lot of promise. Patrice wanted him to go to college and make something of himself. Go into business. That kid could talk a good game. Terry used to say he could sell anything. But he never could seem to find his purpose. Anyway, fifteen years ago or so, he started trying to be a preacher. He was hanging around Pastor Lennard at Holy Reformer. He kinda took Damon under his wing. I introduced them."

"Then what happened?" I asked.

"Well, people started wanting to hear more of what Damon had to say rather than Pastor Lennard. Lennard was getting pretty old by then. Set in his ways. Damon was charismatic. He got the kids excited about the Word. It was something to see. I thought Patrice would be so proud."

"What can you tell me about the Church of the Living Flame?" I asked.

Evelyn adjusted her glasses. "Pastor Lennard and Damon had a falling out. I don't know what it was about. Wasn't my business. But Damon started holding sermons at his house. Patrice inherited her daddy's farm off Millbury Road. They leased the land to another farmer, but the boys lived in the house. Well, word got out and before you knew it, Damon had his own congregation right out there in the barn. That's what he started calling it, the Church of the Living Flame."

"Where did you fit in?" I asked.

"I started helping out. Damon wanted to print some of his more popular sermons and put them online. He asked me if I'd come over and let him dictate them to me. I knew how to type fast. I was so thrilled to support him, so I said yes. It was good for me too. My Terry passed away, and I needed something to occupy my mind. Plus, I made a promise to Patrice way back when. I told her I'd keep an eye on her boys. This seemed like the perfect way to do it."

"Objection," Trevor finally said. "Your Honor, this is a charming walk down memory lane, but we're not hearing anything relevant to the issues in this case."

"Your Honor, this is foundational testimony," I said.

"Overruled, Mr. Page," Judge Ivey said while yawning.

"Mrs. Bishop, what other tasks did you do for Damon and Lyle King?"

"Well, I'd type up Damon's sermons and upload them to the website he set up. It was kind of fun for me to learn a new skill, you know? Keeps ya young."

"You said you uploaded Damon's sermons to his website. Was there a specific computer you were using to do this?" I asked.

"Sure thing," she said. "Damon had a computer at the house. A laptop. I'd go there to do it. I didn't have a computer of my own in those days."

"You always used Damon King's laptop?" I asked. "Did you ever log in anywhere else?"

"No, ma'am," she said. "I'd come out to the house, type up what Damon dictated either directly while I was sitting there, or he'd leave it on a tape recorder for me. When the congregation started to go and Damon started taking up collections, I did the bookkeeping. It got to the point he filed some paperwork with the state to start a non-profit. You know, for tax purposes. I introduced Damon to the lawyer I hired to do Terry's and my will. Then, I'd also do some correspondence for the new church. I'd type up flyers and give them to some congregation kids to pass around. You know, to get the word out about Damon's church. At that time, he was still holding services in the barn. We were starting to look at places to expand. It never got to that point though."

"Mrs. Bishop," I said. "Were you happy with your work for Damon?"

She looked down. "I was. At first. But then Damon started taking a turn."

"How so?"

"At first it was all about including people. You know? He was speaking to those kids in a language they understood. He made the Word more relatable and vibrant to them. As time went on, the whole tone of his sermons changed. It made me uncomfortable."

"How so?" I asked.

"Well, I started to feel like Damon believed he was the Savior. It went to his head. And he started talking about the fire of redemption. Sin and damnation. Every week just got darker and darker. Damon started preaching about how the only true way to let the Holy Spirit into your life was through fire. That all sinners had to suffer to be saved. And it got ... literal."

"How so?" I asked.

"One Sunday, he called a young boy up to the pulpit. The kid was maybe fourteen. Damon had overheard his mama talking about how she'd found some nudie pictures on his computer. Damon got the kid to admit it in front of everyone. Then ... Damon took a lit candle. He handed it to Lyle. Lyle made the boy hold his hand over it until it seared his skin. Burned him pretty bad. I mean, I could smell it. You know?"

"Then what happened?" I asked.

"I overheard Damon and Lyle later that night. I was doing the end-of-the-month books. Lyle seemed upset about what had happened with the boy. He asked Damon, why did he have to do it?"

"Damon said he has to burn for his sins. They all have to burn for their sins and he, Damon, was the only one strong enough to lead them to salvation. There was more after that.

Damon said he would root out the sinners in this town. He was going to bring the fire to them. He was building Lyle up."

"Objection," Noel said. "The witness is speculating about Mr. King's so-called motivations."

"Sustained," Judge Ivey said.

"Mrs. Bishop, can you focus on exactly what you overheard?"

"Yes, ma'am," she said. "It was late one night, about a week after the candle incident. And maybe a week before those poor kids went missing. Lyle was getting agitated. He wanted to know when they were going to save the sinners. He asked his brother where to find them. Damon said, and this really sticks in my mind. He said we'll root them out at the source and purge the earth of the stench of their sins."

"The source," I said. "Did he say where that was?"

She shook her head. "He just kept saying he knew where to find the sinners. He knew where they would be."

"Was there anything else that upset you?" I asked.

"Well, I was in the study off the kitchen. Damon and Lyle were in the kitchen. From a crack in the door, I saw Damon hand Lyle a piece of paper. He told him he'd already started to find the sinners. He said, and I quote, 'These will be the first to burn.'"

"Did you see what was on the piece of paper?" I asked.

"I did," I said. "Damon and Lyle left the house then. I fished it out of the trash. Or at least a piece of it. Damon had ripped it up, but I found a big enough piece to read. It was something he'd printed out from the computer I worked on. That printer had some ink on the drum and it used to print a line right down the center. The list had that line. So, I fired up the computer and found it. It was a document he'd saved earlier in the day. Didn't have a title, but I knew how to pull up recent documents. Anyway, it had a list with I think it was twelve names on it. I recognized some of them. The mayor was on it. The president. But there were other names. Mostly people who came to the church."

"Mrs. Bishop," I said, "I'm handing you what's been marked as Exhibit 14, can you identify it?"

"Yes. This is the kill list."

"Objection!" Trevor jumped up.

"Mrs. Bishop," the judge said, "Please don't editorialize. Just answer the question as asked."

She let out an exasperated huff. "This is the list I saw on Damon's computer with the names I saw written on it. The bottom third of it is what I retrieved from the trash."

"Mrs. Bishop," I said. "Can you read for me the fifth and sixth names on that list?"

"I sure can," she said. "It says Charlie Brinkman and Kristin Nadler."

"Thank you," I said. "Mrs. Bishop, tell me again when you first encountered that list?"

"It was about a week before those two kids went missing."

"Thank you," I said. "What did you do when you heard about the disappearances of Charlie Brinkman and Krista Nadler?"

"I about had a heart attack," she said. "For a day or two, I was just in shock. I think the second day is when they said in the paper that the police were suspecting foul play. And then, my God. When they found them. And it was at the quarry. And they were burned ... that's when I knew I had to speak up. A few days later, they put up a hotline. I called the police. I told them everything I just told you this morning."

"Do you know who you spoke with?" I asked.

"They shuffled me around a bit. But I ended up speaking to Detective Gus Ritter."

"Thank you," I said. "Thank you very much, Mrs. Bishop. I have nothing further."

Trevor Page was right behind me when I turned to go back to my table. He was chomping at the bit.

"Mrs. Bishop," he said. "How much did Damon King pay you for your services?"

"What? Um ... I think ten dollars an hour."

"Isn't it true that you asked him for a raise roughly two weeks before the King brothers were arrested?"

"I did," she said.

"How much did you ask for?"

"I don't remember. Maybe five dollars an hour more. I wasn't trying to get rich off of them, but I knew how much money they were taking in at that point. And I was having to spend more and more time on administrative stuff. It was more than just dictation, which is what I agreed to help with."

"You didn't get your raise, did you?" Trevor asked.

"No, Damon turned me down."

"And that made you angry, didn't it?"

"Well, I wasn't happy, no. My kids were pushing me to quit."

"You didn't quit though, did you?" he asked. "And even when you said you were becoming disturbed with the tone of Damon King's sermons, you didn't quit."

"No."

"You just asked for more money," he said.

"I asked for fair compensation."

This all came out at the original trial. Trevor was almost following Damon's original defense lawyer's cross to the word. It hadn't swayed that jury. I knew it wouldn't sway this one.

"Mrs. Bishop, was that computer you worked on password protected?"

She paused. "It wasn't. No. You just logged on."

"Isn't it true that during the day, there were plenty of other people in that farmhouse?"

"Well, I don't know what you mean by plenty. There were often people around, yes."

"In fact, the King brothers often took in homeless parishioners."

"Yes," she said.

"You didn't like that either," Trevor said. "Did you?"

"I don't know what you mean."

"I mean, isn't it true that you in fact warned Damon not to take in any more strays? You told him they were going to steal from him."

"I don't remember if I said stealing. I remember wanting him to be cautious and not trust strangers."

"So, you don't know who else might have had access to that laptop, do you?" he said.

"I didn't take it home with me," she said.

"And you didn't live in the house with Damon and Lyle. You didn't guard that laptop twenty-four seven, did you?"

"Of course not. But if you're trying to imply Damon didn't make that list, you're wrong. I saw him with it. I heard him tell Lyle it was his starting point. It was Damon's list. I don't care who else might have had access to that laptop. And Damon said all sinners must burn when he handed Lyle the list. End of story."

I tried to hold back a smile. Trevor Page slammed his notebook closed. "I have nothing further for Mrs. Bishop today."

"Mr. Stamford?" the judge said.

"Mrs. Bishop," Noel started. "You study the Bible, don't you?"

"Yes, sir," she said.

"Do you believe that passages from the good book should be taken literally?" he asked.

"What do you mean?" Evelyn questioned.

"I mean, isn't it true that the Bible can be construed as allegory?"

"Objection," I said. "Lack of relevance. This isn't theology 101."

"Sustained," Judge Ivey said.

"Damon took it literally," Evelyn shouted over us. "I just told you I watched him literally burn that kid for his sins."

"Mrs. Bishop," Judge Ivey said. "I'm going to need you to wait for Mr. Stamford to ask you a question before you answer."

Evelyn gave Judge Ivey what I assumed was her stern librarian look.

"Mrs. Bishop," Stamford said. "Did Lyle and Damon share a cell phone, do you know?"

"Damon had one," she answered. "I don't remember Lyle having one."

"You testified that the name Kristin Nadler was on this list you claim Damon wrote, not Krista?"

"Yes," she answered. "But if you say Krista Nadler real fast, I suppose that's what it sounds like."

I covered my mouth to hide my smile. Noel Stamford took a great breath, shook his head, then walked back to his table. "I have nothing further."

"Ms. Brent?"

"Nothing more from me, Your Honor."

With that, Evelyn Bishop stepped down from the witness box.

❧ 19 ❧

Most people hated Detective Gus Ritter. He liked it that way. They invented the word gruff just for him. But if I could choose the detective working on my murder cases, I'd pick Gus every time.

His right side hitched up on him as he climbed into the witness stand. He had a bad hip he was refusing to take care of. Pain made him even saltier, and we were in for a long day. Still, someone could shoot old Gus in the leg and he'd sit there and do his job.

"Good morning, Detective," I said, gathering my notes.

"Ms. Brent," he said.

I quickly took him through his foundational testimony. Gus had been a violent crimes detective for close to twenty years. It made him the most senior member of that particular department in Waynetown.

"Detective Ritter," I said. "What was your role in the Brinkman and Nadler homicide case?"

"It was my case," he said. "Back then, I served as lead investigator. I still do."

"Can you tell me how you first became involved in the case?"

"Sure," he said, settling in. "We received a report of a missing person. Krista Nadler's mother was concerned her daughter hadn't come home after a date with her boyfriend, Charlie Brinkman. She came into the station to get help. I caught the case."

"So you were the first person to speak to Ms. Nadler?"

"After she explained her concerns to the desk sergeant, yes."

"What did you do then?" I asked.

"I brought Stephanie, um, that's Stephanie Nadler, Krista's mother, into an interview room. She hadn't seen her daughter since five o'clock the evening before. It was ten in the morning on August 12th when we started talking."

"What were your initial reactions?" I asked.

"Well, anytime you have a report of a missing teen like that, it's of course concerning. In speaking with Ms. Nadler, I was trying to get a feel for whether Krista was prone to running away, what kind of crowd of friends she hung around with. That's the starting point. Based on Ms. Nadler's statement, it was clear she didn't feel Krista would just run away. She checked in with her mother."

"I see," I said. "So what did you do next?"

"I got in contact with Charlie Brinkman's parents as he was the last person ... at least at that point in my investigation ... who was seen with Krista. He picked her up in his vehicle and they left to go to dinner at the Olive Garden on Jefferson Street."

"Then what did you do?" I asked.

"The Brinkmans were also concerned about Charlie's whereabouts. Stephanie tried to get in touch with them herself, but didn't have a phone number for them. I interviewed the Brinkmans extensively as well. I was trying to find out who Charlie and Krista might have seen that night. Who were their group of friends? Coaches. Teachers. Employers. I started building a list of canvassing interviews that had to be taken."

"Did you personally interview all of those potential witnesses?" I asked.

"Most of them, yes. Eventually. That first morning, I was able to speak to a handful before Officer Wilburn found the bodies. But in those early hours, what emerged pretty quickly was a picture of two good kids who stayed out of trouble."

"What do you mean by that?" I asked.

"Well, you can never say never. But every person I interviewed had a similar story. The consensus was, Charlie Brinkman was admired among his peers. He played on the high school football team. Volunteered at church. He wasn't into drugs and didn't hang around with a criminal element. Same with Krista. They were both college-bound, straight-A students. Now that doesn't mean they didn't do things they shouldn't, but fairly quickly, I became convinced I wasn't dealing with runaways."

"Okay, so how did that guide your investigation from that point on?"

"Well, from almost the outset, we began searching. Stephanie and the Brinkman parents provided a list of places Charlie and Krista liked to hang out. I had officers canvassing in those areas. There is a wooded area behind Waynetown High School with a running trail Charlie used. The football parents' group started organizing a search out there, and my lieutenant had some crews assisting with that. I searched their social media profiles. Got warrants for their cell phone data. This all happened fairly quickly, but it took a couple of hours for the tower data to come back."

"What were you looking for?" I asked.

"I was looking to see where the last place Charlie or Krista's cell phones pinged."

"What did you find out?" I asked.

"Around three thirty that afternoon, I got the preliminary report back on Charlie's phone. Unfortunately, Krista's appeared to be dead. As in, her battery died. Her mother later told me Krista had issues with that and was going to take it into the cell phone store later that week. Anyway, it appeared Charlie Brinkman's cell phone pinged the tower on Quarry Road."

"What did that tell you?" I asked.

"It told me Charlie's phone was likely in a roughly two square mile area in the northwest corner of town. So, I got out a map."

"What did you see?" I asked.

"I saw Belitzer Quarry within that area. So, I got on the radio and dispatched a crew out there."

"What happened next, Detective?" I said.

"At approximately four thirty, the afternoon of the 12th, Officer Deena Wilburn radioed in that she'd found what appeared to be the remains of two human beings up on a hill at the Blitz."

I paused. The jury knew the rest. I raised my eyes and focused hard on Gus. It was subtle. Likely nobody else would have noticed, but I knew Gus Ritter and his mannerisms. He'd given testimony in at least a hundred trials for me over the years. A tremor went through him, and I knew Gus Ritter was struggling hard not to cry.

"Tell me what happened next," I said.

"I arrived on scene at four forty-four p.m. Officer Wilburn had followed standard protocol and secured the scene. There were two other field ops crews there guarding it. The crime scene unit arrived two minutes after I did. We searched Charlie's truck. The keys were missing. But we didn't find any blood or evidence of foul play there. Everything happened up the hill."

I pulled the crime scene photos up on the overhead once again. This time, the jury knew to brace for it.

Gus went into exacting detail, describing what steps the crime scene unit used to collect evidence. One by one, I introduced photographs of them doing their grim work.

Later, I would call the medical examiner to the stand. He would describe how Krista Nadler had been beaten over nearly every square inch of her body. He would theorize that the weapon used was a bike chain. Tiny indentations along her charred flesh were the telltale sign of it. Her face had been pulverized. Teeth broken. Jaw shattered. And worst of all, he would theorize that Krista had been alive for most of that, until one final, fatal blow to the side of her face that crushed her skull. There had been no evidence of smoke inhalation. She was dead by the time her killer set her on fire.

For Charlie, the opposite was true. He suffered no beatings. No broken bones. Instead, he'd been forced to kneel, facing Krista, as he watched helplessly and likely begged for her life as well as his own. Only then was he doused in kerosene and burned alive.

"I'd never seen anything like it," Gus said. "You couldn't make this thing up in the most gruesome horror films."

"Objection," Trevor said. "Can we admonish the witness to stick to the facts?"

"Those are the facts!" Gus snapped.

"Move on, Ms. Brent," Judge Ivey said.

I locked eyes with Gus. He was struggling. I let my gaze serve as a lifeline to him. We were in this together. And we had to get through it.

"Detective, did you have any suspects at that point?"

"We didn't," he said. "From my interviews, Charlie and Krista didn't seem to have a single enemy. They weren't using drugs. There was no paraphernalia found in their vehicle. No alcohol. Nothing found in their system when toxicology came back. No motive for the crime that I could identify at that point. We'd reached a dead end."

"Then what happened?" I asked.

"A few days after the bodies were found, I received a call. She wanted to remain anonymous at first, but I fairly quickly convinced her to come in for an interview."

"Who was that caller, Detective?" I asked. Of course, the jury already knew.

"That was Evelyn Bishop."

I let that sink in for the jury. They knew the story up until now. Gus briefly recapped it, focusing on Evelyn's testimony regarding Damon's sermons. Baptism by fire. The need for parishioners to burn for their sins.

"What did you do with the information you received?" I asked.

"I secured a search warrant for Damon and Lyle King's phones, computer, laptops, all of it. I had them brought in for questioning."

"Let's focus on the electronic data," I asked after introducing the warrant itself into evidence.

"As Mrs. Bishop described, there was a single laptop in the King house. It was registered to Damon King. I was able to pull up a variety of things. First, we found the list Mrs. Bishop described. It had twelve names on it, including Charlie Brinkman and Krista Nadler. After that, I zeroed in on the search history on that computer."

"What did that reveal?" I asked.

"That computer had been used to search both Charlie Brinkman and Krista Nadler's social media profiles. Extensively, actually."

"How so?" I asked.

"Well, for Krista. In the week preceding her disappearance, her name had been googled ten times. Her Facebook profile had been pulled up fourteen times and each session, the user spent a fairly long time stalking her profile."

"What do you mean by fairly long?" I asked.

"Well, in one session, it was fifteen minutes. Then forty-five. The third time her profile was pulled up, the user spent over an hour on it. Pictures from Krista's profile had been screen grabbed and downloaded on this laptop. Charlie's too. But the vast majority of the time was spent on Krista."

"What else did you find?" I asked.

"We found two cans of kerosene in the attached garage. One was almost empty."

"Detective," I asked. "Back to the laptop for a moment, did you examine it for fingerprints?"

"We did," he said. "We found just two distinct sets belonging to Evelyn Bishop and the defendant, Damon King."

"All right," I said. "Did you then have occasion to question either Damon or Lyle King?"

"Both of them," he said. "Lyle refused to talk. But Damon King had some interesting things to say."

"Like what?" I asked.

"Well, by the time I had Damon brought in for questioning, I had the reports back on the cell phone registered to him. It also pinged the tower on Quarry Road within the same time frame as Charlie Brinkman's phone."

"Why is that significant?" I asked.

"Well, you have to understand a little about cell phone technology. Your phone, even back then, is looking for the closest tower to ping. It doesn't skip. So if your phone pings a tower at Quarry Road, that means the phone itself is in the roughly two square mile triangle nearest that tower. The phones were in roughly the same place at the same time."

"Okay, so what, if anything, did you learn from your interview with Mr. Damon King?"

"Well," Detective Ritter said. "I asked him where he was from the time frame of approximately midnight to two a.m. on the morning of August 12th. He told me he was in Perrysburg, on his way to visit a sick parishioner. When I spoke to that parishioner, Larry Winfrey, he couldn't corroborate the story. He wasn't even home that night. He worked at Baylor Tool and Die third shift and reported to work that night."

"Perrysburg," I said. "And were you able to correlate that with the cell phone data you had for Damon King's phone?"

"Objection," Trevor said. "Lack of foundation. Detective Ritter isn't qualified to conclude if the phone in question was Damon King's."

"Ms. Brent?"

"If you'll allow me," I said. Judge Ivey nodded.

"Detective, you've indicated the phone was registered to Damon King?"

"Yes, that's correct."

"When you took possession of the phone, was it password protected?"

"It was," he said. "Using a four-digit code which we were able to bypass."

"Thank you; now, regarding the phone registered to Damon King, were you able to establish whether Mr. King's statement regarding his trip to Perrysburg tracked with your cell phone data?"

"No, I was not able to correlate the locations Mr. King gave me with the cell phone data on that phone."

"Can you elaborate?" I asked.

I moved for admission of the cell phone data records and projected a blow-up so the jury could see. Detective Ritter then used a laser pointer to emphasize each cell tower hit on the night of August 11th to the morning of August 12th.

"At approximately seven p.m., the phone pinged the tower at New Haven."

I used a split screen displaying a map of the cell towers in and around Waynetown.

"The New Haven tower serves the area closest to Millbury Road near Damon King's residence. The phone was at that location for almost eighteen hours, including throughout the night before. Mr. King's residence is a quarter mile from that tower, so I was able to infer that the phone was at his residence."

"Now," Ritter went on. "At approximately ten fifteen p.m., the phone is on the move. It pings the tower at Redmond Junction off I-75. Ten minutes after that, it pings at the Northfield tower here. It tracks north, right along the interstate at Fletching, then Shire Woods. Finally, at two minutes past midnight on August 12th, the tower here at Quarry Road gets pinged. As I testified earlier, that is the closest tower to Belitzer Quarry. The phone doesn't come off that tower until two forty-seven a.m., where it then follows the opposite trajectory, going all the way back to the tower closest to Mr. King's residence. He went home."

"Objection," Trevor said. "Assuming facts not in evidence."

"Sustained," Judge Ivey said, but Gus had already driven his point home.

"What can you conclude from all of that?" I asked.

Gus let out a sigh. "The most immediate conclusion was that Damon King was lying about where he was the night Krista Nadler and Charlie Brinkman were murdered. His phone went nowhere near Perrysburg. It lined up perfectly with a trip from his residence to Belitzer Quarry at the exact time Charlie Brinkman's phone also pinged from that tower. That tells me those two phones, and their owners, were in the same place at the same time."

"What was your next investigative step?" I asked.

"When I laid out that information, including the cell phone records, Mr. King ended the interview at that point. I told him I'd need him to wait for a few moments in the interview room. I then went to talk to Lyle King again. I told him Damon had just told me he went to Perrysburg to visit a sick parishioner. Lyle said, 'Then that's where we went.' I asked him if he had been with his brother the whole night. Lyle said he had and that the two of them went to Perrysburg, just like Damon said."

"Then what happened?" I asked.

"I tried to lay out the same cell phone data to Lyle King. He stared straight ahead and stuck to the same story. Over and over, he repeated that if Damon said they went to Perrysburg, then that's what he did."

"What did you do next?" I asked.

"At that point, I believed I had probable cause to arrest Damon and Lyle King for the murder of Charlie Brinkman and Krista Nadler. I got a warrant and executed it. The pair was placed under arrest, booked, and processed."

"Was your investigation over at that point?" I asked.

"Not by a long shot," he said. "We continued to collect evidence from the scene. I continued interviewing potential witnesses, including other parishioners of Damon King's. I was able to get copies of Damon's most recent sermons."

"How long did all that take?" I asked.

"The King brothers were arraigned on September 8th, 2008," he said. "As I recollect, their bail was set at a hundred thousand a piece. They couldn't make it, so they stayed in county lockup. On October 1st, I received a call from a lawyer representing Aaron Clyde."

"Who was he?" I asked.

"Aaron Clyde was Lyle King's cellmate. He was awaiting his own bail hearing on a drug possession charge. The lawyer's name was Gabby Margolis. She was a public defender for Maumee County at the time. At any rate, Ms. Margolis called and told me her client had information he wanted to share relating to the Brinkman and Nadler murders."

"What was that information?" I asked.

"Aaron Clyde claimed Lyle King had confessed to the killings."

"Objection," Noel said. "Aaron Clyde, as I understand, is available to testify as a witness. As such, his statements to the detective are hearsay."

"Your Honor, we're not introducing Mr. Clyde's statement for the truth of the matter asserted at this point. The detective is testifying on how he acted on it, how it affected the trajectory of his investigation."

"Overruled, Mr. Stamford. You may continue, Ms. Brent."

"Detective," I said. "What did you do next?"

"I interviewed Mr. Clyde in jail. He was cooperative and forthcoming. He was able to provide details about the crime scene that had not been made public."

"What kind of details hadn't been made public?" I asked.

Gus shifted in his seat. "At the time I interviewed Aaron Clyde, the press had been made aware that Charlie and Krista's bodies were badly burned. We had not made it known what type of accelerant was used. It was kerosene, not gasoline. The public was not aware of our theory on the murder weapon for Krista. That her wound patterns were consistent with having been made by a bike chain of some sort. We had not provided details on the positioning of the bodies. Only those directly involved with the investigation were privy to that knowledge."

"So you met with Aaron Clyde," I said. "What then?"

"I preserved his statement, and turned it over to the prosecuting attorney, Phil Halsey."

"Then what happened?" I asked.

"At that point, because of the nature of Mr. Clyde's statement and the details he provided, I felt confident that I had enough evidence that I could conclude my investigation. So I did."

"Thank you, Detective Ritter," I said. "I have nothing further."

Gus Ritter cracked his knuckles. I could see the glint in his eye as he got his second wind. A detail missed by Trevor Page as he passed me on the way to the lectern.

✵ 20 ✵

"**D**etective," Trevor said as he stepped up to the lectern. "You indicated you arrived at the crime scene at approximately four thirty on the afternoon of August 12th, correct?"

"Yes," Gus said. "And it's in my report."

"Right," Trevor said. He paused for a moment and thumbed through Gus's report. He canted his head to the side as he stopped at a particular page.

"You have a supplemental here provided by Officer Wilburn," he said.

"Is that a question?" Gus asked.

"So if Officer Wilburn wrote in her report and also testified that she arrived on scene at approximately three thirty, that means the scene went unprotected for nearly an hour, doesn't it?"

"It absolutely does not mean that. As I testified, Officer Wilburn followed standard protocol for securing the scene."

"And what is that standard protocol?" Trevor asked.

"She immediately radioed for backup. She requested a detective and the crime scene unit. She cordoned off the area with crime scene tape ..."

"Crime scene tape," Trever interjected. "Is that something a field operations officer would have on their person?"

"They carry it with them, yes," Detective Ritter said.

"I mean on their physical person. Are you telling me she would have had a roll of tape on her belt, right next to her service weapon, her radio, and her taser?"

"Objection," I said. "Counsel had an opportunity to cross-examine Officer Wilburn himself."

"She's right, Mr. Page," Judge Ivey said. "I will overrule the objection for now, but hurry up and make your point."

"I will," Trevor said. "But I believe this witness does have direct knowledge of how a field operations officer would access her crime scene tape."

"Detective?" the judge asked.

"She probably had it in her patrol car," Gus said. "That would be standard."

"Okay," Trevor said. "So, in your report, Officer Wilburn's supplemental indicates that she cordoned off the area with crime scene tape. She indicated that a backup field operations officer, Officer Raylon, arrived about ten minutes after she did. That's in her report. That you signed off on."

"It is," Gus said.

"Where was Officer Wilburn's car parked when you arrived on scene?" Trevor asked.

"There were two patrol cars parked in tactical positions at the base of the hill leading up to the clearing where the murders took place."

"Explain what you mean by tactical positions?" Trevor asked.

"I mean the patrol cars were parked in such a way as to block entrance to the trail leading up that hill so no one else could easily get in or out or try to drive up there."

Trevor paused. Melody leaned in and wrote a note.

"Where's he going with this?"

I waited a moment, so as not to draw too much attention to my movements by the jury. "Straw grasping," I wrote. "It's all he's got."

"And you parked your vehicle alongside those patrol cars, correct?" Trevor asked.

"Yes."

"And you then had to walk up that hill on foot to get to the crime scene?" Trevor asked.

"Yes. I didn't fly."

This got a few smiles from the jury.

"How long of a walk was that?" Trevor asked.

"About a minute or less," Gus said. "I'm more spry than I look."

"So if Officer Wilburn had to walk back down to get her crime scene tape, she then had to walk back up with it."

"You're catching on," Gus said.

"Your Honor," I said. "This entire line of questioning is pointless and calls for speculation on the witness's part."

"Mr. Page, you've made your point; move on."

"So," Trevor said, completely ignoring the judge. "The crime scene, before you got there, was left unattended by Officer Wilburn for several minutes. We know that."

"Unattended doesn't mean unprotected," Gus said.

"Okay," Trevor said. "You've made quite a deal about cell phone towers in your direct testimony. But you're not able to determine who was actually using that phone in the time frame that you testified to, correct?"

"There were no incoming or outgoing calls made on Mr. King's phone between the hours of ten p.m. and I believe it was noon from August 11th to August 12th."

"So you only know where the phone was, you don't know where Damon King was, correct?"

"That was a piece of the evidence, not the whole pie, Mr. Page," Gus said.

"Sure," Trevor said. "But you don't know if Damon had that phone on him, do you?"

"No, I don't," Gus said.

"And you don't know if Lyle had that phone on him, correct?"

"No, I don't," Gus said.

"It's possible someone else could have had that phone during that time frame, isn't it?"

"Possible, but not likely," Gus said.

Trevor took a breath. I knew the question he wanted to ask. Why not likely? But despite some of the more glaring issues I had with the choices he was making, he was a fundamentally good lawyer. He left the question unasked.

"Detective, you served an extensive search warrant on the King residence, didn't you? I mean, it wasn't just about phones and computers?"

"We served multiple search warrants, yes," Gus said.

"You said you found kerosene cans in the garage," Trevor said. "But you never found a murder weapon. You don't know what implement was used to beat poor Krista Nadler with, correct?"

"The medical examiner theorized it was a bike chain due to the nature of her injuries," Gus said.

"Did you find a bike chain at the King residence?" Trevor asked.

"We did not," Gus said.

"Charlie and Krista were bound with plastic tubing. Hogtied, as Officer Wilburn testified. But you didn't find any length of tubing matching what was used in commission of this crime at the King residence, did you?"

"No," Gus said.

"You searched Damon King's car. You didn't find any tubing in there, did you?"

"No."

136

"In fact, you didn't find a single piece of physical evidence connecting either Damon King or Lyle King to that crime scene, did you?"

"No," Gus said.

"No tire tracks leading up or down?" Trevor said.

"Well," Gus said. "As you enjoyed belaboring, you have to get up that hill on foot, Mr. Page."

"But you didn't find tire tracks matching Damon King's car at the base of that hill, did you?" Trevor asked.

"No," Gus said.

"You didn't even find footprints leading up or down or around that crime scene that weren't supposed to be there, did you?"

"Well," Gus said. "As you can see from the photos, this is mostly a grassy area. There's not much dirt or mud around it. I wouldn't have expected to find well-defined footprints in grass like that. Plus, you have a killer that might well have covered their tracks. That's kind of what that saying means, Mr. Page."

"Okay," Trevor said. "So, until Evelyn Bishop came forward with her story about fire and damnation, you didn't have a single suspect in this killing, did you?"

"I wouldn't say we didn't have a single suspect. We were still exploring leads."

"But once Mrs. Bishop came to you, you never entertained the idea that anyone else was responsible for this crime, did you?"

"That isn't really a fair characterization. Mrs. Bishop provided me with another avenue to explore. She was a lead. I followed that investigative lead. From there, well, are you asking me to repeat every step I took that I just testified to on direct exam? Because I'd be glad to."

Trevor's face turned crimson. Gus was doing incredibly well. He usually did. When he caught my eye, I tried to keep my expression neutral, but wanted to convey a simple message. Quit while you're ahead.

Gus could be intractable. That was the exact point Trevor Page was trying to put in the jury's mind.

"Detective," Trevor said, regaining a bit of his composure. "Did you ever speak to a woman by the name of Sierra Joy in connection with this case?"

"I did not," Gus answered.

"You testified that your investigative role in this case ended when a witness came forward claiming he had a so-called jail-house confession from Lyle King, correct?"

"No, I said I interviewed a witness who heard that confession. I found his story credible. He provided details about the crime scene that hadn't yet been made public. And still haven't, other than the first trial."

"Did it ever occur to you that witness might himself have been involved in the killings?" Trevor asked.

"No," Gus said. "The witness's knowledge was secondhand. I verified he was incarcerated in the Maumee County jail from August 1st of that year. You could say he had an airtight alibi."

Trevor smiled. "He got out though, didn't he?"

"Excuse me?"

"Your jailhouse witness, he didn't just come to you out of the kindness of his heart, did he? He cut a deal with the Maumee County prosecutor."

"I don't have direct knowledge of that," Gus said. "I took his statement. That was my role."

Trevor tapped his fingers on the lectern. He chewed his bottom lip, looked at the jury once, then raised his chin toward the judge.

"Your Honor, I have nothing further at this time."

"Mr. Stamford?"

Noel shook his head. "We defer cross."

"Ms. Brent?" Ivey said.

Gus was tight on cross. Almost tighter than he'd been on direct. Anything I asked him would open the door to recross by Trevor.

"Detective," I said. "Just to be clear, what was the time frame of Charlie Brinkman and Krista Nadler's killings?"

Gus took a breath. "They were last seen alive by Krista Nadler's mother at approximately five o'clock on the evening of August 11th. Their bodies were found by Officer Wilburn just shy of twenty-four hours later on August 12th."

"Your warrant to search the King brothers' property and electronic devices was issued on August 27th?"

"That's correct," he said, catching the importance of my question. "They did not become the focus of my investigation until almost two weeks later."

Trevor wanted to make an issue about the lack of physical evidence. Later, this time gap would become important. It wasn't as if Gus had the benefit of catching them within hours of the act.

"Thank you, Detective," I said. "I have nothing further."

With that, Gus Ritter had done his job. Judge Ivey put us in recess for the day.

"Come on," Sam said. "You know you want to hug him."

Sam was teasing. I showed up in his office at eight o'clock the next morning, right after roll call. Sam and Gus Ritter had cubicles adjoining each other in the detective bureau's bullpen.

Gus sat with his arms folded, rolling his eyes as Sam ribbed him.

"He's not wrong," I said. "You were terrific yesterday."

Gus answered with a harrumph, then hunched back over whatever case he was working on.

"I don't get it," Sam said. "Page just doesn't impress me. Noel Stamford is a flat-out idiot. This is what the Servants of Divine Justice's money bought?"

"There's still a lot of trial left. And the worst is yet to come. That's what I wanted to talk to you about." I leveled a stare at Gus.

"What do you need?" he asked, not looking up from his computer screen.

"I've got the M.E. later today. Ivey's handling a few other matters, so we're in recess until one o'clock."

Gus finally looked up and leaned back in his chair. "No surprises there."

"I'm not expecting any, no. But I'm putting Aaron Clyde on tomorrow. That's what I wanted to talk to you about."

"I'll leave you guys to it," Sam said.

"No," I said. "Actually, I wouldn't mind having your brain on this one too."

Sam shot a smug look to Gus. The two of them had complementary personalities. Gus was a block of granite to anyone he didn't know well. Sam was far more gregarious and quick to charm. Though Sam had every bit the killer instincts Gus did. He'd learned from the best.

"Let's go into one of the interview rooms," Sam suggested.

Gus's chair made a loud squeak as he scooted it back and followed Sam and me down the hall. Sam chose one of the largest interview rooms with a long table and six chairs around it. It was also the cleanest, and I appreciated the gesture.

There was a pot of coffee brewing in the corner. Sam poured himself a cup and offered me one, which I gratefully accepted. Gus mainlined the stuff all the way until three o'clock I knew.

"Clyde's been evasive," I said. "Lots of one-word answers when we did witness prep. He's cooperative and his story hasn't changed, but ... I don't know. There's just a lot riding on his testimony."

"Everything is riding on his testimony," Gus offered.

"Is what I'm saying," I said as I took a seat opposite him at the table. Sam stayed on his feet, leaning against the far wall as he blew over the top of his coffee cup.

"Clyde's been in and out of jail pretty much his entire adult life," Gus said. "He's a punk. Or he was. Time has mellowed him a little. Having said all of that, he's good on the stand."

"He was good in the first trial," I said.

"He's smart," Gus said. "It's a waste, really. He came from a good, hard-working family. I actually knew his uncle. A machinist. His mom worked as a bank teller. He had a brother that died young. Motorcycle accident, I think."

"So they pinned a lot of hopes on Aaron," I said.

"Yeah," Gus said.

"When are you putting the girl on?" Sam asked.

"You mean Sierra Joy?" I asked. "I'm not sure. Kenya wanted me to put her on early. I thought about it, but I still think we're stronger if the jury understands how awful this crime was and the strength of the evidence against the Kings. So yes, Gus. I'd like to hug you."

Finally, Gus Ritter cracked a smile.

"Clyde will be all right for you," Gus said. "And you just need him to stick to his story. He will. That's one of the reasons I knew he was telling the truth. He was solid. I tried to trip him up a hundred different ways. Couldn't. Just keep him focused. He'll hold up on cross."

My coffee had finally cooled down enough for me to take a sip.

"How are you holding up?" Sam asked.

"I'll just be glad when this trial is behind me."

Sam and Gus exchanged a look. I realized he wasn't talking about just the trial. I couldn't help it. I blushed.

"Thanks," I said. "But I'm okay."

"You moving to D.C. after this is all over?" Gus asked. Sam probably didn't mean for me to see it, but he nudged Gus's leg with his foot.

"It's okay," I said, smiling. "Really. I know everyone's thinking the same thing."

Sam finally moved off the wall and took a seat next to Gus.

"Sorry, Mara," he said. "It's just ... yeah. We all know you're going through a lot. And with everything that happened with Phil, nobody would blame you for wanting a change of scenery."

"You know," I said. "Waynetown was supposed to just be a

stop along the way. It's Jason's hometown. He grew up here, I didn't. But now ... I don't know."

I let my eyes meet Sam's. Worry lines creased his brow, and I found myself choking up. It almost took my breath away. I wasn't expecting it.

"You're good at this," Gus said. "We uh ... we kind of like having you around."

I took another sip of coffee, trying to use the gesture to conceal my quickly watering eyes.

"Stop it," I said. "You trying to make me cry?" I tried to play it off. The way Sam and Gus were acting, I realized this was something one or the other of them had been trying to figure out a way to tell me for a while.

I drew in a sharp breath, staving off whatever emotions threatened to unravel me. "I like my work," I said. "I gotta be honest, it's the one thing that doesn't fail me. I mean, besides Will."

"I get that," Gus said. Oddly, I knew he probably did more than anyone. Gus had been married and divorced twice. Never long enough to have kids, from what Sam had shared with me. He was married to this job. That came with its own beauty as well as sadness.

"We're family," Sam said, smiling. "And you know if you need anything ... well ..."

"Thanks," I said. "I know. But I don't know exactly what my next move is. To be honest, I'm not really thinking about that." It was a lie. But it was all I was willing to give just now.

"How's Will handling all of it?" Sam asked.

"About as well as can be expected," I answered. And it was the truth. "We've really tried to keep the impact on his day to day as minimal as possible. He's pretty well protected at school. Grantham was worth every penny."

"He's a good kid," Sam said. "And he's lucky to have you for a mom."

Now I wanted to hug him as much as Gus. But Lord, we made a heck of a trio. I supposed I should have a girlfriend or two that I could confide in. I didn't have siblings either. Instead, I had Gus and Sam and at the moment, I knew this was what it must feel like to have a pair of protective older brothers.

It felt good. But I knew I couldn't go too far down that emotional road right now.

"So, Sierra Joy," I said. "Do you have anything else I can use on her?"

"I wish we did," Sam answered. "She's been clean though for about the last eight years."

"But you know her record," Gus said.

"And I don't think it's going to matter. I can't go in there and discredit her by trying to call her what, a slut? No way. Not my style. Never mind if the jury would hate me for that. I'd hate myself."

"But you gotta get her past in," Gus said.

"I do," I said. "She had incentive to try to leverage her story to get a plea deal from Phil. That's my angle. I don't have to tear the girl apart for trying to survive. I just don't know if it's going to be enough to discredit her. You sure there's nothing you found at the bar when you recanvassed this year?"

"Neutral," Gus said. "The owner said he half remembers Lyle King hanging out there. He can't back up the dates Sierra says she worked. They don't keep records that far back. The manager she said wanted to hire him as a bouncer croaked like five years ago. It's her word and hers alone."

"Great," I said. "So if the jury believes her, I'm sunk."

"That's about the size of it," Gus agreed.

"I need something," I said. "Lyle's alibi doesn't exonerate Damon. It's still possible we could get a split verdict if the jury believes Sierra."

"You gotta break those two up," Sam said.

"Maybe," I said. "And you sound just like Jules Smith."

"The shrink?" Gus asked.

"Yes. He thinks the key to cracking this whole thing is peeling Lyle away from Damon. So far, nobody's been able to do that. Not even Page and Stamford."

"It's insane," Sam said, shaking his head.

"Gus," I said. "You have to have a theory. Why do you think Damon targeted Charlie and Krista specifically? They didn't go to his church. There's no evidence he even knew who they were prior to about two weeks before their murder. You have his search history, his stalking of their social media profiles. But why? What put them on his radar?"

"I tried for months to figure that out," he said. "Came up empty every time. I interviewed just about every person who ever went to hear Damon King preach. Nobody ever mentioned Krista or Charlie. They didn't travel in the same circles. Hell, most of his congregation was made up of true lost souls. A lot of homeless people. Drifters."

"Evelyn said the same," I said. "It's what bothered her. She was worried at first Damon was the one who might get hurt. Robbed. Mugged. Something."

"Right," Gus said.

"You have a working theory though," I said. "I know you do."

"It's a crappy one," he said. "Unprovable. Believe me. I tried. I mean, it wasn't a secret that kids went out into those woods surrounding the Blitz to fool around. Smoke pot. Drink. Whatever. If he's hunting sinners, it was as good a place as any to set up a blind, you know?"

"So he just happens to spot Charlie and Krista there one night? Fine, except how does he know their names to look them up online?"

"Right," Gus said. "It's a stretch. And nobody ever reported seeing either Lyle or Damon in or around the quarry that summer. Or ever. The cell phone data puts him there the night of the murders, but not any other time before that."

"Someone told him about Charlie and Krista," Sam said. "We just don't know who."

"Well," I said. "I appreciate your insight. I mean, if you think of anything else on it, let me know."

"Always," Gus said.

"And thanks guys. For ... all the rest of it. It's nice knowing you're in my corner."

This time, I swear I saw Sam Cruz start to blush. Gus looked away and darn it if I didn't see the glimmer of a tear in that man's eye.

"Oh the hell with it," I said. I came around the desk and gave old Gus Ritter a hug, whether he liked it or not.

✣ 2 2 ✣

Friday morning, at the end of the first week of trial, Aaron Clyde took the stand. Hojo had taken on the task of cleaning him up for the occasion. New suit that fit him well. A trip to the barber. From my vantage point behind the lectern, I'd swear the kid even had a manicure.

Well done, Hojo, I thought. He sat at the table with me today for this. Among his other charms, Aaron Clyde turned out to be a bit of a misogynistic pig. Enough that it crossed my mind to let Hojo handle his direct testimony. But no one knew this case better than I did. I could leave nothing to chance.

"Mr. Clyde," I started. "If you don't mind, why don't you tell us a little about yourself. How long have you lived in Waynetown?"

"Moved here when I was nineteen," he said. "I was, I grew up in Adrian ... um ... Michigan. Couldn't seem to keep myself out of trouble. So, when my mom took a job down here at the hospital, she talked me into coming with her. And my uncle, Mom's brother lived here. I needed a change."

"Why is that?" I asked. Aaron Clyde was far from a perfect witness. Better to get his flaws right out in the open.

"I was hanging with a crowd that wasn't good for me. Doing drugs. Pot mostly, at first. But it moved on from there. Started when I was in junior high."

"Did you find work when you came to Waynetown?" I asked.

"It was hard," he said. "I didn't have a high school diploma. Finally got my G.E.D. a few years ago, actually. I worked odd jobs. At one of the gas stations off I-475. Did some construction work. Day work. I had an uncle who was trying to get me in at his machine shop. I just ... I couldn't stick to any one thing for very long."

"Mr. Clyde," I said. "I want to focus on the summer of 2008. How old were you at that time?"

He thought. "I was twenty-seven. Well, I turned twenty-eight that August."

"Were you working then?"

"No," he said. "I'd just gotten fired from a job I had helping pour concrete for a pool company."

"Why were you fired?"

Aaron looked down. It took him a moment to muster up his answer. When he did, he raised his chin and looked straight at the jury.

"I fell into some bad habits again. I'm not proud of that. I moved to Waynetown to get away from trouble. It found me. No. That's not fair. I went looking for it. I started using again. I'd been clean for over a year. But I met a girl. She had a habit, too. One thing led to another. It can take hold of you that way. I ... I stole some cash from the office. The secretary figured it out. She called the cops."

"Then what happened?" I asked.

"I got arrested. Petty theft. I took like two hundred bucks from the office. But they found me with some dope. And I had an outstanding warrant for passing a bad check a few months before that. So, they threw me in county lock-up."

"When was that, if you remember?"

"I was arrested on July 30th. I got arraigned a couple of days later. My ma ... at that point, she was working with a drug counselor. She wouldn't post bail. So, I got processed into the Maumee County jail. That was, um, August 1st. They set a trial date, but it was like ninety days out. So, I knew I was going to spend pretty much the rest of the year in jail."

"Mr. Clyde," I said. "Did you have occasion to meet either of the defendants in this case, Damon King or Lyle King?"

"Sure," he said. "They were processed in a while after me. Late September, early October."

"Did you know them prior to that?"

"No," he said. "I kept to myself."

"Had you heard about the murders of Charlie Brinkman and Krista Nadler prior to your entering the Maumee County jail?" I asked.

Clyde shook his head, then leaned into the microphone. "No. I don't remember that. I was pretty selfish back then. I'm not gonna lie. I was wrapped up in my own problems. That summer, I cared about one thing, how I was going to score next. It led me to do a lot of dumb things. I was making good money at the pool company. My uncle lined that up for me too. I pissed it away. It's taken me a lot of years to own up to that. But no, I didn't know anything about those kids. I don't remember that."

"Okay," I said. "What was your interaction with either Damon or Lyle King when they first entered the jail?"

"It wasn't much. I seen them in the chow line. The yard. They were together all the time. That's the thing I remembered. And Damon was always the one doing the talking. Lyle was ... well ... I figured he was slow. That was the rumor flying around. That's the only thing on my mind when they put Lyle King in a cell with me. I remember kind of rolling my eyes."

"Why was that?" I asked.

"I thought he was going to be a problem. Like maybe he'd be tough to train."

"What do you mean train?" I asked.

"Just basic stuff. Cleaning up after himself. Keeping away from my shit. Um ... stuff. Everybody said he was ... um ... dumb. But that's not the word they used. I don't want to say it. It's not very nice. But it started with an R."

"That's fine," I said. "I'm not asking you to say it. Did you and Lyle become friendly?"

"Kind of," Aaron said. "He was real quiet at first. I was surprised. He was kind of ... well ... I've been in and out of the system over the years. Lyle King was probably the best cellmate I ever had. Real clean. Real considerate. Overly so. And he apologized all the time. You know. If he so much as farted. He was kind of ... I don't know ... sweet. And after a few days, he kind of warmed up to me and we started to talk."

"Mr. Clyde, what kinds of things did you and Lyle King talk about?"

"Well, on his part, it was all about his brother. Damon this, Damon that. Damon had big plans. He was going to make them rich. He was going to get them both out of jail and they were going to live in a big mansion. That's what he said. He said everybody loved Damon. They wanted to pay him big money to talk about Jesus. I kind of laughed at first. Because it was clear to me Lyle didn't give a rat's rear end about Jesus."

"Objection," Trevor said. "Calls for speculation."

"Mr. Clyde, please answer only what you've been asked," Judge Ivey said. "Go ahead, Ms. Brent."

"Mr. Clyde, did Lyle ever say he didn't care about Jesus?"

"Yeah," Aaron said. "I'm not speculating. He said it. He said, Damon likes to sell Jesus and everyone wants to buy. He told me his brother was taking in hundreds of dollars a week. He said people would come to the house to hear Damon read them the Bible, and they'd hand over wads of cash."

"I see," I said. "What else did Lyle talk about?"

"He only ever talked about Damon. I started to challenge him. I asked him if he does everything Damon tells him to do. I think I asked him if he'd jump off a bridge if Damon told him to. I mean, I kind of snapped. He even used to eat what Damon told him to."

"What do you mean?" I asked.

"After a couple of weeks, the guards were trying to keep Lyle and Damon separated. I didn't ask why. Anyway, Lyle would come over with tuna fish sandwiches and he'd tell me he hated them, but Damon liked them so that's what their mom would make. Like ... it didn't seem to occur to him that he could damn well pick out his own sandwich. So I said that to him. I wasn't very nice about it. We got into an argument back in the cell one night."

"Then what happened?" I asked.

"Well, Lyle kind of snapped. It was the only time I'd ever seen him do that. He was pretty chill. I mean a chatterbox about his brother, but he was always smiling. Always in a good mood. But that night, when I pushed back about the stupid tuna fish, he lost his temper. He said I didn't have the first clue how powerful his brother was. So, I asked him what he meant."

"What was Lyle's answer?" I asked.

"He said, Damon can send you to heaven or he can send you to hell."

"Those were his exact words?" I asked.

"Yes," Aaron said, leaning into the microphone; I almost thought he meant to swallow it. "Then he told me he could prove it."

"How did he prove it?" I asked.

Aaron folded his hands in his lap. "He told me he watched Damon send two kids to heaven. He said it was out at the Blitz. A boy and a girl. Charlie and Krista."

"He said their names?" I asked.

"He did," Aaron continued. "He said he and Damon went up a trail to the woods. He said Charlie and Krista were parked in a blue Ford Ranger. They were in the bed of it. Um ... having sex. Lyle said Charlie was on top."

Aaron paused. Sweat trickled down the side of his face. He reached for his water bottle and drank some.

"Aaron," I said. "What else did Lyle tell you?"

"He said Damon told him to come up behind them. The kids were really going at it so they didn't hear Lyle coming. Lyle hit the kid in the head. Didn't knock him out, but knocked him a little senseless. Then Lyle jumped in the bed of the truck and dragged him off the girl."

I had Aaron's original trial testimony in front of me. So far, he'd barely changed a detail. Ten years ago, he'd said Lyle knocked Charlie's lights out.

"Did he tell you anything else?" I asked.

"He told me everything. It was like Lyle had this need ... like he'd kept all this stuff inside himself for however many months. He said Damon told him to keep his mouth shut. It was like I unpopped some cork. Once he started, he just kept going."

"What did he say?" I asked.

"Lyle said Damon told him to drag the boy up the hill. He was kind of dazed still. Lyle had gotten a pretty good punch into the back of the kid's head. The girl was quiet. Lyle had a bike chain. He said he threatened to hit the girl with it if Charlie didn't cooperate. Damon had the girl by the arms and they marched up the hill."

"Then what did he tell you?" I asked.

"Damon tied them up," Aaron said. "Lyle was real specific about that. I don't remember what he said he used. Did I say that the last time?"

I showed Aaron the transcript from the first trial. "Yeah," he said after refreshing his recollection. "It was just some plastic tubing they had. Anyway. They made Charlie get on his knees. Damon prayed over him."

"Prayed over him?" I asked.

"Yeah. Lyle quoted some Bible verse. He will baptize you with the Holy Spirit and fire. He said it over and over to me. All about how you can only get to heaven or see the Holy Spirit if you purge your sins by fire. Lyle said Damon told him to make the girl suffer. He said he wanted Charlie to watch. That that would be his penance."

"Watch what?" I asked.

"Lyle said he beat that poor girl. He said he used the bike chain he had, and he whipped her with it. Over and over again. Her legs. Her arms. Her torso. Finally, her face. He bashed her in the head with it. He said she cried and screamed at first. Then she went quiet. But Lyle said Damon told him it wasn't enough. She needed to suffer the pain before she burned. The whole time Lyle said Damon kept Charlie's head up. His hand on his chin, making him watch the whole thing."

A few members of the jury began to cry.

"I'm sorry," Aaron said, his own voice choking up. "But you have to know."

"Aaron," I said. "What else did Lyle say?"

"Lyle got into it."

"What do you mean?" I asked.

"I mean, he was excited like when he was telling the story. Almost like he was seeing it again in his mind. He was getting off on it."

"Objection!" Trevor said.

"Mr. Clyde," Judge Ivey said. "Again, you need to stick to what you actually heard. Not editorialize. The objection is sustained."

"Sorry, Judge," he said.

We were almost to the end. I took a sip of my own water. So far, Aaron had been a rock star. I knew what was coming on cross. Page would do some damage, but I felt confident it wouldn't matter.

"What else did Lyle tell you?" I asked.

"He said Damon was praying over Charlie the whole time. And then Damon poured kerosene all over him. The girl was a mess, Lyle said. Hamburger meat."

Aaron had used that phrase in the first trial. I tried not to, but I flinched.

"She was dead," Aaron said. "I mean, Lyle said he thought she was dead. That's when Damon told him to start the fire. So, Lyle did. He poured the kerosene over the girl. He said he lit a match and threw it on her. He said he went over to Charlie. He was still alive. Lyle said he waited for Damon to give him the word. He said Damon nodded to him. Then Lyle said, you're not her lucky boy now, are you, and lit a match and threw it on him."

He paused, then Aaron said, "Lyle said they watched those poor kids burn for a minute or two, picked up the bike chain and the kerosene, then walked on down the hill."

The jury sat stunned. I glanced over my shoulder. Damon King folded his hands in prayer. His lips moved as he murmured something. Lyle looked at the ceiling, almost as if he were completely unaware of what was going on.

I felt hollowed out as I ended my questions for Aaron Clyde. As Trevor stepped up to take my place, my hands seemed frozen to the sides of the lectern. I wanted to stop time. No. I wanted to rewind it. Because that was the moment those first tentacles of fear wrapped themselves around me. My mind raced, trying to connect the dots. For I knew when they did, they would prove Aaron Clyde was a liar.

❦ 23 ❦

Trevor and Noel tag-teamed Aaron's cross. They covered the same ground the Kings' original lawyer had. Aaron had a history of lying to people in authority. He'd lied to his boss at first about stealing money at the pool company. He tried to pass forged checks off as his own. He didn't drop out of high school; he was expelled. A minor distinction, but Page and Stamford had to make the jury think if Aaron had a habit of playing it loose with the truth, he could be lying about Lyle's confession too. Aaron withstood all those questions. Almost four hours of them. When he finally left the witness box, even Judge Ivey looked spent. He adjourned court for the weekend just after three in the afternoon.

It was Gus and Sam I wanted as I tore through the crowd, heading out of the courthouse. Melody had to run to keep up with me. Hojo ran interference with the press line. He would say a whole lot of nothing, and I made a mental note to send that man a bottle of his favorite tequila for the weekend.

The Divine Justice protestors had grown considerably. They now took up the whole courtyard across from the courthouse and wrapped around the block. When they saw me come out yesterday, about ten of them in the front row had held up signs in unison that spelled out "Sinners" in red lettering. Today, I would duck out a different exit.

As I made another turn down the hall, Sam's dark hair was easy to pick out over the crowd, as tall as he was. He'd just finished testifying in a case downstairs.

"Mara," Melody said breathlessly as she reached my side. "That was great. Clyde was great. I thought ..."

The rest of Melody's words drifted into the background as I turned my phone back on. I had seventeen missed calls. Five were from Will's school, and the burn of panic flared through me in a way only parents get.

"Melody," I said. "I've gotta go. Just do me a favor and track down Detectives Cruz and Ritter. I need a brainstorming session tomorrow. I'd like you to be there."

"Okay," Melody said, looking confused. I didn't wait to explain anymore. I slipped out the service entrance and ran across the street to my car.

Will's teacher had left two voicemails. I peeled out of the lot, hurriedly swiping my keycard through the gate as my Bluetooth speakers kicked on and I played the first message.

"Mrs. Brent," she said. "This is Tara Whitney. Listen, Will's okay and I know you're in trial today. But there's been an incident and we'll need you down here as soon as possible. I'm trying to get a hold of Mr. Brent, but he's not picking up. Neither is his Aunt Kat. Those are all the emergency contacts we have ..."

I punched my steering wheel. What in the world could be going on that both Jason and Kat went AWOL on me?

Grantham Elementary was only a fifteen-minute drive from the courthouse. I'd get there right as school let out, but Will stayed after for an hour on Fridays for robotics club.

I had to weave through the parent pickup line and outgoing buses as I turned down the street. I had to park almost at the end of campus and hot-foot it in my heels. With each step, the air felt thicker. Something was definitely wrong.

I had to swim upstream past hundreds of grade schoolers pouring out of the building. Will wasn't among them. Even when he left with the other students, he had an aid with him. Will didn't do so great in crowds. We were working on it.

Finally, I broke through the line and made a turn down the short hallway toward the office. I recognized Ms. Whitney right away. She was standing in front of another office, the guidance counselor's. I didn't see Will anywhere.

When I opened the office door, I caught Ms. Whitney's eye. She was about my age, mid-thirties, but somehow she always looked so much younger to me. Pretty. Blonde. She wore heavy makeup and false eyelashes.

"Mrs. Brent," she smiled.

"What's happened?" I asked.

Immediately, the other office staff gave us some purse-lipped glances. I didn't like it one bit.

"Where's Will?" I asked.

"Can we have a word in private first?" Tara Whitney asked. "Let me just tell you what's going on. I think you'll appreciate a heads-up."

"Okay," I said. But I was getting angrier by the second. I wanted my kid. Now.

"Mrs. Brent," she said. "There was ... um ... gosh, this is hard. When the kids got back from lunch and recess today, there were some signs taped up in Will's locker. News articles. And some pictures."

I'd spent the day facing down double murderers. But now, my knees felt weak. It was as if every pore on my body opened up at once and a cold sweat trickled down.

Tara Whitney handed me a stack of crumpled papers. They stuck together with tape. I had to pull them apart. They were printouts from a couple of tabloid websites. Some were older articles. One was new. It had a grainy picture of Jason in the arms of Abigail Morgan. I'd seen the more graphic versions of these the day Abby texted them to me.

Oddly, none of that was what stopped my heart. Scrawled in red lettering over several of the pictures was the word "sinners" in red lettering. Just like the signs I'd seen from the Divine Justice protesters.

Will didn't know. Jason and I had been careful to shield him from the reasons why his dad and I had separated. Will was nine years old, for crying out loud.

"Would you like to sit down?" Tara asked.

"No," I snapped. "Do you know who did this?"

"They were ... I'm sorry ... these were taped up in Will's locker. We're reviewing security footage. We'll figure out who did it. But when Will came back from recess and lunch, these were in there. He ... he didn't take it well."

"Ya think?" I snapped. In the back of my mind, I knew it probably wasn't fair to take it out on Tara Whitney. At the moment, I bloody well didn't care.

"He had an episode," she said.

Episode. That was a neat way to put it. I knew my son. He would have been scared. Confused. Horrified. Embarrassed. The last episode, as Tara called it, Will had flailed against the lockers until a janitor got a hold of him and kept him from hurting himself.

"Did his friends see?" I asked.

"Well, I mean, yes. There were a few other children around. They were all putting their lunch bags away and ..."

"I get it," I said. "Where is my son?"

"He's waiting in the health room. We tried to call. Mr. Brent and his sister wouldn't pick up. We called your office too."

I moved past Tara Whitney. The health room was down the short hallway. It was the office I'd seen her standing in front of when I first walked in.

I tried to put a neutral expression on my face. Will was sitting on one of the beds they had set up for sick kids in the nurse's office. Kenya sat beside him, holding a magazine. Will looked so small. His face was still reddened from tears he must have cried. But he was still. He had a lopsided grin on his face as Kenya pointed to a picture in the magazine.

"Hey, buddy," I said. I clenched my fists to keep Will from seeing them shake. "I see you've met my ... my friend."

"I like Kenya," Will said. "She's funny."

I smiled. Kenya Spaulding was a lot of things. I don't know if funny was a term I'd ever used. I took a seat on the other side of Will.

"The school called the office," Kenya said, her voice calm, quiet. She set the perfect tone. "Caro told me what was going on. I was in the neighborhood. I thought I'd come sit with Will while his mom finished up in court."

"She tries to get the bad guys," Will said as he thumbed through the magazine Kenya had. Warmth flooded me as I realized what it was. It was an old issue of *National Geographic* featuring big, full-color images of the wreck of the *Titanic*.

"Had this one sitting in the lobby at the office." Kenya explained. "Can you believe that?"

"I've been looking for this one," Will said. "Somebody stole the library's copy. It's a fifty-dollar fine if they ever catch the person who checked it out. Do you think you could take them to court too?"

Kenya smiled. "Well, if they don't pay the fine."

"Thank you," I said. It was more than that. It meant Kenya paid attention. I might have mentioned just once or twice Will's obsession with the *Titanic*. Kenya had a stack of *National Geographic* in her office. She must have hunted for this specific one before she came to the school.

"I'll tell ya what," Kenya said. "We'll let the library worry about their thief. But you can have this one, okay?"

Will regarded her. "But that will devalue your collection."

"It's okay," she said. "I wasn't planning on selling them. People just like to look through them and I like the way they look on the shelf. They've got that nice yellow binding."

"Not this one," Will said. "It was a special collector's edition. It was only sent to subscribers. I don't think you could have even picked it up at a bookstore."

"It'll make me happy if you have it," she said.

"Will," I said. "Do you mind if I talk to my friend Kenya for a few minutes? Then we'll head out. If you're hungry, we can stop through a drive-through."

"Papa Leoni's," he said. "Stuffed crust pepperoni."

"Done," I said.

I gestured to Kenya. The nurse gave me a pleasant smile and a knowing nod. Will was calm. He'd be fine for a few minutes.

I ran a hand down my face as I shut the door and Kenya and I moved into the hall. Tara Whitney stood waiting.

"Thank you," I said, nearly choking on my words. "Kenya … you didn't have to …"

"Yeah," she said. "I did. And I don't mind a bit. I said I'd have your back. This is what that means, Mara."

I nodded. Speechless. Kenya squared her shoulders and turned to Tara Whitney.

"Now, where's that surveillance tape? Get the principal out here."

No sooner had she said it before the rotund form that was Mr. Hampton came down the hall, his tie flying behind him like a flag, his cheeks flushed.

"Mrs. Brent," he said. "I'm so sorry. We had no idea. I promise we'll find out what happened."

Kenya grabbed the stack of pictures out of Tara's hand. She waved them at Mr. Hampton. "Every surface in that boy's locker was covered with these. That took time. You mean to tell me you let students roam the halls unattended for long enough to do something like this?"

I realized with sick clarity what was going on.

"This wasn't a student," I said. "This was an adult." I spared a glance for Kenya, not wanting to say my suspicions about the Divine Justice group to anyone but her just yet.

Hampton looked like he was about to throw up. "We're handling it. That's all I can tell you right now."

An adult did this. A staff member. Oh God.

"We had a temp working in maintenance this week," Dan Hampton said. "They all go through background checks, I assure you. The safety of these children is our top priority."

"Where is he?" I said.

"Um ... she ..." Hampton corrected me.

"Where is she?" I said through tight lips.

"She had already left for the day. We have the footage. We're in touch with the school's liaison officer, Deputy Wise. I promise you, nothing like this will ever happen again. We'll be pressing charges."

"So will we," Kenya said.

"I'm taking my son home now," I said through clenched teeth. I could barely think. Barely breathe. A grown woman had papered my son's locker with this crap. Here. At his school. Where he was supposed to be protected.

"I think that's best for now," Hampton said. "I mean, of course you have our full support. We can have a meeting to ..."

"Not now," I said. "Now, I just want to get Will out of here."

Kenya followed me back to the health room. Will was still engrossed in Kenya's magazine.

"Ready to go?" I asked. "I mean ... if you don't want to miss robotics, I can stay ..."

"No," Will said, sliding off the bed. "We can skip it today. I'd rather have stuffed crust pepperoni just this one time."

A shudder went through me. For Will to volunteer to alter

his routine meant he was still pretty upset. I grabbed his backpack. I let my son lead the way. Kenya and I closed ranks behind him and left the school together.

Once I got Will situated in the back seat, I turned to Kenya.

"Thank you," I said, trying not to choke up. If I fell apart now, Will would see. He'd had enough trauma for one day.

"It was my pleasure," she said. "In fact, if you're comfortable with it I'd like it if you put my number down with the school as a backup. You've got a pretty great kid in there."

"You're something else," I smiled.

"Don't let it get out," Kenya said, smirking. "I've got a reputation to protect."

"Your secret is safe with me," I said.

Kenya's smile widened. "I mean what I say, Mara. I've got your back."

"Back at ya," I said. I slid behind the wheel. Kenya waved to Will. He looked up from the magazine long enough to wave back. I took a breath and started the car.

A long weekend loomed ahead of me. And I'd just had to add another battle to my war.

24

William was quiet about what happened. He was still asleep at six a.m. the next morning when Jason pulled up. Saturday. It was his weekend. They had plans to go to the art museum. I waited for him at the kitchen island.

"Mara," he said. His face had no color.

"He's doing fine," I said. "Thanks to Kenya. He hasn't wanted to talk about what happened."

"He didn't ask any questions?" Jason asked.

"Not so far. I called his therapist. We're both of the opinion that we wait for him to ask when he's ready and answer him truthfully when he does. Nothing's changed as far as that goes."

"What about whatever bastard hung those pictures?" Jason asked.

"The school wants a formal meeting with us next week. They're reviewing security footage, but it looks like it was a temp they'd just hired in maintenance. Kenya's working with the sheriff's office to figure out what kind of charges can be brought. But I want to keep this out of the press."

"I agree," he said. "It's the last thing any of us need. God. Mara, I'm so sorry."

"I know," I said, then hesitated. Part of me didn't want to bring the next part up. "Jason. I don't know for sure yet, but I suspect that this is connected to my trial You're aware there have been protestors outside the courthouse. Damon's supporters. The signs they carry, their messaging is similar to what was written in Will's locker. The bit about sinners needing to be punished."

A nerve twitched near Jason's eye. "You're telling me this was the King brothers?"

"I think it's likely connected, yes," I said.

"But they wouldn't have had the ammunition to do this if I hadn't given it to them," he said.

I went quiet. I couldn't tell Jason not to blame himself. I didn't. But I just wasn't big enough to let him off that particular hook. Jason stood with his hands curled into fists. I knew him. He wanted to fight something. To punch something. So did I.

"Don't," I said. "Please don't tell me everything's going to be okay. Or that you're going to find a way to make it okay. He knows. Will knows what happened."

"You mean he knows what I did to you. To us. Mara ... give me a chance to try and fix this."

My head pounded. "You can't fix it."

"This wasn't supposed to touch you," he said. Lord, I knew he believed that. There was something else unsettled between us.

"Jason," I said. "Was it you? Did you plant that story about Abby Morgan? Did you put those people up to accusing her of child abuse?"

His answer came so quickly. "I don't know anything about it, Mara."

Plausible deniability. He neither admitted nor denied anything. If Jason were capable of the things Abby said, what else might he do? For the first time since I met Jason, I felt a little afraid.

"Will's expecting you," I said. "He's been looking forward to going with you. He misses you."

"I've got it handled," Jason said. "You could ... why don't you come with us? I mean, it's going to be okay."

I didn't know if it was. I just knew our best shot was keeping Will to the routine we'd set up. He picked up on my emotions. He didn't need to be in the middle of added tension between his father and me.

"I'm meeting with Gus and Sam downtown," I said. "I'm still in the middle of a murder trial. Will understands that. He's been planning his day with you. I don't ..."

"Of course," Jason said. "I get it. You're right. We have to figure this out. Not just you and me and Will, but me and Will." He tried to reach for me as I got up to leave. I grabbed my briefcase and turned my back to him.

As much as it pained me, I had to find a way to let go and let Jason handle this. He was right. I couldn't buffer their relationship. They had to find their way together. And I had to decide if I could find my own way out.

❧ 25 ❧

By the time I pulled into the visitors' lot at the sheriff's department, my worry began to ease. Jason might be a crappy husband, but he was a good dad. I needed to give him space to be that. Somehow.

Melody was waiting for me in the lobby. I wondered if the drama at Will's school had reached her ears. She didn't say anything. So either Caro and Kenya were discreet, or Melody was.

Sam came down and ushered us up to the third floor where Gus waited in an interview room. He had the Brinkman/Nadler case file spread out in front of him.

"Thanks for doing this," I said. "I just ... I'm in the home stretch with my case in chief. I don't want to miss anything. And Aaron Clyde's testimony just ... I don't know. Something was off. I can't figure out what."

"He was perfect," Sam said. "Neither defense lawyer could trip him up."

"I know," I said. "There were a lot of high fives yesterday. I get it. It's just ... I don't know. Something was ... off."

Gus came in, two-fisting his coffee. "He's a punk."

"And he didn't want to testify," I said. "He skipped town the minute the King brothers were granted a new trial."

"I think you need to count your blessings," Gus said. "He held up on cross. He stuck to his story. The jury believed him ten years ago. They'll believe him now. They want to convict. I can feel it."

"I'm glad you think so," I said. "I just don't know how they're going to feel once Sierra Joy gets her say."

"You know she's lying," Sam said. "They will too."

"I want more." I reached across the table. "May I?"

Gus pushed his file toward me. I opened it and began to lay out the crime scene photos again. This was the complete set. Over a hundred photos. We'd only used a third of them or less as actual trial exhibits. One by one, I spread them out on one table. Melody stood over my shoulder.

I fanned them out on the table, placing them like puzzle pieces. The whole crime scene unfolded. There were the bodies, of course. But every inch of the area had been painstakingly documented in full color. Blood on blades of grass. Krista's melted flip-flop. Her necklace on the ground. I'd seen her mother wearing it a few months ago at Krista's gravesite. It was all she had left of her.

"Gus," I said. "Where are your notes from Evelyn Bishop's statement?"

"Right here," he said.

"How many of Damon's followers did you interview?" I asked.

"Lord," he said. "It had to be a couple of dozen. They all fawned over the guy. Said they finally felt like they'd found a place that accepted them for who they were."

"Mostly young people," I said. "The disenfranchised of Waynetown and surrounding areas."

"He had people driving up all the way from Findlay and

Fostoria. And they were coming down from Monroe and Washtenaw counties in Michigan."

"But there's no list," I said. "That's the part I've always had trouble with. Damon claims he wanted to operate the thing as a non-profit. Wanted to expand the tent. But he's not collecting emails or anything. Or even snail mail addresses. How's he getting the word out?"

"He was leaving a lot of that to Evelyn," Gus said. "I always got the impression she was doing her best just trying to keep up."

I tapped my pen against the table. There was something here. I could feel it. I stood and leaned over the photographs. If I closed my eyes, I could see the events play out just as Aaron Clyde relayed Lyle's description. His testimony lined up with the crime scene investigator's theory of the case.

"He pulls Charlie off of Krista in the truck," I said, trying to watch the scene unfold in my imagination. Gus placed the pictures of the truck's interior on the table. No keys in the ignition. The passenger side visor pulled down.

"We've got scuff marks, drag marks in the grass," Gus said, pulling the pictures near Charlie's truck.

"He gets them up the hill," I continued. "Charlie drops to his knees or is forced to them. They take Krista a few yards away from him, on the north side of the hill. Lyle starts to beat her while Damon keeps Charlie under control."

As I spoke, Gus rearranged the pictures to go with my chronology.

"Blood spatter pattern," Gus said. He pulled the pictures, showing blood droplets in the grass.

"Then finally, she's dead. Lyle sets her on fire. Presumably Charlie is still alive for that but already soaked in kerosene, waiting for his turn."

"He doubles over, but dies kneeling," Gus said.

I turned my back to the pictures and began to pace. "How does he know?" I said. "It's planned. Calculated. Aaron never asks or Lyle never tells him how they picked that spot at that exact time. It wasn't random. It couldn't have been. That is what's been driving me nuts about this case. Why these two? Specifically."

"Aaron's telling the truth," Gus said. "He knows way too much about this crime scene, Mara. I testified to all of that. We never released info to the media about how Charlie was found kneeling. The public didn't know how Krista was killed. The bike chain theory. None of that. But Aaron knew it all."

"Could he have been there?" Melody asked. "I mean, the one thing that always bothered me is how no one caught them. Your medical examiner thinks this might have taken up to an hour. Could Aaron have been a lookout?"

"No," I said. "Aaron Clyde was already in the county jail at the time of the murders."

"Oh. Right," Melody said.

"You're overthinking," Gus said. "I told you. Aaron was solid."

"There's something," I said. "Gus, you did everything right. I'm not saying that. But Clyde's lying. I know it. I feel it in my bones."

"I know a liar when I hear one too, Mara," Gus said. "Clyde wasn't lying. He talked to someone who knew that crime scene. There are only two people it could have been, and we know it wasn't Damon. It was Lyle. He confessed. He relished in it. Bragged about it. That's usually how these prison confessions go. Big talk. Chest thumping. Captive audiences. I've seen it a million times. Relax."

"He can't be lying," Sam said. "I think Gus is right, you're overthinking."

"Yeah," I said as I kept pacing around the table. I looked at every photo from every angle. Round and round.

"He doesn't change a word," I said. "I mean barely. Not

from the original trial. Not from what he gave you in his statement when you interviewed him ten years ago. He's reading from a script. That's what's bugging me so much. He forgets nothing? Not one single detail? I don't have to refresh his recollection once?"

"He's got a good memory," Sam said. "That's what you want in a witness, Mara."

I'd combed through Clyde's statements, his trial transcript. I'd prepped him. There were no holes. On paper... and yet.

"Mara," Gus said. "You know that saying about not looking a gift horse in the mouth? Aaron Clyde's your gift horse..."

I froze. Afraid to move. Afraid to breathe. The answer was there, trailing in the winds of my mind. If I thought too hard. If I voiced it, I knew it would flitter away.

I had it. God help us all. I had it.

"You're not such a lucky boy anymore," I said, repeating what Aaron testified Lyle told Charlie before he lit him on fire.

"Lucky Boy," I repeated. My blood started to heat. "Lucky Boy!"

I had turned away from the table and pictures. Lucky Boy. Lucky. I was afraid to turn back around. The pendant. The damn necklace!

I picked up one of the photographs at the end of the table. It was of the necklace Krista had been wearing. The one her mother wore now. It was as if wires connected in my brain, giving off a spark.

"This," I said, waving the photograph in front of Gus. "Look at this."

"Lucky Boy," he said. He turned his head sideways as he stared at Krista's necklace in the photograph.

"It was her horse, I think," Gus said. "One she used to ride when she was a little girl. Stephanie told me about it."

I pointed to the picture of the necklace. Only it wasn't on Krista's neck. It had fallen to the ground.

I grabbed another photograph. This was of Krista's body before the M.E.'s office moved her into an ambulance. The necklace was still around her neck.

Gus took the photos. Sam looked over his shoulder, his eyes widening as he began to track my train of thought.

"It fell off," Sam said.

"Gus?"

"Yeah." Gus scratched his chin. "When they moved her, the chain had weakened to the point of breaking. It fell on the ground."

He looked through his notes. "Here," he said.

Sure enough, the crime scene unit officers had made a notation.

"The pendant fell face down," I said. "It says Lucky Boy on the back, Gus. Not the front. When Krista wore it ... the way Lyle would have seen it ... the horse, the front, would have been visible, not the back."

The photograph of the necklace on the ground showed the minute details of the back of the pendant as it lay. I'd seen the same pendant around Stephanie Nadler's neck. I hadn't been able to see the back of it. Even if I had, I doubted I would have been able to read the inscription without holding it close ... or seeing it blown up in a photograph.

"Son of a bitch," Sam whispered.

"Exactly," I said.

I sank down into my chair with a thud.

"I don't get it," Melody said.

I leaned back, covering my eyes with my hand. All of a sudden, the overhead lighting was too harsh.

"I think Aaron Clyde has seen these crime scene photos," I said. "Lucky Boy."

"He could have seen them at the first trial," Melody offered.

"No," Sam, Gus, and I spoke the word together.

"That photograph was never entered as an exhibit," I said.

"Nobody should have ever seen it except the people actually at that crime scene. The people in this room ..."

"Or Phil Halsey," Melody said. It was her turn to slump in her seat.

"If he weren't already dead, I'd kill him," Gus said. "Mara, you know I sure as hell didn't show Clyde any of these photos when I interviewed him."

"I know you didn't. But I knew there was something," I said. "It was there, in the back of my mind after Aaron testified."

"It doesn't mean Lyle didn't confess," Sam said.

"It means he was coached," I said. "It means Phil showed him these pictures. It wasn't just some accident. He didn't make those kinds of mistakes."

"What now?" Melody asked.

"I don't know yet," I said.

I saw a look pass through Gus Ritter's face.

"Gus," I said. "We have to..."

He pounded a fist on the table. "Son of a bitch. That son of a..."

Worry lines deepened in Sam's face as he watched Gus. "This could be nothing," Sam said. "That's also a possibility. A coincidence. I mean it's a stretch..."

"Sure," I said. "But Clyde was cocky on the stand. That's what bothered me. He went too far. And Lucky Boy. He said you're not her lucky boy anymore. That's not something people just say."

"Page didn't see it," Sam said. "He didn't pick up on it. Neither did Stamford. Have they seen all of these?"

"I'm not sure," I said. "I have to go back and look at exactly what photos were requested and shared in discovery. But it doesn't matter. I have to follow through on this. I have to know if I'm right."

I put my hands on the top of my head as if it might pop right off. "I don't...I don't even know where to start."

"I do," Gus said. "You need to talk to Gabby Margolis. Right now. She was Clyde's defense lawyer back then. If anyone knows what was going on, it'd be her."

Sam was one step ahead of him. He typed furiously into his own laptop. "She's got a current address listed over on Baldwin Street. I'll take you. That's a dangerous neighborhood. I'm not letting you go alone, and this is still a police matter. Besides, if she's gonna talk at all, she won't do it with Gus there. She's lost too many cases he was on the other end of."

"Fine," I said. "Melody, keep working the church angle with Gus. I need something. Anything that helps us figure out how he targeted them."

"Any suggestions?" Melody asked.

My head was pounding. "A money trail, maybe. Talk to Evelyn Bishop again. Look hard at that donor list we were provided. See if there's a pattern. Krista didn't come from money, but Charlie did. Maybe there's a friend of a friend. An ex-girlfriend. Somebody who had a grudge."

"I'll give it another look," Gus said. "Just go."

"You can take my car back to the office," I said to Melody. I knew she took a bus into town every day. I tossed my keys to her.

I grabbed my briefcase and followed Sam out. With each step I took, I felt victory slipping further and further away.

26

"She lives here?" I asked.

Sam drove me to one of the most rundown neighborhoods in Waynetown. Most of the homes here had been built at the turn of the last century. With the decline of the automotive industry, most had just moved on. The neighborhood high school had been consolidated to the center of the city.

Sam pulled into an overgrown driveway with cracked cobblestone and a detached garage. The once purple shingles hung crooked on the two-story Craftsman-style house. A dog barked further down the street.

"You never try any cases with Gabby?" Sam asked.

"Never had the pleasure."

"I got in her crosshairs a few times when I was a new detective. But it's been at least fifteen years."

I'd looked up Gabby Margolis's status in the bar directory. She'd had her license suspended eight years ago for embezzling client funds.

"Why do I feel like this is all just going to make me sad?" I said.

Sam shrugged. "I think her issue was cocaine," he said.

"Don't tell me," I said. "Gus ended up busting her. Is that the dust-up he was talking about?"

"Probably," Sam said. "Come on. I see some lights on. She's home."

I blew out a hard breath through puffed cheeks, said a silent prayer for courage, then followed Sam up the crumbling walkway.

"Gabby?" Sam said, rapping on the screen door with his knuckle. "Ms. Margolis? It's Detective Cruz."

I heard something crash to the ground deeper inside the house, then a good amount of cursing. Finally, Gabby Margolis made her slow way to the front door.

Barely.

Gabby trailed an oxygen tank behind her. I'd seen her picture on the local bar website, but that woman was long gone. The one before me had lost most of her hair. Her skin sagged and had a grayish tinge to it. Her sunken eyes looked both Sam and me up and down. She brought her hand up, took a long, slow drag on a cigarette I hadn't previously noticed, then snuffed it out on the plant ledge beside her.

"Come on in," she said. "I wondered when one of you would show up."

Sam and I exchanged a look. Gabby moved inside. Sam opened the door and held it for me.

Gabby plopped down on a recliner in the corner of the room. She gestured to a couch across from her.

"You're here about the Kings," she said.

"I'm sorry to have to bother you," I said. "I wasn't even planning on calling you as a witness or anything. But I need ... there were some things Aaron Clyde said on the stand that bothered me. You brokered his plea deal with my predecessor. I was hoping you could shed some light on something that's been kind of sticking in my craw about what he had to say."

Gabby reached down and turned off her oxygen. She

grabbed a pack of cigarettes from the table and took out a fresh one.

"You sure that's a good idea?" Sam asked.

"I hope not," Gabby answered.

Sam made eye contact with me. We hadn't really discussed how we wanted to approach Gabby beforehand. But he gave me a little nod that told me he was fine with me taking the lead.

"Surprised you're still working," she said to me.

"I'm sorry?"

"Well," she said. "Phil really did a number on you didn't he? Blowing his brains out like that. Were you really an eyewitness?"

I couldn't tell if she was just trying to rattle me or was genuinely curious. "Yes," I said, deciding to be straightforward.

"He say anything before he did it?" she asked.

"Say?"

"Last words? Confessions?"

"Honestly?" I said. "I don't remember exactly what he said. It was a shock."

"You getting help?" she asked. "Counseling? You gotta be careful. Things like that can creep up on you. You think you're fine. You go about your business. Then bam. You drop your basket over nothing."

"I'm fine," I said. "Thank you for asking. Really."

She shook her head. "Brass balls on you then. You'd have to lock me up in the nuthouse."

"Gabby," I said. "I wanted to talk to you about Aaron Clyde. He said something on the witness stand that gave me pause. That, quite honestly, should have given the Kings' defense lawyers pause ten years ago."

"Spit it out, sister," Gabby said. "If you haven't noticed, time isn't something I have in abundance anymore."

She knew. I felt it in my bones. She blew smoke into the air, waiting for my question. A beat passed. I decided not to ask one.

"Lyle King never said a single word to Aaron about Krista Nadler or Charlie Brinkman's murder."

I stared Gabby Margolis straight in the eyes, refusing to blink.

"He was coached," I said. "Fed information. Lucky Boy. Aaron said Lyle stood over Charlie Brinkman and said something to the effect of, you're not her lucky boy anymore, are you?"

I took the photograph of Krista's pendant as it lay face down on the ground beside her. I tossed it to Gabby.

She didn't so much as bat an eye as she looked at the thing upside down. She just kept right on smoking her cigarette. It was as much as an admission.

"The inscription on the back of Krista's necklace," I said. "Lyle King probably never even knew it was there. That necklace fell off when the M.E. moved her body. It was around her neck while Lyle was beating her to death. It's tiny. He didn't tell Aaron about it. Aaron saw that particular photograph and remembered it. Lucky Boy. The only people who had access to it were Gus Ritter and Phil Halsey. So, I need to know what you know."

She put her cigarette down.

"No," she said.

"No?"

"I don't think I want to talk with him in the room," Gabby said, gesturing to Sam.

"Gabby, if what ..."

"Sam," I interjected. "Maybe give me ten minutes."

His jaw dropped. "Are you serious?"

"I'm serious," I said. "I'll come get you."

He clenched a fist but swallowed back whatever argument he wanted to make.

"Ten minutes," he said, then headed out the front door.

"No more games," I said to Gabby.

"Not going so great for you, is it?" she said, smiling. "He really screwed you over."

"Phil was desperate," I offered. "The King brothers were going to make his career. That conviction got him national press. Two years later, he won his election in a landslide. Everyone remembered who got those monsters off the streets for good."

"Nice story," Gabby said.

"Except it's all a lie. Phil wasn't who I thought he was. You know he literally self-destructed right in front of me. For what? Because of some pills? Gabby, I know now what Phil was willing to do to further his career. He would have let another killer go free to cover up his sins."

She took the last puff of her cigarette, then flicked it into a waiting ashtray. "Honey, you don't know shit."

"So tell me," I said. "I need to know. Because I still believe Lyle and Damon King are guilty. But I won't win this way."

"You sure about that?" she said. "Not about their guilt. You're right. Those boys are killers. I just don't think you really do want the truth."

"I do," I said. "It's all I've ever wanted."

"Must hurt a lot," she said. "I know about you too, Mara. Everyone lies to you, don't they?"

"You're stalling. Tell me what you know. Please."

Gabby went still and silent. There was nothing between us but the ticking of a grandfather clock in the hallway. She started to sweat. For a moment, I worried she'd keel over then and there. I think she wondered too.

"I want something," she said.

"Tell me," I said.

"Not sure you have the power to give it."

"Only one way to find out," I said.

A full minute passed before Gabby Margolis spoke again.

"You think I got nothing left to lose," she said. "Never had any kids. What family I did have, I drove away. Two husbands. My life savings. My career. Now my health is gone. Three months, maybe. There's nothing left they can do for me. The cancer is in my bones now. Eating away at me."

"I'm so sorry," I said.

"But I do have something left to lose," she said. "I still can go out on my terms. Here. In this house. I don't want to sit in some jail cell. Or worse, some state-run hospital. Just here. By myself, if I can."

"What do you know, Gabby?" I said.

She gave me a grim smile. "Honey, I know everything. The whole operation. You think Aaron Clyde was the only one?"

Her words slammed into me.

"I can give you names. Dates. Cases. But you have to deliver for me. I want full immunity. I don't ever want to have to leave this house again."

"You have to give me something," I said. "I can't agree to a deal if I don't know what I'm getting."

"You still don't understand. You think Phil Halsey blew his brains out because he didn't want people to know he was a drug addict?"

It was all there. Right in front of me. And yet, there was a part of me that wanted to defend him. There was good in Phil. He'd taught me how to prosecute a case. He'd taken a chance on me when all everyone saw was a trust fund brat with a law degree and future trophy wife written all over her.

"There were others," I said. "You're telling me Phil Halsey had a ring of informants?"

She leaned far forward in her chair. "Are you going to give me that deal?"

When I first tried to answer, my throat was too dry. "You have to tell me everything. No matter who else it implicates."

That grim smile again. "You say that now. What if this hits too close to home? Mrs. Brent." She put the emphasis on my last name.

"Every detail," I said. "I'm not afraid of the truth."

"Write it down," she said. "Full immunity."

"I need to make a call," I said.

"Call whoever you want, but it has to be now."

I pulled my laptop out of my briefcase. "You have a printer here?"

"In the study down the hall," she said. "Make your phone call. I'll wait for you right here."

I got to my feet. In a full sweat, I went out the front door while dialing Kenya's number. Sam waited for me, leaning against his car. He read the distress on my face.

"What's up, Mara?" Kenya answered.

Pressing my hand to my forehead, I tried to form words. "I have to tell you something," I said, knowing Gabby's story might ruin both of our careers. "And then I need you to trust me."

❦ 27 ❦

"My God," Kenya said it about fourteen times. I watched my friend age about twenty years in the span of an hour as the breadth of Gabby Margolis's revelation became clear. "Aaron Clyde was part of a ring of informants Phil recruited over the course of about a decade. His main contact was an inmate by the name of Frederick Overton. Big Freddy," I said. With Sam's help, we'd pulled the rap sheets of five of the men Gabby fingered. All of them convicted felons passing through the Maumee County jail en route to the state prison system.

"Whatever he wanted," she said. "Whatever he needed. Mara, these men were involved either directly or indirectly in at least a dozen of the major convictions this office secured."

She picked up one of the rap sheets. Attached to it was a mugshot of a heavily tatted, bald man with menacing green eyes.

"Joe Parsons," she said. "He was involved with some of the worst gang activity we've had in Waynetown. This was my case, Mara. We busted up a main supplier of China White dealing along the river."

"I know," I said. "I remember."

"You're telling me my star witness was one of Phil's informants for hire?"

"That's Gabby's story," I said.

"They'll come after me next," she said. "Maybe you too. Mara, every single one of these cases will have to be reopened. New trials granted."

"I know," I said. "Gabby thinks this is really what Phil was afraid would come out. She thinks it's why he took his own life. It wasn't about his drug problem."

A single tear rolled down her face. "Everything. My whole life. This is all I've ever worked for. It's too much. It's too big."

"You know what we have to do," I said. Kenya lifted her eyes.

"It'll sink the case against the King brothers. They'll walk. We have nothing."

"Maybe not," I said. "I mean, probably. But do you want to sit there and tell me they're not guilty? We know they are. They killed those kids. There's something we're missing. There has to be. So we drop the charges. We can still refile. Double jeopardy won't apply. We can do it right."

"With what?" she said.

"With Gus Ritter and Sam Cruz working their butts off right alongside us. I'm not going to give up. Not ever," I said.

"You won't have a choice," she said. "We'll be lucky if either of us ever tries a case again after this."

She paused. Her eyes hardened. "No. No way. If I have to take the fall for this, I will. I'm not letting you go down too. Somebody has to be left standing to pick up the pieces."

"This wasn't your fault," I said. "You shouldn't be pilloried for it either. We'll ... I don't know. We'll figure it out. We have to."

"Is that a promise?" she said, finally letting at least the hint of a smile light her face. It didn't reach her eyes, though.

"What do you mean?"

"You have an out, Mara. You want to tell me Jason's not trying to get you to go to Washington with him? He might be a snake, but he's in love with you. He's giving you space, but he's not done fighting if I know anything about him."

"Kenya ..."

"No," she said. "I've already heard the rumor."

"Which one?" I said, raising a sardonic brow.

"That you're going to get an offer from the U.S. Attorney's office."

My mouth literally dropped. "No," I said. "I haven't heard that rumor."

"Would you take it?" she asked.

My mind spun in so many directions I didn't even know how to answer. The U.S. Attorney's office. It had been a dream of mine since I started law school. Jason and I had discussed it once or twice when he made the decision to get into national politics.

"I don't know," I said. No, I blurted. It was an honest answer. I didn't know anything anymore. Lord, that wasn't true either.

"I know I still have a job to do. We still have a job to do. Krista Nadler and Charlie Brinkman deserve justice. It's you and me, Kenya. We're the only ones left who can bring it to them. I meant what I said. I'm not giving up yet. Not on this case, and not on you. Phil detonated a bomb. But we're still standing."

"I need to talk to the mayor," she said. "The attorney general's office."

That hollow pit widened in my stomach. Gabby Margolis's words still burned through me. Did Jason already know what Phil had been doing? How high up did this go?

"I need to make a call to Trevor Page and Noel Stamford," I

said. "We have a duty to disclose this. I need your authority. They're going to ask me to dismiss the charges."

"Don't commit to anything yet," she said. "You'll have to meet with Judge Ivey, anyway. I need to ... Christ ... I need to start crafting a response."

"I'll wait to hear from you," I said. "We're gonna get through this. We have to."

Kenya went still. Slowly, she rose to her feet and planted her palms flat against the table. We'd covered it with file after file. It represented Phil's life's work. Part of Kenya's. Part of mine. On the whiteboard behind her, Charlie Brinkman and Krista Nadler's smiling school photos stared down at us.

Kenya's gaze went to them too. She balled one fist, grabbed one of the files, and threw it across the room.

"Go home," she said. "Be with Will."

It occurred to me then how lonely Kenya might be. "I can stay," I said. "We can start doing ... something."

She smiled and straightened her back. "It's almost dinner time," she said. "When did you tell him you were coming home?"

"About five hours ago," I said. "It's Jason's weekend. They went to the art museum. He's been texting me all day. He's okay. That's my one blessing today. Will's hanging in there."

"Good," she said. "But go. We'll both have better heads in the morning. Melody dropped your car off a few hours ago. She took the bus home."

"Melody, I forgot all about her. She was working on combing through Damon King's financials. Do you know if anything popped out at her?"

"She didn't say," Kenya answered.

"I'll be in tomorrow," I said.

"It's Sunday," Kenya said. "Work from home. I'll call you in the morning. Now get out of here. I'm still your boss. It's an order."

I put a hand on Kenya's arm. I knew she wouldn't be leaving tonight. If Jason weren't at the house, I would have asked her to stay with me. Something told me she could use the company. But Kenya was already sifting through more files. I could practically see the gears shifting inside her brain.

I said goodbye and headed out down the dark hallway. Saturday afternoon, there would be no one in the building except a stray sheriff's deputy about to start night shift security for the county buildings. I grabbed my car keys from my desk where Melody had left them.

I closed the door behind me and headed down to my car. Melody had parked it in my usual spot. I took one last look up at the office. The conference room was the single visible light. I could see Kenya's silhouette. She was still hunched over the table.

I pushed my guilt away and unlocked the car door. A shadow fell over me. The hairs stood up on the back of my head. I turned just as Abigail Morgan rushed toward me, her hair flying wildly around her.

❧ 28 ❧

"Did you help him?" she shrieked. "Was this your idea? You know what that makes you?"

I put my hands up, ready to defend myself if Abigail tried to strike me.

"You need to step off," I said. "I have nothing to say to you."

"You need to know what you're married to," she said. "Jason always wins. Don't you get that? No matter what. No matter who he has to run over or ruin along the way. He takes what he wants. Whenever he wants it. You have no idea what he's capable of. How far he's willing to go. You think I'm his worst sin."

"Abigail," I said through clenched teeth. "You really don't want to get in my face right now. Or ever."

"I want what's mine," she said. "That's all. I told you that before. I was an idiot to think you'd have any compassion for me. You're no better than he is. No. You're worse because you're a woman."

"I don't know what you want or what you're talking about," I said, advancing on her. I would not let this girl intimidate me.

"I'm trying to protect my son. That's it. You wanna know what happened to him? They put pictures ... *your* pictures ... all over his locker. You want to tell me you had nothing to do with that? They came from you. Your phone. You're the only one who has them," I said.

I hadn't really thought of Abigail being behind the stunt at Will's school. Now that I said it, I started to believe it. Maybe she had been approached by Divine Justice, or the other way around. I wanted to tear her damn hair out.

"So let me give you a warning," I said. "Stay away from me. Stay away from my kid. Or whatever you think Jason's done is just the tip of the iceberg."

Her eyes widened. Abigail knew enough to be scared. I went full on Mama Bear, backing her against another car.

"Leave," I said. "Get out of Waynetown. I'm sorry your life choices aren't working out so well for you. And I'm sorry it's my son and me who are having to pay for them."

"Mara?" A deep, male voice cut the air.

Sam Cruz came out of the shadows. I saw his right hand playing at his hip holster. I took a step away from Abigail.

"Stay away from us," I said.

"Everything all right?" Sam asked. He came to my side and touched my elbow.

"It is now," I muttered.

"Doesn't look like Mrs. Brent much wants to talk to you," Sam said to Abigail. "Do you have business here?"

She sneered. "Well, if that isn't just perfect."

She straightened her skirt and spun away from us. Then she disappeared back into the shadows.

Sam looked at me. "You okay?"

"No," I said. "I'm really not. Sam, that was. She's ... Jason's." It was the only way I could think to say it. It was enough. Sam gave me a knowing nod.

"I think maybe she had something to do with the pictures they found in Will's locker too." I'd looped Sam in on what happened. Will's school had filed a report with the sheriff's department so I knew Sam would hear about it, anyway.

Sam's face fell. "That's ... crap. That's actually what I was coming to find you about."

"What do you mean?"

"Mara, we were able to ID the temp janitor from the security footage. She used a false name. But we tracked her down. She's local."

"Do you know if she's connected to the Servants of Divine Justice?" I said, my pulse quickening.

"The woman's name was Arlene Smith, but she's used aliases," Sam answered. "She did some volunteer work for Divine Justice. So yeah, there's a connection. Your instincts were right. Of course, they're claiming she acted without their authority. I just thought you should know."

"This was the Kings," I said. "My God. Sam. Damon King had those pictures plastered all over Will's locker? He's making this personal."

Sam dropped his chin. His eyes were kind but filled with an amount of pity I just couldn't deal with right now.

"It's looking likely," he said. "Gus is interviewing the woman now. He'll get us the answers we need."

"Thanks," I said. "I just ..."

"You need to get home to your kid," he said, throwing me a gentle smile.

"Yeah," I said.

"Come on," he said. "I'll follow you home. Make sure you don't run into any more trouble along the way."

I was about to protest, but Sam's dark eyes told me he wasn't asking. Gratitude filled my heart, though I couldn't quite express it in words. Not yet.

I slid behind the wheel and pulled out of my parking spot. Sam fell behind me, the headlights of his cruiser filling my rearview mirror. He stayed close but kept his distance, scanning the surrounding road. With everything that had happened in the last day and a half, it felt good to know someone else had my back.

❧ 29 ❧

Monday morning at seven a.m., Judge Ivey met us in his chambers. Kenya, me, Trevor Page, Noel Stamford, and Damon King. Lyle opted or was told not to show. Damon sat quietly staring at all of us, a neutral expression on his face as I laid out the basic facts as I knew them.

"He was coached," Judge Ivey said. He peered at Gabby Margolis's affidavit and plea agreement through giant reading glasses.

"It appears so, yes," I said. "According to Ms. Margolis, Aaron Clyde was approached by another inmate by the name of Freddy Overton. Freddy was the contact point. When Halsey needed a witness to testify ... um ... a certain way, Freddy had a network within the prison system."

"He's admitting to all of this?" Ivey asked.

"He is," I said. "Aaron Clyde was taken into custody late last night. Detective Cruz typed up his statement. I provided copies to Mr. Page and Mr. Stamford. Yours are attached to Ms. Margolis's affidavit."

"Unbelievable," Page said.

"Mr. Clyde's entire testimony is compromised," Judge Ivey

said. "How far back does this go? How many other convictions?"

"Your Honor," Kenya said. "We're in the midst of an ongoing investigation. I can assure you the prosecutor's office will cooperate fully with the attorney general's office."

Trevor Page barked out a laugh. "Mara never should have taken this case in the first place. Your entire office is corrupt. She's married to the assistant attorney general!"

I whipped around. "You wanna talk to me about conflicts of interest? That's the road you want to go down?"

"Enough," Judge Ivey said. "Fine, we'll confine our discussion to matters strictly pertaining to the case at hand. Your star witness is impeached, Ms. Brent."

"Halsey framed my client," Page said. "That's abundantly clear. We already knew that. Now you're telling me the same sheriff's department that procured Clyde's bogus testimony is currently interviewing him again? Without a lawyer present?"

"He's waived his right to one," Kenya answered.

"Right," Page said.

"Mr. Page, Mr. Stamford," Judge Ivey said. "It seems to me you've got grounds for a mistrial. Let's go on the record and get this over with."

"Trevor," Damon said. "I'd like to speak to my attorney in private."

There was a cold, calm menace in Damon King's voice. Trevor went a little white. He awkwardly cleared his throat. Ivey waved them off.

"Five minutes," he said. "We've taken up enough of the jury's time."

"I only need two," Damon said. It earned him a raised brow from Judge Ivey. If I ever had a doubt who was calling the shots in that relationship, the Demon King just cleared them. Noel, Trevor, and Damon left the room. Only Noel looked upset.

"Your Honor," Kenya started.

"Stop right there," Ivey said. "Not a word out of either one of you. Not without opposing counsel present. You know better. But that's one hell of a dumpster fire your predecessor left behind for you."

I heard shouting coming from the hall. Judge Ivey's door was thick enough I couldn't make out the words, just the sentiments. Trevor Page wasn't happy.

Only a minute went by before the door swung open and Page and Stamford walked in. Noel looked nervous and kept adjusting his tie. Sweat glistened over his brow. What in the world had King said to them?

"Your Honor," Page said. "We won't be moving for a mistrial. We don't want one."

"Mr. Stamford?" Judge Ivey said.

"No, Your Honor," Noel said. "I concur with Mr. Page. Lyle King isn't seeking a mistrial either."

"You're kidding." Ivey and Kenya said it in unison.

"I am not," Page said, then looked at Noel. "If I may, the King brothers have spent nearly ten years in prison for a crime they didn't commit. This isn't just a mistake. This was a deliberate, coordinated conspiracy to deprive them of their freedom and ruin their lives. We want to put the State to its proofs once and for all and let the jury render its verdict."

It was a bold move, but it made a certain diabolical sense. As things stood now, Trevor and Noel could make reasonable doubt in about ten different ways. Sierra Joy hadn't even testified yet. Odds were heavily in the Kings' favor that the jury would acquit. Then, double jeopardy would apply and they could never be recharged or retried for Charlie and Krista's murder.

"Your Honor," I said. "If defense counsel doesn't wish to move for mistrial, the State can. In the interests of justice, we'd ..."

"Save it," Judge Ivey said. "I'm telling you right now, if the defendants don't want a mistrial, I'm not granting one. If I may be so bold, this is your office's shit sandwich. You're stuck with it, as far as I'm concerned. You want to drop the charges, I can't stop you. Under the circumstances, I'm going to grant a four day recess. Figure out amongst yourselves what you're going to do. Otherwise, I'll see you all Thursday morning. For now, I've heard enough. You're all dismissed."

I rose. When I turned, Damon King stared straight through me, grinning. As we left, King and Page went one way, trailed by Noel Stamford; Kenya and I went the other.

I still couldn't believe what I'd heard. I gestured to Kenya, and we ducked into the tiny law library kitty corner to Judge Ivey's office.

"I'll tell you one thing," I said. "King's smarter than Page and Stamford combined."

"I was about to say the same thing," Kenya said. "Because this is it. If we can't salvage this thing and nail the Kings right here, right now, we'll never get another chance."

"We can dismiss," I said. "We can refile. Someone knows something. I'm certain of it. Damon King didn't just target Charlie and Krista by accident. There's proof out there. We just need more time."

"We don't have it," she said. "You heard Judge Ivey, we've got four days."

I wanted to argue. I wanted to sputter off about a dozen 'buts' to Kenya's statement. Except I knew where we would end up. Judge Ivey was right. Phil Halsey had left more than a dumpster fire behind. He'd detonated a nuclear bomb.

"I'm going to have to spend the next two to three years unraveling all the damage Phil did," Kenya said. "That will be my legacy. There won't be any new charges filed against Lyle and Damon King, Mara. It's gotta be this trial. This jury."

I sank slowly into one of the chairs by the wall.

"I don't have much left," I said. "We have Damon's search

history. We have Evelyn Bishop's suspicion and her overhearing, after the fact, of statements about baptismal fires. I have no physical evidence linking them to the crime. No confession now. No eyewitness. And Sierra Joy was going to be my next witness. I figured I'd get out in front of her damaging testimony."

I started to laugh as I got the last words out. It sounded a little unhinged to my own ears. "I'm basically in a position where I was about to beg Trevor Page to file that motion for a mistrial."

Kenya walked to the other side of the room. She paused and pulled a single volume of the *Ohio Revised Code* off the shelf. For half a second, I thought she had some epiphany. She didn't. Instead, she raised the book above her head and hurled it against the far wall.

"They did it," she said. "They killed those poor kids. There's no doubt in my mind."

"I know," I said.

"They're going to get away with it, aren't they?"

I wanted to tell her pretty things. Heck, I wanted to say them to myself. I wanted to be able to tuck my son in at night and promise him there were no such things as monsters. That the good guys always won. Or even that his daddy was the hero he'd always thought him to be. Or ... that I was.

"We still have four days," I said.

Kenya plopped down into the chair beside me. She took my hand and raised it.

"What are you ..."

Kenya looked straight ahead. The third-floor window gave us a clear view of the Waynetown skyline and the Empire Bridge stretching across the Maumee River.

It could have been a canyon, though. She sat to my left as if she were in the driver's seat.

I bit my lip.

"Let's keep going," she said. "Go."

Laughing a bit, I said the next line from the movie I knew she was thinking of. "You sure?"

"Yes," she said.

"Okay," I said. "But I'm not going to kiss you now, Thelma."

"I hear you, Louise," she answered. "But if there's anybody I have to jump off a cliff with, I want it to be you."

I felt a bit of the weight lifting from my shoulders. I knew it was because Kenya shared that weight with me.

"Me too," I said. "But we haven't reached that cliff just yet. We've still got four days' worth of road."

"So let's get busy," Kenya said, squeezing my hand.

Monday evening, I took my files home so I could have dinner with Will. It had been the one constant through this whole trial. Jason was leaving the next morning but had some business in Columbus. He would spend the night here in the guest room, but then our lives would shift once more.

Will was especially quiet tonight. I'd brought Japanese takeout from one of his favorite restaurants. My son might be one of the few nine-year-olds who craved sushi more than French fries. He worked a pair of chopsticks like a pro. Years ago, one of his forward-thinking occupational therapists had used them with him to help him work on his fine motor skills. I had to stick with my fork.

"How did it go today?" I asked. My sister-in-law Kat had picked Will up from school. She said he seemed normal, but didn't want to pry about Friday's drama.

"It went," Will said. "We're starting a solar system unit. I asked Mrs. Whitney if I could build a Lego model."

This was a work-a-round Will often used. Written tests were tough for him. He could build a pulley machine with his father in the garage. He struggled with answering multiple-choice questions about how they worked.

"You sure you're going to have time for that?" I asked. "Nine planets. The sun. And you know you're not going to like it unless you figure out how to build rings around Saturn."

"Saturn isn't the only planet with rings," he said.

"Right," I said. "What about sketching it? You're good at that, too. We can go to the art store and get you some new colored pencils and drawing paper."

Will canted his head to the side as he considered my offer. "That could work," he finally said.

"You want me to talk to Mrs. Whitney? I can email her after dinner."

"No," Will said. "I have to advocate for myself."

I reached for him, smoothing the hair down where it always stuck up in the back. He let me.

"Are we moving?" he abruptly asked.

I set my fork down. "Dad is," I answered. "You know he has to for at least part of the year."

"I'd like to go there," Will said, making my lungs burn with anxiety.

"To D.C.?"

"The cost of living is three times what it is here in Waynetown. You wouldn't be able to afford a house like this one on your salary."

"Will, we've talked about this. You need to let Dad and me worry about how we pay the bills. It's going to be okay. That I can promise you," I said. "But D.C. Are you saying that's where you'd want to live?"

He clicked his chopsticks together, at the same time exposing his bottom teeth in what I used to call his T-Rex face when he was littler.

"Mrs. Whitney is just about broken in," he said. It was the

way of Will sometimes. He might not give me a direct answer, but I learned his mind from the things he did say.

"That's no small thing," I said. "We never did quite break in Mrs. Polaski when you were in second grade, remember?"

Will nodded.

"He did a bad thing," Will said. "Dad. He hurt your feelings."

I held my breath. I tried to remember all the things we'd discussed with Will's therapist. Answer the questions he asks truthfully and simply.

"Yes," I said. "Dad hurt my feelings. Married people can do that. But it doesn't mean they always stop loving each other. And more importantly, it doesn't mean they stop loving their kids or being good parents."

"Have you stopped loving him?" Will asked.

"Parts of him, yes," I said. "I know that's maybe hard for you to hear."

"I know," he said. "I think Mercury might really be the hardest if I were going to stick with the Lego plan."

I folded my hands in my lap. A small sound behind me toward the garage door drew my attention. Jason stood there, frozen, like perhaps he was the one made out of Legos.

"It's very small," I said. "I mean, in relation to the other planets. Where are we on Pluto?"

Will pursed his lips, deepening the dimple in his cheek. "It's complicated," he said. "Can I go take my bath now?"

"Sure thing," I said. Jason walked into the dining room. He kissed Will on the head just as he got up to leave the table.

When we heard the water running, Jason sat down in Will's seat.

"I don't want to talk about that," I said. "Not now."

"I know," Jason answered. "It's been a tough week on all of us."

"She came to see me," I said. "Abby." With everything that had happened with Will and the King trial, we hadn't had a chance to really talk about what happened with Abby in the parking lot the other day.

Jason dropped his head. He knew. Dammit. He already knew.

"I'm sorry," he said.

"Sam," I said.

"He called me," Jason said. "He thought I should know."

"Fine," I said. "Jason, I don't want to have to do it. But I'll get a restraining order. I can't have that woman coming to my work. What if Will's school is next?"

"She won't," he said. "I can handle it."

"We're never going to get out from under this, are we?" I asked.

"We will," he said, reaching for me. "I just need time. Things are so crazy right now. For you and for me. Give it a few weeks and we can carve some kind of new normal. I need you by my side."

"You need me? Or you need the photographs of me literally by your side?" I asked.

"Don't say that."

"Jason, I'm not going to talk about this with you now. If you haven't been paying attention, I've got a bit of a mess of my own to deal with."

Jason sighed. "Halsey."

"Yes, Halsey. The gift that keeps on giving."

Jason shook his head. "It's your whole case. Without Aaron Clyde's testimony, what do you have left?"

"I'm not done fighting," I said.

Jason smiled. "I know you're not. You've got that look you get. Is there anything I can do to help?"

On the other side of the dining room table, I had a stack of paperwork Melody sent over by messenger. She'd gone through Damon King's financial records and made some notes. It was my next chore after making sure Will was settled. Tomorrow, I was going to try one more time with Stephanie Nadler and Charlie and Sharon Brinkman. Maybe there was something ... some tiny detail about what Krista and Charlie were doing that summer that might jar their memories.

"I don't think so," I said. "And I suppose technically we shouldn't even be talking about this. Your old office is still investigating my office."

"I was walled off from anything to do with Waynetown before I left for D.C."

"Still," I said. "I just don't want to do anything that'll give even the appearance of impropriety."

No sooner had I said it, before something else tugged at the corners of my brain. It was Abigail. It was Phil. It was Gabby Margolis's innuendo. It was everything.

"Jason," I said. "Did you know?"

"Know what?" he asked.

"What Phil was doing? I mean, did you have any inkling? You worked with him too. You knew him longer than even I did."

Jason sat with his elbow on the table, his chin resting against his palm. But he didn't answer right away. Instead, Abby's words to me replayed in my mind.

You have no idea what he's capable of. How far he's willing to go. You think I'm his worst sin.

"Jason?"

He snapped back to attention. "Did I know Phil was running an informant ring out of the prison? No, Mara. I didn't know that."

"In all this time. All these cases, you never once suspected anything was going on?" I asked.

"Did you?" He threw it back to me. "Christ. You worked more closely with him than I did."

"Abby told me you planted evidence against her. Or your people did. She denied everything about those child abuse charges. Was it Len Grantham? Was this your campaign people?"

Jason slammed his fist down. "Don't ask me that. We've already had that conversation."

"Don't ask you because you don't want to have to lie? Jason, I'm done. I can't take any more deception. At this point, I'd rather know the truth. For once."

His gray eyes flashed as he stared at me. It wasn't a denial. It wasn't an admission either. My head just ... hurt. How big a fool had I really been? I believed in Phil Halsey. The same way I'd believed in this man. They both betrayed me.

"I'll tell you what," he said. "I'll let you do your job. I promised our son I'd help him talk out some solar system project he's got in mind. It looks to me like you've got a project of your own."

He waved to the stack of papers on the table.

"Jason ..."

"We'll be upstairs when you're ready to come up for air," he said. Then Jason scooted away from the table and stormed upstairs.

I tried to clear my head as I cleared the table from mine and Will's dinner. I threw the trash in the garbage under the sink. Seeing it was full, I took it out, relishing the cool night air as I made my way to the bin we kept on the other side of the garage.

When I came back in, I could hear my husband and my son's voices from the upstairs spare bedroom. Will's was louder, talking a mile a minute. Jason listened, patiently offering a suggestion or two that would keep Will on track, steering him back from the tangents he often took.

His compass. That's how I always thought of Jason. When Will started to go astray, it was his father's soothing voice and guiding hand that would lead him back out of the thickest woods.

❧ 31 ❧

I picked up the stack of papers and began to spread them out on the table.

Evelyn Bishop kept meticulous records of all incoming and outgoing money. Expenses were small. Printer paper. Website maintenance. The utility bills for the farm. I'd combed through all of this before but found it mostly useless.

Damon's receipts were mostly cash donations. No names. Five dollars here and there. Twenty. The people who made up his congregation were poor. They offered what they could. Sometimes it was just loose change. Evelyn started a food bank with it.

I ran my finger down the columns of her balance sheet. I paused at one entry. In late May, the summer of Charlie and Krista's murder, she took in a fifty-dollar cash donation. There had never been anything that large before.

I kept going. One week later, another fifty dollars. The same the week after that. It went on for the whole summer. I pulled up a 2008 calendar on my phone. It was always on Mondays. By the middle of August, it totaled six hundred dollars, if this was all coming from the same donor.

I checked the time. It was only seven p.m. I dialed Melody's number. She answered right away.

"Hey, Melody," I said. "I'm looking at King's ledger. I'm noticing a regular donation. Starting early summer."

"The fifty-dollar one," she said. "I noticed that too."

"It was always cash?" I asked.

"Yep," Melody said. "I asked Evelyn about it."

"Could she shed any light on it?" I asked.

"Not really," Melody said. "She said she remembers it and it was so much larger than what they usually got, so she did ask Damon about it."

"And?"

"And he wouldn't tell her," she said. "Evelyn said he told her just put it in the bank and do her job. She said he started taking a meeting on Sunday nights and Monday morning he'd walk in and hand her a fifty-dollar bill. That's it."

"A fifty-dollar bill," I said. "She was certain of that? It didn't just total fifty dollars?"

"Nope. She said a fifty-dollar bill. Every time. Evelyn worked for Damon around her regular job at the library. So she'd come and do the books for him on the weekends. She said that whole summer he was having Sunday dinner somewhere. She asked him if he wanted to expense that. He said no. And she didn't know where he was going or who he was meeting with."

"Thanks," I said.

"Is there something else you want me to try to run down?" Melody asked.

"Not tonight," I said. "I'll let you know if it ends up being anything. I have one more call I need to make."

I hung up with Melody and dialed Gus Ritter's number. It rang a few times. I knew Gus still carried a flip phone.

"Yeah," he answered.

"Gus," I said. "I need you to check something for me. Pull

your cell phone report for Damon King the summer of 2008. I need to try and figure out where he might have been on Sunday nights starting the beginning of June."

I explained to him what I saw in the ledger.

"Fifty bucks a week?" he said.

"Yeah. I know. It's maybe nothing. And I would think it was nothing. It's just ... Gus ... the last fifty-dollar donation I see in this book happened the Sunday before Charlie and Krista died."

He went silent on the other end of the line. Then Gus's next word encapsulated everything I was feeling just then.

"Shit."

❧ 32 ❧

Sharon and Charlie Brinkman Sr. sold the house they'd lived in when Charlie Jr. was still alive. They spent half their time in a condo on the Gulf side of Florida. Everyone said Sharon wanted to move there permanently, but Charlie Sr. wouldn't go. His son was buried in Waynetown.

Finally, after months of asking and having Sharon blow me off, she agreed to meet with me along with her husband at Denman Metro Park inside the pavilion that stayed open year-round. It was Tuesday. Thirty-six hours before Lyle and Damon King's murder trial would resume.

I came armed with a stack of spreadsheets, dwindling hopes, and a hunch.

Sharon Brinkman had bleach blonde hair. That was different. From the photographs that circulated ten years ago, she'd been a dark brunette. Charlie Sr. looked like he'd aged fifty years instead of just the ten. He walked with a cane now. His clothes hung off of him. I felt as though I were looking at a man who had flat out lost the will to live.

"Thanks for seeing me," I said. We sat at a table near the window. Sounds of laughter and delighted screams came to us from the sledding hills a few yards away. We could see them from a large window. This building was used most often for banquets and weddings.

Charlie's eyes drifted to the kids. For a moment, he smiled. Then it melted into a blank stare. I imagined his grief was like that. He orbited around it.

"We don't have anything new to tell you," Sharon said. "You have our statements to the police. We both testified in the first trial. You have no idea how difficult this is for us. It stirs up too much. Charlie's had two heart attacks."

"I'm so sorry," I said. "I know there's nothing I can say that can ease your pain. I'm just trying to preserve justice for Charlie and Krista."

"Can you?" Charlie asked. "We've been hearing some rumors."

"I suppose you have," I said. "What I'm about to tell you is still under a gag order. But you aren't members of the press. That said, I do need discretion from you. Until this trial is over, I have to ask that you don't repeat our discussion."

"We don't talk to anyone," Sharon said. "That's the thing they don't tell you when you lose a child like we did. You lose your friends too. It becomes too painful for them. You're a constant reminder of this terrible tragedy."

I nodded. "Stephanie Nadler said something very similar to me. Again, I really am sorry."

"What do you have to tell us?" Charlie asked.

"Thursday morning," I said. "The King trial will resume. The jury is going to be told that Aaron Clyde, the man who said Lyle King confessed to him, was lying. I'm so sorry. But Aaron made Lyle's confession up."

I couldn't tell them the rest about Phil Halsey's informant ring. That was still confidential and under investigation. Soon enough, it wouldn't be.

"He didn't kill our boy?" Sharon asked. Her tone was odd. It sounded like relief. The hunch in my gut deepened, throbbing as if it had a pulse. If I were wrong about this, I was about to revictimize Sharon and Charlie Brinkman.

"No," I said. "I still believe he did. It's just that a critical piece of evidence will be thrown out. The jury will be instructed to disregard Aaron Clyde's testimony and Lyle King's so-called confession completely."

Charlie made a choked sound. He dropped his head. "You're telling us those men will go free. Without that confession ..."

I pulled a thin file out of my briefcase and laid it on the table in front of them.

"This is what I need to talk to you about," I said. "The piece that's been missing for me is how Damon King targeted your son and his girlfriend specifically."

"That came out already," Charlie said. "Kids have been going up into the woods around the Blitz to make out since the early seventies."

"I don't think so," I said. "We know Damon was stalking Krista on the internet for a couple of weeks prior to the murders. It wasn't random. If I can establish another connection between Damon or Lyle and Charlie and Krista, we still have a chance. A strong one."

"We're done here," Sharon said. "I've had enough of this. We've been over this and over this. For years."

She started to rise. She tugged on her husband's sleeve. He was like a robot. I don't think he really knew what he was doing. He just started to swing his legs to the side of his chair. His wife told him to move, so he began to move.

I opened the file and laid out the spreadsheets. "I want to ask you what you might have known about the Church of the Living Flame," I said. "Damon King's ministry."

Charlie stopped moving. Sharon didn't.

"You know the theory has always been that Damon was trying to save Charlie and Krista's souls. In his twisted mind, a baptism by fire would purge them of their sins. You know this. He wears a tattoo. Luke 3:16. Are you familiar with it?"

Charlie's hand shook as he covered his mouth with it. I hated that I had to bring him any additional pain.

"I baptize you with water. But he who is mightier than I is coming. The strap of whose sandals I am not worthy to untie. He will baptize you with the Holy Spirit and fire," I said.

Sharon's lips tightened, but she finally stopped moving.

"You belonged to the Holy Reformer church," I said. "Stephanie first told me that. Sharon, you knew Pastor Lennard. Didn't you?"

Nothing.

"Damon liked Matthew 3:10 as well," I said.

This time, Charlie answered, but it was as if he were speaking from very far away. "His winnowing fork is in his hand, and he will clear his threshing floor, gathering his wheat into the barn and burning up the chaff with unquenchable fire."

"Yes. We're tracking a strange donation," I said. "Fifty dollars a week that Damon received in cash every Sunday night for about three months before the murders. They stopped though, that last Sunday the week Charlie and Krista died."

A look passed over Sharon Brinkman's face. Not grief. Not even anger. Hatred.

"Mrs. Brinkman," I said. "Do you know anything about that donation?"

"Why would we know?" Charlie asked. His voice went up an octave. Color came into his cheeks.

"Mrs. Brinkman." I kept my focus on Sharon. "You didn't want Stephanie at Charlie's funeral. She said you blamed her. Why?"

Sharon Brinkman's lips disappeared. In their place was a tight, white line.

"Did you tell her she should pray that the Holy Spirit finally came to Krista?"

"We're leaving, Charlie!" she shouted.

I pushed the spreadsheets closer. "I'm preparing a subpoena," I said. "I need you to understand that time is of the utmost essence. It would be far better if you would simply turn the documents over to me."

"What documents?" Charlie asked.

"Mr. Brinkman, am I right in assuming that for your 2008 tax year, you would have claimed six hundred dollars to the Kingdom Ministries?"

"How could I possibly remember that?" he asked. "We donate thousands every year to church charities. Sharon brings me the receipts and I give them to the tax guy. Sharon has a big heart. Sometimes it's bigger than my pocketbook."

"Right," I said. "But the Kingdom Ministries. Specifically fifty dollars a week, for twelve weeks ..."

"I'm done," Sharon said.

"I'm not saying you did anything wrong," I said. "Mrs. Brinkman, I know you loved your son. I know you just wanted the best for him."

"Sharon?" Charlie said. "What the hell is she talking about? Did you do something?"

"Mr. Brinkman," I said. "The Kingdom Ministries is the 501(C) 3 corporation that Damon King set up for the Church of the Living Flame."

It was as if I'd reached in and removed Charlie Brinkman's spine. He went boneless, crumpling over the table. His sobs echoed through the hall.

Sharon stared me down. I pulled one more document out of my file and slid it across to her.

"I'm going to need you in court Thursday morning," I said. "That's a subpoena compelling your testimony. Though I was hoping you'd just come voluntarily."

Then, Sharon Brinkman finally broke. Tears burst from her eyes and she slowly sank next to her husband.

❦ 33 ❦

Sharon Brinkman looked so small as she sat in the witness box Thursday morning. Judge Ivey started promptly at eight. Within an hour, the jury had heard from Gabby Margolis. She laid out her entire dealings with Phil Halsey and how Aaron Clyde's testimony had been solicited. She had her immunity deal. She explained in meticulous detail how she and Phil showed Aaron the crime scene photos so he could construct a story that made it sound like only Lyle King could have told it.

Aaron took the stand and promptly exerted his Fifth Amendment right not to incriminate himself further. With that, a hole as wide as Texas ripped through my case.

Now, Sharon Brinkman's testimony felt like trying to close a bullet hole with Scotch tape.

"Mrs. Brinkman," I asked. "Can you tell me how you met Damon King."

She hiccupped. I wondered if she'd even get through it. Gus came through for me as well if she started to lie. When he reviewed the cell phone data they had on Damon's phone, he could put him in the vicinity of a diner a mile from Sharon Brinkman's home, every Sunday from seven to eight p.m. that corresponded to the receipt of her fifty-dollar donations. Melody came through and found a manager who still worked at the diner. He remembered Damon coming in that summer on Sundays. He couldn't identify Sharon, but it would hopefully be enough to keep her honest.

"I heard about him from Pastor Lennard," she said. "At Holy Reformer. He was grooming Damon. Then they parted ways. But before that, Pastor Lennard thought my Charlie might benefit from attending one of Damon's sermons."

"Did he?" I asked.

"No," she said. "Charlie, my husband, was set on Holy Reformer. But I wanted to see what the fuss was about for myself before sending my son to listen to Damon. Plus, I didn't think his father would approve."

"Did you attend one of Mr. King's sermons?" I asked.

"Once," she said. "But not out at the farm where he usually preached. In April of 2008, he came to a luncheon I attended over in Fostoria. There was a group of us. Women I'd known since our kids were in preschool together. I liked what he had to say."

"Which was what?" I asked.

"Damon preached about how our young people were losing their way. How we had to learn to speak their language and relate to their struggles if we wanted to help guide them to salvation. And if we didn't, we would lose them. How the internet was the devil's work and it would take over their lives."

"What happened after that luncheon?" I asked.

"I went up to him. I talked to Damon for about an hour after that. I thought ... he was very charming. He seemed to truly care about what we were going through."

"Is that the last time you saw him?" I asked.

"No," she said. Sharon grabbed a tissue from the box and started to wring it with both hands.

"When else did you see him?"

"I started ... I started to seek counsel from him over that summer. I was worried. Charlie was drifting away from us. He was talking about changing his plans. He was all set to go to seminary school after he graduated from High School. In May he told me he'd changed his mind. He thought he might like to try business school. Or even join the military."

"How did that make you feel?" I asked.

"I was so angry. But mostly scared for him. It wasn't like my Charlie. He was different. He ... stopped talking to us. He spent all his time with that girl. She was changing him. He was ... they weren't ... I found ... condoms in his room."

I took a beat. Trevor Page scribbled furious notes. Damon sat quite still, staring at Sharon. She wouldn't look his way.

"What did you do about that?" I asked.

"I needed help. Charlie, his dad, wouldn't listen to me. No one would listen to me. They all thought I was overreacting. I was fighting for my son's life. She was turning him away from God, from his calling. I could see it happening. Day by day. Damon King was the only one who seemed to understand. I told him. I confided to him about what I'd found. I told him I knew they were sneaking off and doing things together. I knew he was taking her to that quarry. We were all scared of that. All the mothers in my group."

"Then what happened?" I asked.

"We started meeting for coffee once a week. I didn't want to go to his church at the farm. I still didn't think my husband would approve of that. He's very set in his ways. So, I would meet with Damon King for about a half-hour after dinner on Sunday nights that summer. At the Sunrise Diner on Rowan Street. I could walk there. That's what I did. I took my Sunday night walks."

"What did you discuss?" I asked.

"We talked about Charlie. About Mr. King's ministry. I

would give him fifty dollars. A fifty-dollar bill every week. A donation."

At that point, I introduced Charlie and Sharon's tax returns showing the six-hundred-dollar donation.

"What else did you discuss?"

"I wanted to hear his thoughts about how to save Charlie's soul. I was losing him. I knew it," she said.

"You told him that?" I asked. "Mrs. Brinkman, I need you to be very clear about what you told Damon King."

"I told him I knew they were sneaking off to the Blitz!" She screamed the last part and became hysterical.

"Ma'am," Judge Ivey said. "Would you like to take a break?"

"No," Sharon sniffled. "No. I'm sorry. Oh Charlie, I'm so sorry. I didn't know. I didn't think. He said he would pray with me. That's all. Pray for Charlie. I was lost. I was desperate. I didn't know he would ... that he would take my boy!"

"Objection!" Trevor Page shouted.

"Your Honor," I said. "I have nothing further for this witness."

Trevor stormed past me, brushing against my shoulder hard enough I almost lost my balance.

"Mrs. Brinkman," Trevor said. "You never once told this story to the police, did you?"

"No," she said.

"And you testified at the original trial against my client, didn't you?" he asked.

"Yes."

"Do you remember being asked by both Phil Halsey and Mr. King's defense attorney whether you knew the defendant?"

"I suppose so, yes," she said.

"And what did you answer?" Trevor asked.

"No," she said. "I told them no."

"And you were questioned by the police before that," Trevor asked.

"Yes," she cried.

"And you never once mentioned that you knew the defendant. Or that you'd been meeting with him. Or that, my God, you claim you told him your son would be at the Blitz?"

"No," she said, barely audible.

"Your son was murdered, Mrs. Brinkman. No. Not just murdered. He was tortured. And you expect this jury to believe that you withheld information about who you say you told about his whereabouts?" Trevor asked.

"I didn't tell them," she said. "No."

"So as a mother who loves her son, you expect this jury to believe that you had pertinent information that you withheld from the police and the prosecutor that in our mind, might have helped convict who you thought killed him ... and you kept it to yourself?" Trevor asked.

"Yes," she sobbed. "I'm sorry. I'm so sorry. I couldn't believe it. It was so awful. I made a mistake. I made so many mistakes. And then he confessed. They said his brother confessed. What did it matter then? I'm so, so sorry. Oh Charlie. I didn't mean it. I swear I didn't mean it."

"I have nothing further for this witness," Trevor said.

"Mr. Stamford?" Judge Ivey said.

"I just have one question to add," Noel said.

"Mrs. Brinkman, was Lyle King ever at these meetings?"

"No," she said.

"Sorry, one more question. You never even met Lyle King, did you?"

"No," she said.

Noel nodded, then turned back to his seat. Damon King's mask of charm slipped for an instant. I was certain I may have been the only person to see it. But his eyes went dead and cold as he looked at Noel Stamford.

"Ms. Brent?" Judge Ivey asked.

By then, Sharon Brinkman was doubled over in tears. The

jury might hate her for what she'd withheld. But they might feel sorry for her, too. I knew I did. It was all just such an awful waste.

"Nothing from me, Your Honor," I said.

"You may step down, Mrs. Brinkman."

She did. The bailiff had to help her. Charlie Brinkman Sr. sat mute in the courtroom, his face wet with tears. He didn't go to his wife when she shrugged off the sheriff. He didn't go to her as she made her way to the back of the courtroom and put her hand on the doors. She would have walked out alone.

But then, a primal shriek echoed through the courtroom. From the gallery, Stephanie Nadler launched herself down the aisle. She descended on Sharon Brinkman like a wraith, grabbing her shoulders and pitching her forward so they both fell through the doors and into the hallway.

The courtroom erupted in chaos. It took three deputies to pull Stephanie Nadler off of Sharon Brinkman.

❧ 34 ❧

Stephanie Nadler let loose a primal cry that ripped through me, awakening my mother's heart.

"Don't hurt her!" I yelled, trying to push my way to her. Sam came running. One deputy had his arms around Stephanie. Three more formed a wall between her and Sharon Brinkman.

Judge Ivey's gavel banged loudly. The bailiff hurriedly ushered the jury back into their waiting room. But of course they'd seen everything.

"They won't hurt her," Sam said as he got to me. "It's going to be okay."

Sam sprang into action, directing the other deputies to usher Sharon and Charlie Brinkman toward the elevator at the end of the hall. I backed away, letting them do their jobs.

Members of the press tried to jostle their way through to get a quote from either the Brinkmans or Stephanie. One pushed past me with enough force that I stumbled.

An arm shot out, catching me before I pitched face first into the wall.

"Thank you," I said, putting a hand out. I'd managed to

carve a small space for myself away from the chaos. His hand was still firm on my upper arm. I looked up.

"It's not safe for you out here," Damon King said. His blue eyes flashed and his lips curved into a smile.

I jerked my arm away. The air in my lungs thickened.

"Are you sure you're all right, Ms. Brent?" he said. "You look like maybe you need to sit down."

I looked up and down the hall. Trevor Page was at the other end of it, managing Lyle King along with Noel.

"I think you need to head back to your seat," I said. "Judge Ivey will reconvene soon."

King's smile curved upward. "Oh, I think he'll give this a little while to simmer down. Don't you?"

"I can't talk to you," I said. "Not without your counsel present. I need to get back inside."

Except there was no good way to do that at the moment. The crowd began to disperse, but the courtroom doors were still firmly shut with two deputies guarding the entrance.

"You're very good at what you do," Damon said. "If circumstances were different, I think I'd very much like to have you on my side."

He was calm, eerily so. Damon leaned against the wall on one shoulder, regarding me with those penetrating eyes.

I thought about Sharon Brinkman. Desperate. Worried. Misguided, for sure. She'd been in a panic when she first encountered Damon. I imagined he'd stayed like this. Cool. Centered. She would have found him soothing, perhaps.

"You're already on your path," Damon said. "That can be difficult for some people to embrace."

"What?"

He picked at lint on his sleeve. "We all are. I'm sorry for what's been done to you."

"What's been done to me? You're sorry for that?" I wasn't entirely sure what he even meant.

"I've prayed for you," he said. "For your heart. For your son."

Anger flared through me. "You can get my son out of your mind," I snapped.

"He's on his path too. It's so hard to see that as he struggles. But the struggle is the path. You should trust it more."

The crowd started to thin. I could just make out Stephanie Nadler's head. She was crying. One of the deputies held her against his chest. He pushed into the crowd with his arm, clearing a space for them as he guided her to the elevators.

"I'm not afraid," Damon said. "Even with everything that's been done to me. I embrace it."

"You should be scared to death," I said, letting my rage get the best of me.

His smile only widened. "You'll have your retribution. You'll have your peace. I told you, I've prayed on it."

"Mara?" Sam's voice cut through. He froze, seeing Damon standing so close to me. Something changed in Sam's face. He launched himself forward, coming down on Damon like a tidal wave.

"What did you say to her?"

"Sam," I said, my voice rising with alarm. Not here. Not now. The last thing I needed was another accusation of prosecutorial misconduct. It didn't matter that it was Damon who approached me.

"Time to go," I said to Sam, tugging on his sleeve.

He towered over Damon, his jaw twitching from clenching it so hard. He had his fists curled. When I tried to move him, Sam stood rigid as if he'd turned to stone.

"Sam!" I shouted. Finally, his eyes flickered, and he became aware of me again.

A couple of the deputies saw what was happening and moved in our direction.

The bailiff poked his head out of Judge Ivey's courtroom.

"Judge is ready to take the bench again," he shouted.

Sam finally moved with me. He put a protective arm around my shoulders, forming a physical barrier between Damon King and me. For his part, Damon never moved from his casual posture against the wall.

As I turned my back on him, Damon's words reverberated through me.

I would have my retribution.

Damn straight I would. I didn't know quite how yet, but I had to find a way to lock that man away for good.

35

We closed out Thursday's testimony with the forensic accountant I'd hired to reconstruct Charlie and Sharon Brinkman's tax returns. I kept it short and simple. By the end of it, I felt confident the jury believed Sharon's story, despite her years of lying and misdirection.

She knew Damon King. She confided in him. The paper trail of donations corroborated everything Sharon and Evelyn Bishop said.

It was good to end the day on a high note. But it still wasn't enough to prove Damon and Lyle committed murder.

Detective Cruz walked me from the courthouse to my office.

"I appreciate it," I said. "But this is overkill. Damon King can't be dumb enough to try to start anything with me in public again."

"Don't care," Sam said. "It's enough if it just makes me feel better."

As it turned out, his presence was necessary. Damon's followers were growing. We walked a gauntlet of shouting picketers all the way down the street. I tried not to read their signs, but a few of them caught my eye.

"We'll Pray for You!" It was the same thing Damon had said to me twice in the hallway. A few of the other picketers held signs that said simply, "Sinners Will Be Judged."

I froze in my tracks, abruptly enough that Sam walked a few steps ahead before he realized I wasn't at his elbow.

"You okay?" he said, looking over my shoulder as he led me away from the protestors.

"I don't know anymore," I said. "I honestly don't. I'm thinking of what happened with Will. For all I know, one of those very people helped bully my son."

"Geez," he said. "Mara, I'm so sorry."

We were at the door to my office. "I can take it from here," I said. I reached for him and squeezed his hand.

"I want you to let me send a patrol car for you when you're ready to leave. Let them follow you home."

"Sam ..."

"I'm not asking," he said. "And we're putting one outside your house. And Will's school for the duration."

"Okay," I said. I think Sam expected me to protest. I couldn't. He was right that I didn't want to ask. But I knew to accept help when it was offered.

"And thanks for today," I said. "For all of it. I mean it."

"Anytime," he said, winking. "That's what friends are for, Mara." Then he turned and walked away.

I found Melody and Kenya waiting for me in my office. For the first time in days, Kenya had a smile on her face.

"Good stuff today," she said. "Real good stuff."

"I suppose," I said, plopping down in my desk chair. I didn't have the energy to move into the conference room where we had all the exhibits laid out. I was flat out exhausted after today.

"I just can't believe it," Melody said. "This whole time.

Sharon Brinkman knew how Damon King targeted her son. She led him to him. And she says nothing? She protects him?"

"I think it was more about protecting herself," I said. "I really think Sharon was in denial for a lot of years. She believed what Damon was telling her. She thought he had all the answers about how to help her and Charlie Jr."

"Answers," Melody said. "I'm a Christian. I go to church every Sunday. The same church the Brinkmans used to attend. Holy Reformer. I knew Pastor Lennard. What Damon King preached was a perversion. He took the Bible's teachings and twisted it to this sick vision of his, not God's. I just don't understand how anybody could buy into that."

"He preyed on people like Sharon Brinkman," I said. "I don't even think it was about money with him. I mean, fifty dollars a week? No. He's after the power. The adoration. That's what drives him."

"What's next?" Kenya asked.

I took a beat. "Sierra," I said. "She's subpoenaed for first thing tomorrow morning. I expect her testimony to take the better part of the day."

"You're calling her in your case in chief?" Melody asked.

"Yep," I answered. "Judge already granted my motion to treat her as a hostile witness. But I need to try and frame her story before Trevor and Noel get a hold of her. It's all going to come down to whether the jury believes her."

Kenya stayed strangely silent. When I said "all of it" I meant the King verdict. But I knew it was more than that for her. For all of us.

"Do you need anything?" she asked.

"A big glass of red wine," I said. "A deserted tropical island, perhaps? A time machine?"

"Sign me up," she said.

"Do you think they'll put either of the King brothers on the stand?" Melody asked.

I shook my head. "They'd be insane to do it. If it were me, I wouldn't even call any witnesses."

"That makes sense, of course," Kenya said. "Except Trevor's never been the one calling the shots. Noel either."

"Right," I agreed. I hesitated, but then decided to tell Kenya about my exchange with Damon King.

"Wow," she said. "The Demon King speaks. Risky."

"He's feeling confident," I said. "Indestructible."

"He thinks he's going to win," Melody said.

I was about to agree with her. Then another thought struck me.

"No," I said. "He thinks it doesn't matter whether he wins or not. He thinks he's just as powerful in or out of prison."

"In prison," Kenya said, "He's a martyr. An icon. The deputies tell me Damon and Lyle got more mail than any other inmate. Fan mail."

"Gross," Melody said, encapsulating my sentiment perfectly.

"Even this trial," I said. "He's in the spotlight again. The press swarms him. The protestors outside. It fuels him. It's why he told Trevor not to seek a mistrial after the Halsey debacle. He doesn't want this to end."

"You're good at this, Mara," Melody said. "I mean it. I think you turned the tide today with Sharon Brinkman. You gave the jury something."

"Thanks," I said. "But you're right. It's just something. Not everything. We've got a long way to go."

"But do you think," Melody said. "I mean, there's still a chance, right? This guy ... he's not ... he won't walk. He can't walk."

For a moment, I felt the mother in me rise up. Melody was genuinely scared of Damon King. So was I.

I reached across the desk and took her hand. "I think I'm not quite done yet. And I think you should ask me again after I get done with Sierra Joy tomorrow."

❦ 36 ❦

Sierra Joy had gotten herself a make-over since the last time we met. She walked into the courtroom wearing a tailored pink business suit and a new, softer haircut. Her hand was steady as she raised it and got sworn in. She seemed cool, calm, confident, but I noticed her eyes dart quickly to the defense table.

I was ready to roll.

"Will you please state your name for the record?" I asked.

"Sierra Jocelyn Joy," she answered.

"Is that your legal name?" I asked. "Your surname?"

"It is now," she said. "I was born Janowicz. Jocelyn Janowicz, but I had it legally changed six years ago. Before that, though, I mean, everyone knows me as Sierra. Even in high school."

"Thank you," I said. "Ms. Joy, how long have you lived in Waynetown?"

"Almost my whole life. My dad moved us here when I was six. We lived with my mom near Pittsburgh before that. She ... uh ... she passed away."

"I'm sorry for your loss," I said. I was. I knew Sierra had had a tough life growing up. Her mother had actually died of a drug overdose. Her father had been in and out of prison and died roughly two years before the Brinkman/Nadler murders.

"And how old are you now?" I asked.

"I'm ... um ... I'm thirty-two," she said, as if that were the worst thing anyone could admit about themselves.

"Let me take you back to the summer of 2008, if I may. Where were you living and working then?"

Sierra got more comfortable in her seat. "I worked a couple of different jobs that year. I was, um, I was a waitress at Scarlett and Lace in Toledo. Once or twice a month I'd also work as a bartender there. I was actually training to become one full-time."

"I see," I said. "You said you had a couple of different jobs. What else did you do to make ends meet?"

I hated this part, but it had to be done.

"That year was a turning point for me," she said. "My dad tried, but he didn't really ever have a steady job. He had a drug problem, like my mom before him. There were ... well, there were a lot of people he brought into my life that weren't the greatest influence on me. I made some bad choices back then. I got the job at Scarlett and Lace through a contact at my previous employer. I worked at the Pink Lady on Telegraph Road in Luna Pier. I was an exotic dancer. There were times I ... I turned tricks."

"I see," I said.

"They fired me for that at the Pink Lady. But I was trying to turn everything around. That's what my job at the Scarlett and Lace was helping me do. They paid for me to go to bartending school in Detroit."

"Ms. Joy," I said. "You said you made bad life choices back then. Is there anything else?" I asked.

"I got arrested a few times," she said. "There were some small things when I was a minor. Shoplifting, mostly. But then

after I turned eighteen, I did get popped for minor drug possession in Michigan. And ... a few prostitution stings."

"Okay," I said. "So in the summer of 2008, were any of those
charges pending?"

"Yes," she said. "I was facing a felony prostitution charge
and one drug-related charge. It was all from the same incident
earlier that year, in February, I think. I got caught up in a sting
they ... uh ... the FBI were doing."

"Okay," I said. "I appreciate you being so forthright about
that. I understand it was a difficult time. I'd like to direct your
attention to late 2008. Isn't it true you reached out to Phil Halsey,
the then assistant prosecuting attorney for Maumee County?"

"Yes," she said.

"Can you tell me what that was about?" I asked.

"Well," Sierra started. "I told you, I was working at the Scarlett and Lace. I saw on the news ... I mean, it was all over the
news ... that they were looking for information about those two
kids who got killed out at the Blitz."

"Did you know Charlie Brinkman or Krista Nadler?"

"No," she said. "I don't think so. I mean, I knew the Blitz.
And I knew kids went out there and fooled around in the
woods. We all did. I did."

"Okay," I said. "So as of the summer of 2008, you were well
aware of the murders and knew the police were looking for
tips."

"Yes," she said.

"But you sent an email to Phil Halsey, the prosecuting
attorney in December, isn't that right?"

"Um, yes," she said.

"Do you recall what your email said?"

"No," she said. "Not word for word."

I moved to admit Sierra's email into evidence. Trevor Page
and Noel Stamford, not surprisingly, had no objections. As I

went to the table to grab a copy for Sierra to read, I glanced at Trevor's table.

Damon King had his stone-faced expression. Lyle King, however, was paying attention. It was the first time I'd seen him so much as look toward the witness box in nearly two weeks of trial. He was smiling.

"Okay," I said, handing the paper to Sierra. "I'd like you to read what you wrote to Mr. Halsey."

Sierra cleared her throat. "I wrote, we need to talk. It's important."

"You didn't mention the Brinkman/Nadler case in this email," I said.

"No," she said.

"Not even in the subject line," I said. "Because that says what again?"

"It says I need to talk," she answered.

"Doesn't mention Lyle King, doesn't mention Krista or Charlie by name. Doesn't even mention a time frame or a case or anything," I said.

"Objection," Trevor said. "The email speaks for itself. The witness has read it. The jury can read it. Ms. Brent, I assume, can read it."

"Sustained, Ms. Brent," Judge Ivey said. "Let's not belabor the point."

"All right, Ms. Joy," I said. "What is it you claim happened as a result of this email?"

"I met with Mr. Halsey," she said. "He called me. I think it was the day after I sent that email. He came to my apartment. We talked in the hallway."

"Was anyone else there?" I asked.

"No."

"Did any of your neighbors come out?"

"I don't remember. I don't think so."

"Did you tell anyone else you were planning on reaching out to Mr. Halsey?"

"No way," she said.

"What information was it that you now claim you wanted to convey?" I asked.

"It was about Lyle King," she said. "I know where he was the night Krista and Charlie got killed."

"What night was that?" I asked.

"August 11th, going into the early morning of August 12th," she answered. "I told Mr. Halsey that Lyle King was at the bar where I worked. He was drinking at the bar for my whole shift."

"Your whole shift," I said. "From when to when?"

"That was a Friday. I always came in at six and we closed at two a.m. If I was lucky, I'd get out at three a.m. And like I told you before when we talked. I remember that night because it was the night Mule McKinney fought."

"And you claim that you remember seeing Lyle King there on that particular night four months prior to when you happened to contact Mr. Halsey, is that right?" I asked.

"That's right," she said. "He was there. I remember it. I told you. Mule McKinney fought on television."

"So you've said," I said. Of course she was right about the date on Mule McKinney. Hojo confirmed it with a simple google search. Which meant it was exactly the kind of thing Sierra could have done too.

"Okay, so let's go back in time a little bit," I said. "You're aware that Lyle and Damon King were arrested on September 8th, 2008?"

"I don't know the exact date of that, no," she said.

"But by December 2008, you were well aware that Lyle was suspected of committing this crime," I said.

"Yes," she said. "I told you, it was all over the news."

"In fact, Lyle King had been sitting in jail for almost three months prior to the time you claim you met with Mr. Halsey," I said.

"I mean, I guess so," she said.

"You guess so," I said. "But you didn't see fit to call the police with your information in September when the Kings were first arrested," I asked.

"I didn't contact the police then, no," she said.

"And you didn't contact the police or Mr. Halsey in October?" I asked.

"No, ma'am," she said.

"Or November?" I asked.

"No, ma'am," she said.

"Even though you were absolutely sure of the date. Because of Mule McKinney."

"I know it was August 11th, yes," she said.

"Right," I said.

I went back to my table and picked up Sierra Joy's four-page criminal record. "Ms. Joy," I said. "You indicated as of the summer of 2008, you were facing prostitution and drug possession charges. In fact, you were set to go to trial on those charges in January of 2009, isn't that right?"

"If that's what that paper you have in front of you says, then yes," she said.

I admitted the court docket into the record. "Ms. Joy," I said. "Let me direct your attention to an entry on January 3rd, 2009. Can you tell me what that says?" I asked.

"It says the case against me was dismissed," she said.

I felt like my world was upside down. This was a tactic defense attorneys usually used to discredit informants. I was in the position of having to do it myself.

"Ms. Joy," I said. "You contacted Phil Halsey because you wanted to work out a plea deal on your own case, isn't that right?"

"Um ... no," she said. "I wanted to tell him Lyle King had an alibi. He was in the bar that night. I saw him. All night."

"You saw him," I said. "Did you know Lyle King before that night?"

"I knew of him," she said. "He came into the bar a lot. He was nice to me. I mean, he kept to himself, but he was nice. He always stayed at the bar, never sat at a table."

"You were working as a waitress that night?" I said. "Was the bar your section?"

"No," she said. "I wasn't bartending that night, no."

"Do you remember if it was a busy night?"

"No. I mean, I don't remember. It probably was. Fridays were always slammed. Wait. Yes. It was busy. Because of that fight."

"Do you remember how much you made in tips that night?" I asked.

"No," she said.

"Do you know if any other waitress reported seeing Lyle King sitting at the bar that night?" I asked.

"No," I said. "I don't know. But Phil Halsey never told anyone I said I saw him. He never even called me at trial."

"About that," I said. "The trial got national attention, didn't it? It was the talk of the town during the spring of 2009, wasn't it?"

"I mean ... I don't know, I guess so," she said.

"But you never told anyone else about your claim regarding Lyle King's whereabouts," I said.

"No," she said. "I just assumed Phil Halsey knew what he was doing. I don't know. It was hard for me to reach out as much as I did. I was raised to keep my mouth shut. Avoid the police or any drama with law enforcement. I'm not ... I don't want to be a snitch, but right is right and wrong is wrong."

"Sure," I said. "But your civic duty only extended to the point you got your own plea deal, is that it?"

"Objection," Noel said. "Badgering."

"I'll withdraw," I said. "Ms. Joy, did you know Lyle King by name back in 2008?"

"No," she said.

"You said you didn't wait on him that night. Had you ever waited on him?"

"I'm not sure. I think maybe. He was just ... I don't know. Nice. Sweet. Polite."

When I turned around, Lyle was positively mooning.

"Was he a good tipper?" I asked. "I mean, in general."

"I don't know," she said.

"How often are you claiming Lyle King frequented the Scarlett and Lace?" I asked. "Let's focus on specifically the summer of 2008."

"I don't know. I mean, he wasn't a regular. But I recognized him. He's big. He's hard to miss."

"What was he wearing the night of August 11th?" I asked.

"I don't remember. I think jeans, maybe. A tee-shirt. Yes. Definitely a tee-shirt."

Sierra straightened in her seat. Her eyes got big and her face flushed.

It happened. If she'd stopped there, maybe the next twenty minutes would have unfolded differently. But she didn't stop.

"How can you be so sure it was a tee-shirt?" I asked. "Your face just kind of lit up there."

"Objection," Trevor said. "It's not up to counsel to characterize the witness's facial expressions, for crying out loud."

"Stick to questions, Ms. Brent," Judge Ivey said.

"Let me repeat my last one," I said. "Ms. Joy, how are you so sure Mr. King was wearing a tee-shirt? Did it have writing on it? You remember the color?"

Maybe I should have stopped. I was violating one of the cardinal rules of cross-examination. Never ask a question you don't know the answer to. But I was following a different rule. Go with your gut.

"Because I saw his tattoo," she said.

"His tattoo?" I asked.

"Yes," she said, gleaming. "It was um ... a spider web or cobweb, I think. On his left elbow."

Now Noel Stamford began to gleam. Lyle King kept smiling. He was currently wearing a suit. Both arms were well covered.

I had that feeling, just as you crest the tallest hill of a roller coaster. My nerves buzzed. On the witness stand, Sierra Joy came into sharper focus for me. My prey.

"You remember a tattoo on his left elbow," I said. "You saw it when he was sitting at the bar on the night Mule McKinney fought?"

"I sure did," she said. "He had his arms up on the bar. It's a big tattoo, I think. It covers his whole elbow. The point of his elbow was the center of the web. Then the webbing crawled all the way up and down his arm. I remember that. Because he leaned over the bar on his elbows like guys do, you know. I saw it. You can't miss it."

I felt my cheeks flush as I rushed back to the table. I pulled Lyle's file out and quickly flipped through it. The jury knew something was happening.

She saw his tattoo. She remembered it. I recognized that look in Trevor's eyes. He smelled victory. And it had been me who'd inadvertently kicked the ball into the wrong end zone.

Except I hadn't. Beside me, Melody started to gasp. I stared down at the various prison ID photos included with Lyle's file. I picked the two I needed.

I walked over to Trevor and Noel's table and showed them the first photo. Trevor kept his face neutral except for those shining eyes. Noel's color drained.

That's when I glanced at Damon King. He knew what was about to happen. For once, I saw his stony expression slip.

"Ms. Joy," I said. "I'd like to direct your attention to this photograph. Do you recognize it?"

"That's Lyle King," she said. "And that's the tattoo I saw. Just there on his left elbow. See? Just like I said. The point of his elbow is the center of the web. I told you."

"Can you read the date of that photo for me, you can see it written on the placard Mr. King is holding, can't you?"

She squinted. "It's March 27, 2015."

"And will you look at the second photo? Do you recognize this man?" I said.

"It's Lyle again," she said.

"Objection!" Trevor Page yelled. Now he was getting it. "This witness isn't qualified to authenticate these photos."

"He's right, Ms. Brent."

"I'm not asking to introduce them into evidence just yet," I said. "I'm just asking if this witness recognizes who's in them. Plus, these are all part of the defendant's prison record. The authenticity of the whole file was already stipulated to by both parties during pre-trial."

"Overruled, Mr. Page," Judge Ivey said. Now he was getting it.

"Ms. Joy," I said. "Do you recognize the man in the second photo?"

"Yes," she said. "It looks like Lyle King."

"Ms. Joy, what is the date of that second photo?" I asked.

"It says September 8th, 2008," she said.

Then Sierra Joy got it.

❧ 37 ❧

Sierra began to hyperventilate. It was as if I'd flipped a switch. Tears burst from her eyes.

"Ms. Joy," I said. "Mr. King is wearing a short-sleeved shirt in this photo, isn't he?"

"Yes," she said.

"From September of 2008," I said. "His left arm is bare, isn't it?"

"Yes," she whispered.

"Do you see a spiderweb tattoo on Mr. King in this photo?" I asked.

"No," she said.

"There aren't any tattoos on Mr. King's arms visible in this photo, are there?" I asked.

"No."

"This was taken less than a month after the Brinkman boy and Krista Nadler were murdered," I said.

"I guess..."

"Less than a month after the night you claim you saw Lyle King at the Scarlett and Lace during Mule McKinney's famous fight, right?"

"I didn't ... that wasn't ... I'm not ..."

"You never saw Lyle King at the Scarlett and Lace on August 11th or the morning of August 12th, did you?" I asked.

"Lyle?" she cried.

I didn't know how yet. I didn't know when. But Sierra Joy had been in contact with Lyle King only recently. He'd only gotten the cobweb tattoo in the last five years. In prison. The Department of Corrections routinely documented new prisoner tattoos.

Trevor Page sprang into action. He threw himself across the table and got into Lyle's face. I couldn't hear what he said, but he was trying to keep Lyle from saying anything. Noel Stamford sat dumbstruck.

"You never saw Lyle King at the Scarlett and Lace on August 11th, 2008, did you?" I asked. "You made that up."

"I didn't ... I was trying to ... I'm sorry. Lyle, I'm sorry. I wanted to help. I can't ... can I plead the Fifth? Isn't that something I can say?"

Trevor Page collected himself. Now Damon had his face in front of his brother's. Lyle was agitated. He gritted his teeth and pounded his fists against the back of Damon's chair, but he stayed silent.

"Ms. Joy," the judge said. "The Fifth Amendment affords you the right against self-incrimination. If you feel you're being asked to provide testimony implicating ..."

"I plead the Fifth," she said. "I'm not going to answer any more of your questions. I want a lawyer."

"Then I have nothing further for this witness at this time," I said. "Though I reserve the right to recall her on rebuttal."

"Naturally," the judge said. "Mr. Page? Mr. Stamford?"

Trevor stormed to the lectern.

I barely paid attention to what he said. I pulled out a pen and scribbled a furious note to Melody. "Give this to Sam," I whispered. "Now!"

Melody scrambled out of her chair. I knew Sam Cruz was sitting in the back of the courtroom.

"Ms. Joy," Trevor said. "Isn't it true that you were intimidated by Mr. Halsey?"

"I plead the Fifth," Sierra said. She was full-on crying now. Her hair became disheveled. She clawed at her own neck. Her skin had become purple and blotchy. The girl was having a panic attack.

Trevor asked a series of rapid-fire questions. He tried desperately to get Sierra to admit she was terrified of my office and the police. He was flailing. The dust would have to settle later. But at that moment, I truly believed Sierra's testimony blindsided him and Stamford. He tried for at last fifteen minutes to get Sierra to rehabilitate herself.

But Trevor Page was the least of my concerns. It was Lyle King who had my attention.

He murmured something. Damon whispered in his ear. Noel tried to get in between them, but Damon literally pushed him away. Damon had been like an ice man at that table for two weeks. Now, his mask had slipped a bit. I couldn't hear his words either, but the Demon King spewed venom in his brother's ear. I was sure of it. I just hoped my next move would provide the antidote.

"I have nothing further at this time for this witness, in light of her invocation of her Fifth Amendment privilege," Trevor said, defeated. He may be down, but I knew he'd come back swinging.

"Mr. Stamford?" Judge Ivey said. Finally, Lyle King said something. He whispered it in Stamford's ear. I watched the man go sheet white. I read Lyle's lips. *You're fired.*

"I have no questions," Stamford said.

I heard the doors swing open behind me. I held my smile.

"In light of the hour," the judge said. "We'll adjourn. We're back here Monday morning at eight. Same admonishments for the jury. You're not to discuss this case with anyone."

Sierra staggered out of the witness chair. Trevor tried to get Lyle and Damon out quickly. Noel sat stunned at the table, fumbling for his notes.

I turned. Sam Cruz stood at the back of the courtroom. He gave me a slow, knowing nod.

The jury filed out. Sierra rushed to the courtroom doors. When she opened them, she was met by two Maumee County deputy sheriffs.

"Ms. Joy," one of them said. "We have a warrant for your arrest on the grounds of perjury and obstruction of justice. You have the right to remain silent ..."

Sierra's cries nearly drowned out the rest of her Miranda warning. The deputies slipped the cuffs on her just as Lyle made it to her side.

Trevor tried to hold him back. Two more deputies had to help. Damon stepped forward and actually covered Lyle's mouth with his hands. Lyle thrashed against them, breathing heavily like a winded racehorse.

As Sierra was led away, Lyle finally settled enough that the deputies let him go.

Sam was right at my side. We waited together as the Kings and Trevor Page disappeared into the stairwell. Noel Stamford finally found his feet and chased after them.

"Thanks," I said to Sam.

"Hope it helps," he said. "Not sure what I just did."

"I threw a Hail Mary pass," I said. "And you just caught it, my friend."

❧ 38 ❧

"It's amazing!" Melody shouted, her face flushed. "Mara, what you did was amazing!"

She, Howard, and Kenya waited for me right outside my office. I unlocked the door, and we all filed in. Howard gave me a literal pat on the back as he passed me. Kenya had a small smile, but still a smile.

"You did it!" Melody said again. She could barely stand still. I set my briefcase down beside my desk and took a seat.

My feet hurt. My brain hurt. It was barely three o'clock in the afternoon.

"She was lying," Hojo said as he plopped down on the couch in the corner. He chewed on the end of a cigar, not lighting the thing. Still, even that felt like too much celebration.

"All I've proven," I said, "is that everyone in this case has been lying."

"But he's got no alibi," Melody said.

"I just wish Ivey hadn't granted bail," Kenya said. "They had to have been writing letters this whole time, Lyle and Sierra."

"I've got a call into my contact at the prison," Howard said.

"He's combing through the last couple of years of visitors either Damon or Lyle have had."

"Have them look for Jocelyn Janowicz too," I said.

"What difference does it even make now?" Melody said. "Sierra admitted to lying. Who cares why? She's toast."

"I know," I said. "No matter what happens, this might never be over. Not for a long time, anyway. If we lose, they'll appeal. The scope of Phil's misconduct isn't done killing us. Page and Stamford have given them about a dozen ways to prove ineffective assistance of counsel already."

"That's the other reason Damon didn't want a mistrial," Kenya said. "He was hedging his bets. Dammit, he's smart. He's been one step ahead of us this whole time."

"Not anymore," Hojo said. "I watched his face. He thought Sierra Joy's testimony would be solid."

"I think he handpicked her," I said. "That's my theory. He could have gotten access to Halsey's plea deals around the time of trial prep in the original case."

"I remember that prostitution sting," Kenya said. "The one they scooped Sierra up in. Before the King murders, this office was getting a lot of mileage out of it. It made the papers. There were a few prominent men among those Johns. A couple of local lawyers, a township trustee, there was even a sheriff's deputy."

"Son of a bitch," Howard said. "I remember it too. Chet Merrick got censured by the bar, I think. I used to work for him before I came over to the prosecutor's office."

"Well then, I think that's our answer," Kenya said. "I'd bet anything the real reason Sierra reached out to Phil ten years ago was to leverage something else she knew about one of those johns or her pimp at the time. I'll do some digging. If Sierra won't come clean on her own, I'll find out what she really gave him. Damon King just had one hell of a stroke of luck that Sierra was just vague enough in that email to Phil."

"I'd bet my next paycheck Sierra wasn't the only one of Phil's informants Damon looked into," Hojo said. "She was just the best one."

"And I'd bet my next paycheck Lyle's in love with that girl," I said. "He couldn't take his eyes off of her the entire time she was on the stand. I think it's probably one of the few times they've been in a room together."

"And you just had her manhandled and arrested right in front of him," Kenya said, her face finally cracking into a full smile.

"It's a long shot," I said. "But I need some chum in the water. Sierra will probably get bonded out in the next day or two."

"Oh," Howard said. "We might be able to stretch that a bit."

"No," I said. "For the love of God, don't. I cut corners enough having her arrested like that. Ivey didn't like it. I'll probably get my rear end chewed out over it in court on Monday. For now, it's enough. I mean, I hope it's enough."

"For what?" Melody asked.

Kenya and I exchanged a look. I folded my hands in my lap.

"Melody," I said. "I don't have anything left up my sleeve. That was it. My last play. Like I said, I've only managed to prove every principal witness in this case has been lying. Including the former prosecutor. Sharon Brinkman lied about her relationship with Damon King. Aaron Clyde lied about Lyle's confession. Sierra Joy lied about seeing Lyle the night of the murders. We still have no physical evidence tying them to the killings. No eyewitnesses. No confession. We have an overzealous, psychopath preacher who thinks he's some instrument of the Holy Spirit who knew two innocent kids were having sex and where. That's it. The jury might not even believe Sharon. She has a motive for lying. She wants to pin Damon for killing her son. If I were Page or Stamford, that's what I'd argue in closing."

"You have the phone forensics," Howard offered.

"Right," I said. "I can prove Damon King's phone was at the Blitz during the murders. But I can't prove he was the one holding it. Or that Lyle was. Trevor Page has done inexplicable things throughout this whole trial. But he's an excellent closer. There's reasonable doubt."

"It's worse than that," Kenya said. "If he manages to shift the jury's focus back to Phil when they head into deliberations ..."

"Game over," Howard said.

"No," Melody insisted. "Just ... no. They can't walk. They just can't."

The room fell silent. Melody stood behind one of the chairs, gripping the back of it. She was young, passionate, fearless. She'd formed a bond with Stephanie Nadler over the past couple of months. I knew this case would stick with her well beyond the outcome next week. It would with me too.

"I think we all need a break," Kenya said. "Get some rest if you can. We'll come at this fresh tomorrow."

"What will he do?" Melody asked. "I mean ... who can the defense even call if they put on a case?"

"I don't know," I said. "If it were me, no one. Recalling Sierra is too risky. Stamford can't control Lyle when she's on the stand. Lyle's in the process of trying to fire him, anyway, I think. Page did what he could with Sharon Brinkman. He can't possibly call either of the King brothers. His best bet is really to wrap it up in a bow on closing."

"You ready for yours?" Kenya asked.

"I will be," I said. "But you're right. I could use a good night's sleep."

We broke for the day. I had a few loose ends to tie up on other cases. I was out the door by four thirty.

The gauntlet of Divine Justice protestors had grown, spreading from the courthouse to right outside my office. I made it just to my car when a particular picket sign caught my eye.

"Sinners will be judged. Only the flame can purge their souls!"

There, blown up to 16 X 20 size, was the same picture of Jason and Abby Morgan they'd plastered all over Will's locker.

I snapped, grabbing the sign from the young girl who held it. She was maybe nineteen or twenty. She immediately dropped to the ground and began to pray.

Hate filled me. I took a step. A breath. Then ripped the sign in half and stomped on it, breaking its wooden handle in two.

I wanted to do more. I wanted to scream at this girl and ask her where her parents were. Did she need me to show her pictures of what Lyle and Damon King did to Krista Nadler?

But it would do no good. Plus, another girl stood off to the side, pointing her phone straight at me. She was recording everything. No doubt she'd post her video on social media within the next five minutes.

I straightened my skirt and turned toward my car. The praying girl rose.

"It's going to be okay," she said. "You'll have your retribution. You can believe."

"Go home, honey," I said. "Just ... go home."

I slid behind the wheel. The protestors locked hands but moved back so I could drive past them.

Retribution. Damon King had used that exact word. I had no idea what he meant and no desire to stick around and find out.

❧ 39 ❧

I got to spend a more or less quiet evening with Will and my mother. She'd flown back in from New Hampshire to stay with us for the next four days. By then, the King trial would likely be finished.

Natalie Montleroy never had a hair out of place nor a wrinkle in her clothes, even when she wore linen, which was most of the time. She sat on the couch with Will as he talked her through one of his favorite nature documentaries. It featured lions of the Serengeti. I arrived just in time. Two scenes from now, my mother was about to learn what an alpha lion would do to a male trespasser and his mate.

"Why don't we pause this one right there?" I said.

"It's nature," Will said, knowing exactly what I wanted to avoid. "He has to ensure only his DNA is passed down. He has to send a message."

"I think Grandma gets the idea," I said. Sure enough, my mother's face went a little green as she worked it out for herself.

"How can you let him watch that?" she said as she followed me into the kitchen. "It's brutal."

"Well," I said. "Like he said, it's nature."

"I guess it's better than those ghoulish JFK assassination ones he normally watches," she said.

"That's the spirit," I said.

I went over to my crockpot. I'd thrown in a pork roast this morning with carrots and potatoes. That, along with shredded chicken tacos, was about as creative as I got in the kitchen. Jason had always enjoyed cooking more than I did.

My mother sat at the kitchen island, watching me test the potatoes.

"Another hour," I said.

"He seems okay," she said, gesturing with her chin toward Will. She couldn't see the television from where she sat. Good thing. Will was about to load one of his "ghoulish" JFK documentaries.

"I mean with that nasty business at the school. He seems ... normal," my mother said.

"He is," I answered. "He had a good weekend with his father. I think it eased his mind a bit about what's to come."

My mother's face changed. She pursed her lips. I realized maybe Will's mind wasn't the one that needed easing. I knew my mother well. And of all the things happening right now, I wasn't in the mood for this conversation.

"I'm still worried about you, Mara," she said. "If you don't want to be with Jason, I understand. But here. This place? Who is going to take care of you?"

I sat on the stool opposite her. I waited until I could hear the late Peter Jennings's voice clearly from the television before I answered.

"I'm doing what I think is best," I said. "And you know I can take care of myself."

"You could still live in D.C." she said. "Even if you don't want to be married. There are opportunities for you. Or come back home. Live in New Hampshire by me. I'm getting old, you know."

"Who are you kidding?" I laughed. "You're never going to let that happen."

"Will said you're going to D.C. next week," she said.

"Is that a question or a statement?" I asked.

"Mara," she said, dropping her voice while raising her brow.

"I don't know yet. I'm in the middle of a murder trial," I said. "That's my professional priority right now."

"Do you hate me for still taking an interest in Jason's career? He's still Will's father. That boy's future is still tied to Jason's. If you'll let me put on my political operative hat for a moment, you have to present a united front," she said. "Otherwise Jason's first congressional term will be marred by this scandal. Can you keep up appearances for just a little while longer? It's not hard, Mara. You put a smile on your face. You stand by his side. You have your picture taken. The end."

"Not my style, Mother," I said. "And it's not the end. You're worried about appearances for the rest of the world. I'm worried about appearances for my son."

"So you've decided, then," she said. "You're actually going to stay here?"

"Not now," I said. "Please. I can't think past this weekend. Really."

"Jason thinks you're trying to punish him," she said.

"Are you having heart-to-heart talks with Jason now?" I asked.

"No," she said. "Well, a little. This girl. Ms. Morgan. I was worried she was going to keep being a problem. I asked around. You'll be happy to know she seems to have faded back into the woodwork for now."

I pressed a hand to my forehead. "I'm not mad at Abby Morgan anymore, believe it or not."

"Well," my mother said. "I am."

I paused. A look went through my mother's eyes that gave me pause. "Mom?" I asked. "Was it you? Were you the one who planted that story about those child abuse allegations?"

The moment I said it, I felt I knew the truth. "Oh God. Mom. Did you?"

She went to the fridge and took out a bottle of wine. "That girl is her own worst enemy."

"That's not an answer," I said. "You did. Didn't you? You paid that couple she worked for off."

She poured herself a glass. "Don't be ridiculous."

It still wasn't an answer. But I knew my mother. She could be every bit as cold and ruthless as Jason could be. In a lot of ways, she took credit for creating him. Of course she'd do anything to protect him. Or me.

"I can't hear this," I said, shaking my head. "Christ. I can't *know* this."

"Don't be vulgar," she said, sipping her wine. "Besides, I told you. Abby Morgan is gone. I checked. Vanished. Poof. Crawled back under whatever rock she came out of."

"I don't wish her ill," I said. "I don't wish her anything. I just wish ... I just don't ever want to have to think about her again."

My mother's face softened. She reached across the counter and touched my hand. "I know. Mara, if I don't say it often enough, I'm proud of you. I really am. I just ... I want you to have everything. The world. Jason's path can open that up for you. Even if you don't walk it with him."

I came around the island and hugged my mother. She stiffened for a moment, then hugged me back.

The pot roast was delicious. Will's documentary, riveting. My mother stopped pestering me about Jason or my plans for the future. It might have turned into the perfect night.

But at ten p.m., just after I tucked Will in, the phone rang. It was Kenya.

I barely squeaked out the word hello before she practically shouted into the phone.

"Mara! You have to come into the office. Meet me there. Right now."

"Kenya, it's ten o'clock on a Saturday night. What could ..."

"Lyle King," she shouted. "Mara, the sheriff's office called. He's locked in a car in front of our building. He says he'll only talk to you."

40

By the time I got to the office, four patrol cars and an unmarked cruiser had pulled up. Lyle King sat behind the driver's seat in a beat-up Chevy Suburban with tinted windows.

I made a beeline for Gus Ritter when I saw him standing off to the side, talking into his radio.

"What gives?" I asked.

Gus shrugged. "Says he wants to talk. He's unarmed. He cooperated enough to come out, let us frisk him, and search the vehicle. After that, he just climbed back in and has been waiting like that."

"Where's Kenya?" I asked.

"Still on the way," he said. Kenya had told me she'd tried to light out for her parents' vacation home in Brighton, Michigan. It was about a two-hour drive. At midnight on a Saturday morning, I didn't suppose she'd hit traffic.

"What do you want to do?" Gus asked.

"Not a thing. Not until I get Noel Stamford down here. Lyle's represented."

Gus shook his head. "Don't think so. King's saying he fired him."

"Please tell me you haven't tried to question him beyond that," I said.

Gus gave me a sideways glance. "Hell, no," he said. "We've got bodycam footage of every exchange we've had with him since he got here. I recorded my own two sentences with him on my phone. We've been waiting for you."

"How long has he been there?" I asked.

"Couple of hours. Night county security spotted him. They didn't recognize the suburban and ran the plates. And here we are."

"Thanks," I said, stepping away from Gus. I tried Noel Stamford's number again. My two previous attempts took me to his voicemail. I left yet another message as I walked up to Lyle's car.

He rolled the window down when he saw me approach. "Just you," he said. "Told all them I only want to talk to you."

"Lyle," I said. I hit the record button on my own camera. "You know I can't talk to you without your lawyer present. I'm trying to get a hold of Mr. Stamford again now."

"Don't care," he said. "Don't want him. I'll sign whatever I need to. I called Noel a few hours ago and fired him. He's not my lawyer anymore. Don't want another one."

I felt sweat forming between my shoulder blades even though it was forty degrees outside. We'd been lucky. Any snow we'd had over the last week had melted except for a few piles in the corner of the lot where the plows had come through.

"What do you want to talk about?" I asked.

"Sierra," he said. "And me. I need your word that you'll take care of her. I know I can trust you. I've asked around."

I turned to Gus. He stood just within earshot.

"Not letting you talk to this lady alone," Gus said. "Not on your life. I don't care what you have to say."

Lyle shrugged. He was calm. Casual. You'd think he was doing nothing more serious than discussing the weather. It was then that my phone rang. Stamford was calling back. I stepped away from Gus and Lyle.

"Noel," I said. "Your client has shown up in my parking lot. He says he wants to talk only to me."

"He's not my client anymore," Stamford said, slurring his words. Just great.

"Are you kidding me?" I said.

"He fired me four hours ago," Noel said. "I'm on my way out of town."

"We need to bring the judge in on this," I said. "You can't just abandon your client in the middle of a trial, no matter what he says. Noel, it's malpractice! You could lose your license."

"I'm done," he said. "I've got a waiver from Lyle. My ass is covered."

"A waiver? Noel, you've lost your mind. Lyle can't waive your own damn negligence. What are you doing?"

Noel laughed. "Saving my ass. Maybe your office should try it once in a while."

Then, he hung up.

Tires screeched at the entrance to the parking lot. Kenya pulled up. She zipped into the nearest space, parking at an odd angle. She raced to my side.

"He's ready to talk," I said. "Noel Stamford just confirmed he's been fired."

"Get him inside," she said. "Before we have any media attention."

"He needs a lawyer," I said.

"Don't want one," Lyle shouted from his vehicle. "I told you. Give me whatever you want me to sign. I know my rights. I want to talk. Just me. Just you. But hurry up, I'm starting to get hungry."

"Gus," Kenya said. "Can you have one of the street guys go get some pizzas or something?"

"No mushrooms," Lyle called out. "Hate 'em on pizza. Too slimy. I like bacon."

"Of course you do," I muttered.

Lyle got out of his car, making Gus and the rest of the cops move in. Lyle put his hands up as he walked toward us.

"Let's talk," he said. "I'm tired of waiting."

Kenya gestured to me. She pulled out her key card, and we started walking to the building.

"Not him," Lyle said, pointing to Gus. "Him I don't trust. I want to talk to Mara Brent."

"And I said you don't get to be in a room with the lady alone," Gus said.

Lyle shrugged. "Fine. Bring one or two of those guys. Cuff me if you want."

"No," I said. "You're not under arrest." Not yet. The simple fact was, Lyle King had currently not broken any laws.

"As long as you understand, you're free to leave at any time," I said. "And you'll sign another waiver."

By way of an answer, Lyle King recited back a standard Miranda warning, word for word. Then, he walked ahead of us and waited at the door.

"Christ," Gus said. "I'll be right out here. You record every damn thing that lunatic says."

"Of course," I said.

So Lyle King, Kenya, two of Gus's handpicked patrolmen, and I walked into our conference room together. Lyle took a seat at the head of the table and promptly asked for a diet soda. Kenya ran to grab it.

"You want me to say the thing again?" he asked. "About knowing my rights and not wanting a lawyer here?"

"Yes," I said. "And I want you to sign it."

"Then let's get going," he said. "How long for the pizza?"

I had Deputies Nick Jaffe and Al Trembly standing at the door. They exchanged a bewildered glance. I knew how they felt. With his thumbs in his belt loops, Al leaned forward a bit and answered. "Uh. Fifteen minutes."

"Good," Lyle said.

We kept video recording equipment in the corner of the room. I went over and turned it on. As soon as I was sure it was recording, I identified myself on camera and had the deputies do the same. Before I could even prompt Lyle King, he leaned forward and looked straight into the lens.

"I'm Lyle King. I'm here on my own. Nobody forced me to come. I'm over eighteen. I want to talk to Mara Brent. I know she's a lawyer. I know she's in the middle of a trial where she's trying to put my brother and me away for murder. I want to talk to her, anyway. I've got stuff to say. I fired my lawyer. Signed all the paperwork. I know my rights. Now let's get this over with."

"Lyle," I said. "What is it you want to say?"

"First, you gotta make me some promises," he said.

"Not happening," I said. "You tell me what you want to talk about."

"That black lady, she's your boss, right?" he asked.

"Kenya Spaulding," I said. "She's the Maumee County prosecuting attorney. She's the head of this office. Yes, she's my boss."

Kenya picked that exact moment to appear in the doorway holding two cans of diet soda. She stepped in and handed him one of the cans of soda. He thanked her and popped the top.

"Good," Lyle said. "I'll tell you what I want. Then you can ask me any question you want. I want Sierra safe. You don't go after her for what she said on the witness stand. You make her trouble go away. Full immunity. That's for one thing. For another, I don't want the needle. Whatever happens to me, you wanna put me back in prison, fine. I'll go. I don't hate it there. Maybe there's where I should be, anyway. After what I done. After what Damon made us do. He said it was God's will. That we were helping. I don't know anymore. Sierra says ... well, she got me thinking."

"Lyle," I said. "We need to know what information you have first."

Lyle King looked up from his soda can. He fixed his stare. He looked so much like his brother. But with Damon, there was a cool calculation behind his eyes. Lyle's eyes were merely hard. He had to outweigh his brother by at least forty pounds. He had big, beefy hands. He would have towered over Krista Nadler and Charlie Brinkman. I could imagine them begging for their lives. I knew now that Lyle had simply given them the same stone-cold look. He'd made up his mind.

"Can you give me what I want?" he asked, looking at me, then Kenya. "Immunity for Sierra. No needle for me. And ... we want to get married. I already asked Sierra, and she said yes. So maybe, if I could get to be alone with her sometimes. I know other guys get to do that with their wives. That wouldn't be so bad."

Kenya took a seat beside me. "Sierra's facing perjury and obstruction of justice charges. Yes, depending on what you have to say, I have the power to grant her immunity from prosecution."

"And the death penalty? You make that go away?"

My skin crawled. Lyle wasn't asking for immunity for himself at all. In some dark corner of my mind, I knew it was because he understood how awful his deeds truly were. Was it possible he had a conscience in there somewhere?

"Yes," Kenya answered. "But I can't promise you conjugal visits. That's not up to me."

"With Sierra's history," I said, "she's looking at years in prison, Lyle."

He let out a groan. "I'll take it."

"So what do you have to give?" I asked.

Lyle paused. He tapped his fingers on the table. I had an

odd thought, wondering whether he had ever jumped off the cliff at the Blitz as a kid.

"Everything," he said abruptly. "I can give you everything."

Another deputy came to the door, bearing three pizza boxes. My stomach turned. As Lyle settled in, I knew we were in for a very long night.

❧ 41 ❧

Monday morning, January 14th, I called Lyle King to the stand to testify against his own brother.

For the past thirty-six hours, I'd kept him at a safe house under police protection. The Servants of Divine Justice threw bricks at him when he tried to walk into the courthouse this morning. Seven had already been arrested.

Lyle wore the same wrinkled brown suit he'd sported for most of the trial. His hair was combed. His face, clean-shaven. He'd been solid all weekend as we went over his story multiple times. Sierra Joy had been released from jail and deposited in her own safe house a few miles from here. I just prayed Lyle wouldn't cave the second he got in a room with Damon again, even with a layer of deputies between them.

"Mr. King," I said as I stepped up to the lectern. "Can you tell the jury how it is you've come to testify today?"

"It was time," he said. "I needed to tell the truth. Sierra Joy ... what happened with her wasn't her fault. She's my friend. She's more than my friend and she was only trying to help me."

"What is your relationship with Sierra Joy?" I asked.

"My brother Damon told me about her a couple of years

ago. He showed me her picture from the internet and thought we should both write her a letter. I did. She wrote me back. Not him. We became friends. We wrote each other all the time. She visited me twice a few years ago. We ... we're going to get married."

"Whose idea was it for her to come forward and testify about this case?" I asked.

"It was Damon's," Lyle said. "Once me and Sierra started to be friends. He wanted to be her friend, but Sierra didn't really like him. Only me. She was afraid of Damon. He said wouldn't it be great if she could say how she saw me the night those kids died. He knew she worked at the Scarlett and Lace. He knew everything about her. So, I asked her. I told her Damon said it could maybe help us get a new trial if she told someone that she tried to give me an alibi all those years ago. He told me to tell her to get a newspaper from the night those kids died. So she could say something that people would believe she remembered the date. I told you, Damon knew all about her. I don't know how he knew. But Sierra said she met with Mr. Halsey the prosecutor about her case around the time we were getting ready to go to trial."

"Objection," Trevor said. "Statements made by a party are non-hearsay, Ms. Joy isn't the defendant here. This witness can't testify about what Ms. Joy said or didn't say outside of court."

"I'll withdraw," I said.

"Mr. King," I said. "Were you in the Scarlett and Lace bar on the night of August 11th, 2008?"

"No," he said. "I wasn't there. That wasn't true. That was something Damon cooked up so we could get a new trial. He said it was how we were going to get free. I wasn't at the Scarlett and Lace that night. I was never there. I don't like those kind of places. I was at the Blitz. Damon and me, we killed those kids. We killed Krista Nadler and Charlie Brinkman."

It was as if a thunderclap went through the courtroom. Not even the jury could keep silent.

Judge Ivey banged his gavel, attempting to restore order. When he did, I adjusted the microphone at the lectern and asked my next question.

"Mr. King," I said. "Why don't you take us through that night. What happened on August 12th, 2008?"

"Well," Lyle said. "It's funny. I never said a damn word to Aaron Clyde. Barely even talked to him. He was the one who wouldn't shut up. Couldn't stand him. But what he said up here? I'll be damned if it wasn't just about what I would have told him."

"In what way?" I asked.

"Well, see, Damon said he was going to get us into heaven. I was ... I was always worried about our mom. She died when we were pretty young. I miss her still. I want to see her again. I know my dad isn't in heaven. He was a mean son of a bitch and there's no way he's anywhere but hell."

I expected Trevor to object that Lyle was being unresponsive to questions. He didn't. If anything, Trevor Page looked smug.

"Anyway," Lyle continued. "It mattered to me. I wanted to talk to Jesus. I wanted to talk to my mom. I tried often enough. But I could never hear anything. Damon always said he could. He said she came to him all the time. Guiding him. Telling him she still loved us. He promised me he'd tell her things for me. It was better when she was still alive. I never had to worry about anything. She took care of me. Got me through school. Made sure I knew where I was supposed to be."

"Mr. King," I said. "What about Charlie Brinkman and Krista Nadler?"

"I'm getting to that. It was good Damon could talk to our mom. He told me things I knew only she would have said. She was taking care of me through Damon. That felt good. It still does. But then Damon started talking to Jesus for other people. Making them feel better. Feel loved. It was just a few people we were friends with first. Then, more and more started coming around the farm. Kids, mostly. And they paid us money. That felt good. But what felt best was knowing I could always talk to my mom through Damon. He had her ear. He had the Holy Spirit."

"Let's focus on the summer of 2008," I said.

"Sure," he said. "Damon really started helping people. If they had a problem, he could solve it. It was God talking to him. I know it. And all these people, they just wanted what I wanted. They wanted to be with the loved ones they lost. They wanted to make sure they could get into heaven instead of the other place. Damon said they could, but only if they burned for their sins. The Bible says it. So, when Damon told me we had to help Mrs. Brinkman, I knew what he meant."

"Tell me about that," I said. "Tell me about Mrs. Brinkman."

"Damon said he met with her a couple of times out at that diner. Just like she said they did. She seemed real nice. I didn't ever go in. But I would wait in the car sometimes for Damon. Mrs. Brinkman looked real rich. She'd always buy. One time she saw me waiting and Damon let her order a burger for me and brought it out to the car when they were done talking. I remember she smelled good. I don't know why she said she didn't remember me. But she was worried about her kids, he said. They were turning to the devil. She wanted them to get into heaven too. So finally, Damon said he'd help her."

"How did he help her?" I asked.

"That Friday, the 11th of August," Lyle said. "We drove out to the Blitz. I knew there were always kids back there fooling around and sinning. Damon had a picture of Charlie's truck. Mrs. Brinkman gave it to us. I even remember the license plate. Knight 14. Mrs. Brinkman said that was the number Charlie played. You know, on his football jersey."

I reintroduced the crime scene photo we had showing Charlie's truck and his vanity plate. Mrs. Brinkman failed to mention that little detail during her testimony.

"Then what happened, Lyle?" I asked.

"I pulled Charlie off that girl. He was ... I mean, they were doing it. Fornicating. Sinning. We tied him up. Damon marched him up the hill and left me with the girl. She was crying and begging me not to hurt Charlie. I took her by the arm and helped her up that hill."

One by one, I laid out the crime scene photos. One by one, Lyle described how he positioned Krista. How Damon told Charlie it was time for him to pray.

"Then what happened?" I asked.

"I didn't think I could do it," Lyle said. "That girl was crying so hard. She asked for her mom. That got me. But Damon said we were going to make sure she could always be with her mom. They would be able to see each other in heaven. He told me I would be able to see my mom too because I helped purge them of their sins. It would get me into heaven. So, I did what Damon told me to. I had a chain from an old Schwinn I'd been working on fixing. I used it on the girl."

"Used it how?" I asked.

"I flogged her for her sins," Lyle asked. "While Damon made Charlie pray. He saved him. Made him confess his sins. I set her free. Through suffering, our sins are forgiven. She suffered. And now she's free."

"You killed her," I said, my voice breaking.

"Yeah," Lyle said. "Because Damon said it was how she'd get into heaven. Now, I don't know. I think I just wanted to believe that. I knew it was wrong. I think maybe that was my mom. She was talking to me after all. It was wrong. Killing is wrong. But it felt good. It made me feel important."

"Then what happened?" I asked.

"Then, it was time for them to burn. Damon brought a can

of kerosene and he poured it over Charlie and then Krista. She wasn't really moving by then."

"Then what happened?" I asked.

"Damon came over and lit a match and threw it on Krista. She was already dead, though. I mean, she didn't even have a face anymore."

"What was Charlie doing?" I asked.

"He was crying."

"What did you do then?" I asked.

"Well, I think I said. Did I say? I poured kerosene on Charlie. Damon came over. He asked Charlie if he had anything else he wanted to atone for. I don't remember if he said. Then Damon gave me the matches. I lit one and threw it on Charlie Brinkman. He kind of crumpled over. But he stayed like that. Like you see in those pictures. It took him a couple minutes to die, I think. I didn't want to watch."

I turned away. Most of the jury were in tears. The rest were so repulsed they couldn't even look at Lyle King anymore.

I stopped. I let the echo of Lyle's words die down. It was unspeakable. Unforgivable.

When the silence settled over the courtroom, if I listened hard enough, I believed I could hear Charlie Brinkman's final scream.

❧ 42 ❧

Trevor Page took a moment as he organized himself at the lectern. No matter what happened after this trial, I wondered if he'd be able to hang on to his law license, let alone his reputation.

"Mr. King," he said. "What was your bargain?"

"My what?" Lyle asked.

"Your bargain," he said. "Ms. Brent asked you what brought you here today to testify. It was Sierra Joy, wasn't it?"

"She doesn't deserve to go to jail. She was just trying to be my friend. My girl."

"Right, but it was you who asked her to lie for you, wasn't it?" he asked.

"I told her what Damon said. I told her it would maybe help if she said she saw me that night. I wished I hadn't. It was wrong."

"I see," Trevor asked. "And you think you know the difference?"

"I know wrong can send you to hell," he said.

"Mr. King, do you still believe your mother talks to you through your brother Damon?" he asked.

"I don't know anymore," Lyle said, dropping his head. "Sierra doesn't think so. She thinks Damon just said that to get me to do what he wanted."

"So isn't it true you're sitting here today because Sierra Joy told you to?" Trevor said.

"She didn't tell me anything. She just tried to help. She loves me," Lyle said.

"Mr. King, back in 2008, did you use a cell phone?"

"I had one," Lyle said. "Yeah. Damon gave it to me."

"What was the phone number?" Trevor asked.

Lyle paused for a moment, then rattled off the number associated with the phone registered to Damon King.

"Did Damon have a separate cell phone?" Trevor asked.

"No," Lyle said. "I didn't have one of my own. Damon let me use his. We couldn't afford two."

"Okay," Trevor said. "So you're telling me it was commonplace for you to take that cell phone and carry it with you?"

"Yeah," Lyle said. "I told you. We shared it."

Melody nudged me.

"Isn't it also true that on the night of August 11th, you were in fact carrying that phone?"

Lyle furrowed his brow. "I don't know. I don't remember that. Maybe."

"Let's talk about Sierra Joy again," Trevor said. "She means a lot to you, doesn't she?"

"Yes. I said that. We're going to get married," he said.

"She doesn't like Damon very much, does she?"

Lyle shook his head. "She thinks Damon isn't taking care of me as much as I think he is."

"In fact, she's the one who put you up to this, isn't she?" Trevor asked.

"I don't know what you mean," Lyle asked.

"She told you to tell everyone lies about your brother, didn't she?" Trevor asked.

"I'm not lying," he said.

"Do you think your mother is watching you now?"

"Objection," I said. "Despite being irrelevant, that question is ludicrous."

"Your Honor," Trevor said. "This witness has just spewed a story about how his perception of his mother's judgment has informed his actions. I'd like to explore that a little."

"Overruled," Judge Ivey said.

"Answer the question, Mr. King," Trevor said.

"She's always watching," Lyle said.

"So she knows you're the one who killed Charlie Brinkman and Krista Nadler, doesn't she?"

"She knows," Lyle said, growing agitated.

"You swore to tell the truth. You put your hand on that Bible. Do you suppose your mother could hear that too?"

"Yes."

"Do you suppose you'll ever hear anything from her again after today?"

"Your Honor?" I shouted.

"Enough, Mr. Page," Judge Ivey said. "Let's get back to the realm of the living, shall we?"

"I'm telling the truth!" Lyle shouted. His eyes went a bit wild. "Damon told me those kids would go to heaven if they suffered for their sins on earth. We were helping. I thought I was helping. Mama, I thought I was helping. Talk to me too. I want you to talk to me too!"

"You talked to the prosecutor, didn't you Lyle?"

"I talked to Mrs. Brent," he said.

"And you love Sierra Joy, don't you?" he asked.

"We love each other."

"You'd do anything to be with her. You'd do anything to protect her, wouldn't you?"

"Of course," he said. "I want Sierra to be my wife."

"And she'd do anything, say anything to protect you,

wouldn't she?" Page raised his voice. "In fact, she'd lie to protect you! You've admitted you both lie for each other, didn't you?"

"Your mother didn't like liars, did she Lyle? What do you think she'd have to say about Sierra Joy? Do you think she'd approve?"

He banged his fist against the side of the witness stand. I turned to look at Damon. He was smiling. It was smart of him to get Lyle to think he was the only conduit to their mother. She may be the only thing left that might bring Lyle back under his control. I wished I could have had Sierra Joy in the court-room with me.

"You tell the truth, Damon," Lyle shouted. "You tell them what we did. You tell them about Barclay's field. Ask him. Ask him right now."

Damon's smile faded.

"What's Barclay's field?" Melody whispered to me.

My stomach dropped. "I have no idea," I whispered back through gritted teeth. "He never said anything about it to us."

Damon threw a look to Trevor Page. From the panicked look on Page's face, I knew he had no idea what Barclay's field was either.

Murmurs spread through the gallery. Gus Ritter and Sam Cruz sat on a bench in the back. They had their heads together. Sam had his phone out, hopefully googling Barclay's field as Lyle spoke.

"I have nothing further for this witness," Trevor said.

"Ms. Brent?" the judge asked.

My knees knocked together as I stood. Did I ask? Did I take the leap?

It was almost as if someone else took over my body as I walked up to the lectern. Twelve years of legal training pulled at me, telling me to quit while I was ahead and sit back down. But I swear, the ghosts of Charlie Brinkman and Krista Nader pressed me forward.

"Mr. King," I said. "What's in Barclay's field?"

"It's where we took everything," he said. "After we were done. You'll see I'm telling the truth."

"What did you take there?" I asked.

"The bike chain. The matches. Our clothes. Everything we did is out there. Go see. If you need me to, I'll draw you a map. Damon told me to burn it all."

Lyle King's eyes went vacant. A smile crept across his face as he repeated himself. "Damon told me to burn it all. Only, I never did."

❧ 43 ❧

Seventy-two hours. Judge Ivey granted a continuance until Thursday morning after Lyle King left the stand. When he did, he was taken back into custody. He was going away for first degree murder. A life sentence. No possibility of parole. His one other stipulation was that we let him see Sierra Joy. The deputies were arranging it, but they would not leave his side.

As he walked out of the courthouse in shackles, Gus Ritter was ready with a map on his phone. "You tell me where, you son of a bitch," Gus said. "Or you'll never see your girl again."

Lyle took one look at it, pointed out a spot. "Now let me see Sierra."

"Not until you show us where," I snapped. I felt the urge to do violence rising within me. It scared me. I think Sam saw it in my eyes.

"Mara," he said.

"I want to go with you," I said to him, my voice breaking. "Sam, I want to see it for myself."

"Not this time," Sam said. "You let us do our jobs. This could take a while. It's been ten years. Go home. Be with Will. I will call you the minute we know anything. I swear. You did your job, Mara. Now let us go do ours."

I trusted him. I trusted Gus. I went home and waited. Sleep was impossible. I took a page from my mother's anxiety play-book and started cleaning my kitchen.

It was four a.m. before Sam called to tell me they'd found what they were looking for. Over the next two days, there was no sleep for me. And none for Detectives Gus Ritter, Sam Cruz, or the Maumee County crime scene unit. They, along with agents from the Ohio Bureau of Crime Investigations, descended on that small strip of land adjacent to Damon King's farm and processed the second crime scene. One that had been hidden to us for a decade.

Thursday morning, the jury reconvened, and I recalled a bleary-eyed Gus Ritter to the stand.

My own frayed nerves had me swaying on my feet. I'd downed seven cups of coffee, gearing up for what might be the most important direct examination of both Gus and my careers.

"Detective Ritter," I started. "Thank you for being here this morning. I know it's been a long week. So let's get right down to it."

Gus was mainlining his own tumbler of coffee.

"Detective Ritter, I know we covered this the first time you took the stand and I don't want to rehash it, but can you remind the jury what your role is pertaining to the murders of Charlie Brinkman and Krista Nadler?"

"I was assigned lead detective to their case back in 2008. I remain the lead detective on that case," he said.

"You were present in the courtroom Monday morning for Lyle King's testimony?" I asked.

"I was," Gus answered.

"Can you tell me what investigative steps you took incident to Mr. King's testimony?" I asked.

"Well, as you likely remember, Mr. King made a statement at the conclusion of his testimony, on cross-examination by Mr. Page, about the existence of a possible crime scene at Barclay's field. He testified that he'd been instructed to dispose of items by burning after the killings of Charlie and Krista at that location, but admitted that he never did."

"What did you do next?" I asked.

"I got out a map," Gus said. "Mr. King indicated a spot of roughly a ten-yard-square area in the southeastern property owned by one Daniel Barclay. Mr. Barclay's farm abuts property owned by Damon and Lyle King along roughly a one-and-a-half-acre strip. Though it's separated by a densely wooded area."

"Did you search that area in 2008?" I asked.

"We did not," he said. "We fully searched the King property and the adjoining lands going in maybe a hundred yards, or the length of a football field. But there was no indication of anyone having been through there at that time. We found no physical evidence on the King property connecting either defendant to the crime in 2008. There was no probable cause to seek a search warrant for Mr. Barclay's or anyone else's property."

"What about now?" I asked.

"Daniel Barclay gave us permission to walk every inch of his property if we needed to."

"Did you need to?" I asked.

"No," he said. "At the conclusion of Lyle's testimony, I showed him my map of Barclay's farm. I pulled it up on my phone. Lyle pointed to a very specific location ... where I just described. I got a warrant anyway so that I could search the King property again. I assembled a team, called in B.C.I. down from Columbus, and we went out to secure the scene in Barclay's field."

Gus then went on to describe in detail all the detectives on scene and their methods of evidence collection. He was precise. Thorough. Methodical.

I pulled up a satellite map of the area and admitted it into evidence. Gus marked off with red arrows the bare patch of ground beyond the tree line separating Dan Barclay and Damon King's farms. We then identified a dozen pictures taken at the scene just thirty hours ago.

"Here," Gus said, using a pointer. "We got a hit with our metal detectors almost exactly in the spot Lyle King pointed out. He accompanied us to the site and directed some of our efforts in terms of where to dig. We started digging. Approximately three feet deep, we hit metal."

B.C.I. had recorded the entire sequence. I kept the sound off to avoid any objections from Trevor Page. The jury sat riveted as Gus and his team cleared away dirt and pulled a tangled mess of metal out of the ground.

I switched to the next picture in my slide show.

"Detective," I said. "Can you tell us what it was you found?"

"We found a standard bike chain of two feet in length. It was fairly heavily rusted. After processing at the crime lab, the links of this chain matched the wound patterns found on Krista Nadler."

I let that sit for a moment. The jury's eyes were glued to the image of the muddy, rusted bike chain as it lay stretched out on a blue tarp with evidence tags all around it. I knew they could imagine how it was used. The pain it would have inflicted.

I grabbed a box off the evidence table. "Detective Ritter, do you recognize what's been marked as State's exhibit 143?"

"Yes," he said. "That's the chain we found in that hole."

I moved to admit it into evidence. Trevor objected. He was overruled. Using a pair of latex gloves, I pulled the chain out of the box and stretched it out between my hands. I walked in front of the jury with it. It was rusted. Filthy. But you could see it. You could imagine the damage it did to Krista's poor body. No. They didn't have to imagine it. They had seen the pictures.

Carefully, I laid the chain back in the box.

"Detective Ritter," I said. "Can you tell me what else you found in that hole?"

"We found two sets of clothing. Jeans and two tee-shirts. They were fairly degraded. Rotted from being in the ground for ten years."

"Objection," Trevor said. "The detective is assuming facts, not in evidence. He has no idea how long any of these items were in the ground."

"Detective?" Judge Ivey asked.

Gus looked at me. I gave him a small nod. It was okay. The bigger gun was coming next.

"No," he said. "We haven't been able to independently determine how long the bike chain or the clothing items were in the ground, but the man who admitted to burying them has been in jail for ten years since he did it."

"Okay," I said. "What else did you find?"

"We found a set of keys."

I paused for a beat, then pulled the keys in question out of the box. Like the bike chain, they were covered in dirt and rust. The leather fob on the key chain was mostly eaten away, but you could make out part of a name. Dunning. I knew most of the members of the jury would recognize it as Dunning Ford over on Lassiter Street. Half of them had probably purchased vehicles there in their lifetime.

"Detective," I said. "What, if anything, were you able to determine about these keys?"

"Charlie Brinkman drove a 1999 Ford Ranger. The keys for it weren't in the ignition or on his person when we recovered the bodies. It was a mystery we hadn't been able to solve. Until now."

"How so?" I asked.

"Well," Gus said. "As you can see, there were scorch marks on the metal. Part of the plastic on two of the keys appears melted." I had a blown-up picture of the keys I held on the screen next to Gus. Gus pointed to the marks on the photograph.

"Detective," I asked. "Were you able to determine whose keys these were?"

"The keys in the pit on Barclay's field belonged to Charlie Brinkman, Jr.," Gus said.

"How can you be so sure?" I asked.

"Well," he said. "Charlie and Sharon Brinkman kept Charlie's truck. They never sold it. I took the keys to them and asked for permission to use them on the truck. It started right up. There are two other keys on this chain. Though the Brinkmans no longer own the home they lived in when Charlie died, the new owners never changed the locks. The smaller key with the goldish trim unlocked the garage service door to that property. The larger key with the silver tinge opened their front door. These were Charlie's keys. The lab found fibers embedded in the plastic parts of the keys. Denim. They matched the fibers stuck to Charlie's body. It appears they were in his pocket when he was set on fire. Most likely, they fell to the ground and for whatever reason, Lyle or Damon picked them up before they left the scene."

"Objection," Trevor said. "Move to strike. The detective is once again assuming facts, not in evidence."

"Sustained," Judge Ivey said. "The jury will disregard the detective's theory on whether the defendants took possession of the keys. You may continue, Ms. Brent."

I closed my binder. "Your Honor," I said. "I have no further questions."

"Mr. Page?" the judge asked.

Trevor and I traded places. I sat down next to Melody.

"Detective," he said. "You claim Lyle King pointed out this patch of property on Barclay's farm, correct?"

"That's correct," Gus said. "He also took us there in person."

"To be clear, you have absolutely no idea when any of these items were buried on that property, or even where they came from?" Trevor asked.

"Well, as far as the keys, I know they were in Charlie Brinkman's hands on the evening of August 11th, 2008, and haven't been seen since," Gus said.

"But they could have been buried there last week, isn't that correct?"

"This wasn't a fresh hole," Gus said. "Grass and brush had grown over on it. It had been there for years. So no, these items weren't buried there a week ago."

"You found no physical evidence on this bike chain, did you?" Trevor said.

"No," Gus answered.

"No blood."

"No."

"No skin tissue."

"No."

"No bone."

"No."

"Not even any fingerprints."

"No, but like I said, this stuff had been down there for years. I would have been surprised if I had found anything like that."

"Likewise," Trevor said. "You found no physical evidence in the form of DNA, blood, hair, nails, fingerprints, etc. on the clothing you pulled from the hole."

"No, sir," Gus said.

"And no physical evidence on the keys," Trevor said.

"Nope," Gus said.

"In fact, you still have no physical evidence linking Damon King to that crime scene, Barclay's field, Charlie Brinkman's truck, or anywhere else, do you?" Trevor's voice raised to a crescendo.

Gus stayed calm. "No," he answered.

"You have no other witnesses who claim to have seen Damon King at the Blitz on the night of the murders."

"No," Gus said.

"And you have no witness who claims to have seen Damon King dig this hole on Barclay's property," Trevor said.

"No," Gus said.

"You only have Lyle King's story," Trevor said.

"Well, that, and the murder weapon and keys belonging to the victim," Gus said. He never raised his voice. Never changed his casual posture in the witness chair. But with one sentence, he'd just skewered Trevor Page. I knew my best strategy was to stay out of his way.

"You don't know it's the murder weapon," Trevor said. "That's an assumption, isn't it?"

"We have a confessed murderer telling us he used it to kill the victim, then he buried it on property he had access to and it was found with the belongings of one of the murder victims," Gus said. "It's not a mere assumption, Mr. Page."

"You have no idea how many perpetrators there were in this crime, do you?" Trevor asked.

"Excuse me?"

"I mean, Lyle King is the only one saying he had help," Trevor asked.

"I'm commenting on the evidence," Gus said.

"There might have been one murderer, isn't that possible?" Trevor asked.

"I don't think the evidence supports that theory," Gus said.

"But you don't know that for sure," Trevor said.

"Your Honor," I said. "This has been asked and answered. The detective is qualified to draw a conclusion after his investigation. He's done that. He's testified to it."

"Move on, Mr. Page," Judge Ivey said.

"Detective," Trevor said. "There could have been three perpetrators, couldn't there?"

"Perhaps," Gus said. "But once again, that's not what the evidence shows, in my opinion."

"And the bulk of your opinion now comes from the word of Lyle King, isn't that right?" Trevor asked.

"He is a crucial eyewitness, yes," Gus answered.

Trevor paused. He took a great breath as if he were going to launch into something else. Then, he simply closed his notepad and looked at the judge.

"I have no further questions for this witness," Trevor said.

"Ms. Brent?" The judge looked at me.

I rose from my seat. "Your Honor, at this time, the prosecution rests."

I waited, rocking back on my heels. Trevor had barely made it back to his table.

"Mr. Page, you may call your first witness for the defense."

Trevor leaned down and whispered something in Damon's ear. I couldn't hear what he said, but Damon's response was clear. He mouthed the word no.

Trevor rose and faced the judge. "Your Honor, the defense also rests."

I couldn't read the judge. I did my best to keep my expression neutral as well.

"All right," he said. "It's eleven a.m. We'll take forty-five minutes for lunch. Then let's see if we can't get this case to the jury by the end of the afternoon."

Judge Ivey banged his gavel. Gus caught my eye and winked at me. He was good. Devastating. But I knew I was far from home.

❧ 44 ❧

Melody, Hojo, even Sam and Gus buzzed around me. We found an empty jury room on the second floor and commandeered it. I sat in the corner of the room with an unopened turkey sub in front of me.

I couldn't eat. I couldn't get caught up in everyone else's expectation.

It was Sam who sensed my mood. He sat beside me, staring straight ahead.

"Is there anything else you need?" he asked. I smiled at him. In this light, his eyes appeared so dark, as if he only had pupils.

"Ask me again when this is over," I said.

"Why isn't he calling any witnesses?" Melody asked from across the room.

"Because he doesn't think he needs to," Sam answered for me.

"Because you've nailed them?" Melody beamed. "You've nailed them both."

Hojo gave her a high five. That's when Sam rose.

"Come on. Let's give Mara a second to clear her head. Our work is done, but hers isn't."

I mouthed a thank you as he herded everyone back out of the room. I caught Gus's eye just as he left. I saw the weight of this case pressing against him. Ten years. It was one thing to see the crime scene photos, but he'd been out there. He'd smelled the bodies. It had been his arms Stephanie Nadler collapsed into when he had to tell her her daughter had died, and how.

He quietly closed the door. I hung my head. The clock on the wall ticked the seconds. I didn't know if I wanted them to slow or speed up. I just knew this case wasn't like others I'd tried. It mattered more. It wasn't just Charlie and Krista, though they were enough. They mattered. It was a decade's worth of work from my office and Gus's. It felt like the world.

I tossed the sandwich in the trash and slid the strap of my briefcase over my shoulder. It felt like battle armor. A shield.

As I walked down the hall, I could hear the clamor of protestors through the window on the street below. I tried to drown it out as I took the stairs back up to the third floor.

I found Trevor Page there, standing in front of Judge Ivey's courtroom. Further down the hall, Damon King sat. He had a cell phone to his ear. He gave me a cold smile.

I brushed past them both and took my seat at the prosecution's table.

I was ready.

Moments later, the rest of the world filtered in. I didn't hear them. I didn't even hear Trevor and Damon take their seats. I felt Melody fall in behind me. She'd be ready with exhibits when I needed them.

Judge Ivey retook the bench and called the jury in. Then it was all up to me.

I walked slowly to the lectern like I'd done hundreds, maybe thousands of times over the years. I took a breath and argued for the souls of Charlie Brinkman and Krista Nadler in the only way I knew how.

"Ladies and gentlemen," I said. "This case hasn't unfolded

the way any of us thought it would. On a personal level, I've had to face the truth about people I used to trust. A mentor. Someone who was sworn to uphold justice and the public trust did something unforgivable.

"Phil Halsey wasn't what we thought he was. I, more than anyone, know that. There will be a reckoning for him. I will make sure of it. That's a promise. But the defense wants you to believe this trial is Phil Halsey's reckoning.

"Don't let him. He's going to try to get you to focus on all the lies that were told in this case. Aaron Clyde lied. Sierra Joy lied. Sharon Brinkman didn't lie, but she withheld the whole truth. I'd like to tell you that none of that matters. It does. Of course it does. When we ask someone to sit in that witness chair and swear to uphold truth and justice, we need to trust that they will. In this case, many of them didn't.

"It matters. But Charlie Brinkman and Krista Nadler matter more. You have to silence all the noise in this case. There was a lot of it. But one simple truth has emerged and you can't look away from it."

I pulled the crime scene photo showing Charlie and Krista up one last time.

"It's hard to look at. Everything about this case has been hard to look at. I know it. I feel it. It will stay with me long after you render your verdict. But we have to look. We have to see what's real.

"Lyle King told you what's real. He made it plain. Damon King had manipulated Lyle for years. He made him believe Damon alone held the memory of their dead mother. He made him believe only Damon could bring Lyle back to her when the time came for him to meet God. Lyle believed Damon. He did everything Damon told him to do. And he killed for him.

"Damon preyed on lost souls. His brother Lyle was lost more than most. It was Damon who planned these murders. You know that because it was Damon who met with Sharon

Brinkman. You know that because it was Damon who stalked these poor kids online. And it was Damon who conceived of the idea to punish them for their so-called sins.

"Lyle told you the truth. He testified against his own interests. Lyle King is going to spend the rest of his life in prison. You cannot let Damon go free.

"Damon King was the mastermind behind one of the most brutal killings I've ever seen in my years as a prosecutor. He left you a roadmap in the sermons he preached to those lost enough to follow him. Lyle laid everything out in his confession. He did not act alone.

"Mr. Page is going to want you to walk away from this thinking Damon had nothing to do with this. He'll talk about the lack of blood and DNA as if it matters in this case. It doesn't.

"Lyle was telling the truth, ladies and gentlemen. He told you what he and Damon did at the Blitz. He told you Damon was the one who directed him to light the match that consumed Charlie Brinkman. Killing him in the most horrific way possible. He told you what happened afterward. I think maybe Lyle knew someday he'd need a way to make sure people believed him. He led us to that burial pit. There is no doubt. You have the murder weapon. There *is* physical evidence connecting the Kings to this crime. You have Charlie Brinkman's keys in the same pit as the bike chain Lyle used to beat, torture, and kill Krista Nadler. You have it all. You have the truth. There is no doubt.

"I ask that you look past the noise. The lies. The people who tried to obstruct justice in this case. You must render a guilty verdict. You must ensure that Damon and Lyle King can never hurt another soul again. Thank you."

Trevor Page came at me like a racehorse out of the gate when the judge gave him the go ahead. He bypassed the lectern and went straight to the jury box.

He threw up his hands and shook his head. "Ms. Brent just told you she's never seen anything like this case in all her years as a prosecutor. I've been at this longer than she has. She's right. Because there is no other case like this one.

"This one will keep me up at night for the rest of my life. I imagine for some of you, you'll find the same. Charlie Brinkman and Krista Nadler didn't deserve to die. They didn't deserve to be tortured. It wasn't just their lives that were ruined that night.

"Sharon and Charlie Brinkman's lives were ruined. Stephanie Nadler's life was ruined. But Damon King's life was ruined too. He did not commit this crime."

Trevor paused.

"Mara Brent is good at her job. I, for one, am glad that Maumee County has her. I wish she was the one who prosecuted this case when it was first tried. If she had, Damon King wouldn't even be sitting here.

"But she wasn't here. Phil Halsey was. The extent of his misconduct is something we are only beginning to unravel. But one thing is clear. He made a name for himself with this case. He had to get a conviction. He had what he thought was the perfect villain. The Demon King. You all heard it. It was straight out of a movie. Phil Halsey vilified Damon King to suit his ends and launch his own career.

"Think about that. Phil Halsey was willing to sacrifice justice for Charlie and Krista so he could win an election. An election! He, in essence, revictimized those poor kids by his actions.

"Let me tell you what's not in dispute in this case. There's no dispute that Phil Halsey coerced an elaborate lie out of Aaron Clyde to secure a wrongful conviction against Damon King. Clyde admitted it. His lawyer admitted it. The prosecution in this case admitted it. Because of that action, Damon

King has spent the last ten years in prison for a crime he didn't commit. This never should have even gone to trial.

"What else do we know? We know you already have your killer. Lyle King murdered those kids. He admitted it. In horrific, gory detail. He told you what happened. He told you what he did with the evidence of his crime. But he only did that when his first lie began to unravel.

"Think about that. Lyle also admitted that he put Sierra Joy up to falsifying an alibi for him. They're in love. They've been corresponding for years. It was only when that lie was revealed that Lyle started spinning his new lie. It's the act of a desperate, sadistic man. The only way he can try to save his own skin is by lying about Damon's role in it.

"Fact. There is no physical evidence tying Damon King to this crime. No blood. No DNA. No hair or clothing fibers from the victims on his person. None. There is only Lyle King's word. That's all. Detective Ritter is a good cop. A decent man. But even he can't tell you what really happened on that hill overlooking the Blitz. Was it one killer? Two? Five? He doesn't know. He's only taking Lyle King's word for it.

"Your task in this case is to decide whether the State has proven Damon King guilty of these murders beyond a reasonable doubt. I put it to you that you can't. It's not even close. The only thing they've shown you is that a phone registered in Damon's name was near the Blitz that night. But there are no calls or texts to or from Damon on that phone that night. Lyle and Evelyn Bishop admitted to you that Lyle had possession of that phone as much as or more than Damon did.

"Damon King is an innocent man. But more than that, he is also a victim. He is the victim of an overzealous prosecutor who would stop at nothing to win a conviction. Who subverted justice by procuring false testimony from a two-bit drug dealer looking to peel time off his own sentence. Damon is the victim of a vile, intense, false media campaign painting him as the devil himself. He has lost his freedom. His livelihood. His reputation.

"You know who killed Krista and Charlie. He has confessed. He will be punished. But Damon King is innocent. It's not a reasonable doubt that you have before you. There can be *no* doubt. Lyle is your killer. Damon King is just another victim. I know that you can see the truth. I know you'll do the right thing and hold the system accountable for what's been done. I know you'll return the only just verdict of not guilty on all counts. Thank you."

I looked over at Damon King as Trevor turned his back to the jury to reclaim his seat. Damon wasn't looking at them as I thought he would be. Instead, he was looking straight at me.

❈ 45 ❈

I didn't want to leave the courthouse. I didn't want to stay either. Outside, I'd find press, protestors, and well-wishers. I found I didn't have the stomach to be around any of them.

Trevor Page ushered Damon out a side door as I gathered the rest of my files and slid them inside my briefcase. It was two o'clock in the afternoon. Jury instructions had taken a little over an hour. Melody had gone on ahead. Kenya thought it might be a good idea to order pizza for the office and try to decompress while we waited for the jury to come back.

Slow footsteps drew my attention. Looking up, I smiled.

"Come on, kid," Gus Ritter said. "Let's get the hell out of here."

Sam stood behind him. I realized Gus and Sam were pretty much the only two people I could stand to be around right now. Everyone back at my office had expectations. Their own careers might hinge on what I'd done in this courtroom. We fought a war together, but right now, Gus and Sam felt like brothers.

Sam stepped forward and offered to carry my heavy briefcase.

"I'll love you forever if you carry these stupid heels," I joked, sticking a leg out.

"Your feet probably stink," he teased. "But no worse than Gus's. You can kick them off when we get back to the office. I can't offer you lunch, but we've got some birthday cake left over from somebody's party."

I followed them the two short blocks to headquarters. Each step weighed me down. I was beyond tired.

I found myself in the detective's break room a few minutes later. Sam cut me a piece of cake. Mine had a giant red frosted balloon on it. The portion left read "Happy B."

"So, whose birthday?" I said, taking a bite of cake so sweet I felt fuzz on my teeth.

"Uh, one of the computer lab guys," Gus said.

"Sure he won't mind you stole his cake?" I asked.

"He doesn't know. Keep eating and we won't have any evidence left," Sam answered.

I kicked my shoes off. I could feel my feet swelling already. The thought of trying to stuff them back into my three-inch pumps made my bones ache.

My phone started ringing. I checked to make sure it wasn't my mother or Will's school, then clicked it to silence. It earned me a raised eyebrow glance from both Gus and Sam.

This was perfect. Other than slipping under the bubbles in a hot bath with a waiting glass of wine, I couldn't think of anywhere else I wanted to be. Neither Gus nor Sam asked me the questions I knew I'd get if I were back at the office.

Had we done enough? I didn't want to rehash any of it. I wanted to get through the day and maybe never think of Damon King again.

"Divine Justice," Gus said. Even from here, we could see a group of picketers outside police headquarters. "You know, he wins no matter what."

"What do you mean?" I asked.

"He's a martyr to these nut jobs. He's famous again. He'll want to grant interviews. Write a book."

"He can't profit off these murders," Sam said.

"No," I said. "But Gus is right. He'll funnel whatever he makes back into the Church of the Living Flame or the Servants of Divine Justice."

"He'll appeal," Sam said.

"Of course," I said. "And I'm sure someday he might even bring Lyle back under his wing. Some lawyer, somewhere, looking to make a name for herself or himself will try to argue Lyle was never competent to stand trial in the first place."

"He's a whack job," Gus said.

"No," Sam said. "Mara, you were smart. You covered your bases. Lyle said over and over again on that witness stand that he knew right from wrong. It'll go nowhere. He's never getting out."

I didn't say the thing all three of us feared. If Damon was acquitted, he would kill again.

"I wish I had just five minutes alone with him," Gus said in a voice so low I wondered for a moment whether he meant to utter it out loud.

"No," I said. "You don't want it to go down that way. That's not who you are."

Gus Ritter met my eyes. He didn't blink. His expression told me everything I needed to know. Damon King may be a monster, but this was a man I didn't want to cross either.

"I'll take another slice," I said, surprised I had that much of an appetite, and for stale birthday cake, no less.

"What's Kenya gonna do after all this?" Sam asked. "Is she still putting herself on the ballot for the special election?"

"I hope so," I said. "I hope the people in this county don't hold Phil's misdeeds against her."

"But they might want new blood," Gus said. "You know that, right?"

I did. I also knew he didn't just mean Kenya. It was possible everyone in our office who'd worked with Phil might be forced out.

I leaned back and put my feet up on the chair beside me. "I don't want to think about any of that now. I just want to think of warm weather. Sunny skies. Maybe a beach somewhere."

"Not an even bigger river?" Sam asked. Once again, I saw a look pass between them. Gus had nudged Sam under the table. He was asking me a question both of them still had.

"A river?" I asked.

"You know," Sam said; leaning forward, he scraped off my discarded frosting with his fork. "Say ... the Potomac?" His eyes darted to Gus, and he shrugged as if to say that was as smooth as he could be.

"Not again with you guys," I said. "I've been getting enough of that question from my mother."

"Saw the swearing in on cable news," Gus asked. "You didn't go."

"I've been kinda busy," I smiled.

"Said it before and I'll say it again," Sam said. "Jason is a fool. But I hope his loss is our gain."

It was a cheesy remark, but heartfelt, I knew. "Thanks," I said. "Now give me more of that cake."

"Where the hell does she put it all?" Gus said. He cut me another piece and slid it over.

"It's ..." I didn't get to finish my answer. My phone vibrated with a text. Gus and Sam's phones went off about three seconds later.

"They can't ..." Sam started.

I grabbed my phone. The text came from Judge Ivey's clerk.

"Christ," Gus said, rising to his feet. "They're back already."

"Let me find out," I said, dialing the clerk's number.

"This is Mara," I said into the phone.

"Mara, we have a verdict," the clerk said. "Judge wants you back in the courthouse. How fast can you get here?"

"Uh ... ten minutes," I said. "I'm just with Gus and Sam Cruz ..."

"Okay ... the defendant is already here. The bailiff caught him and Mr. Page before they left the building." She clicked off.

I dropped my phone to the table. Gus looked at his watch.

"Seventy-two minutes," he said. "They've only been out for seventy-two minutes."

"Come on," Sam said. "Let me get some deputies. I don't want you walking into that courtroom again without protection. We don't know how this is going to go."

I went on autopilot. I barely remembered to put my shoes back on. Sam and Gus led me down a service elevator closed to the public. As we stepped outside, he had a patrol car waiting.

It was only three blocks, but Gus, Sam, and I rode up to the mailroom entrance far away from the protestors. Two other patrol cars were already waiting.

As I got out, it felt like half the Maumee County sheriff's department had formed a wall around me. But we made it in the building unaccosted. I couldn't help but wonder what would happen on my way back out.

46

"All rise!"

I kept my hands on the table. The jury had come back so fast, there'd been no time for most of the public to make it back in. There were only two or three reporters struggling to get an internet connection on their phones.

Damon King was already there when I took my seat. Gus and Sam sat on the bench behind me, giving me their silent strength. Kenya texted, saying she'd stay back at the office. Poor Melody was going to miss it altogether. She'd started driving to her parents' house where she meant to have dinner.

The jury filed in. I looked over my shoulder. Stephanie Nadler sat in the back surrounded by a few of the Silver Angels advocacy group. The Brinkmans weren't here. I'd heard Charlie Sr. had packed Sharon's things and thrown her out of their condo.

So many victims.

"Madam Foreperson," Judge Ivey said. "Have you reached a verdict?"

"Yes, Your Honor," the woman said. She was a retired

history teacher. A grandmother of seven. Her husband was a volunteer firefighter.

She handed the verdict form to Judge Ivey. He silently read it and handed it back to the clerk.

Her name was Denni Milton. Jason had gone to high school with her. He said she'd been in the marching band. Now, a few words from her would change everything.

"We the jury in the above-entitled action on the count of first-degree murder of Krista Nadler find the defendant, Damon King, not guilty."

Stephanie Nadler broke. I kept my eyes straight ahead. I still had a job to do. Her sobs echoed through the courtroom. Murmurs rose as those who had made it here in time moved to surround Stephanie.

"We're not done here." Judge Ivey banged the gavel.

I squeezed my eyes shut. When I opened them, Damon King stood straighter. Trevor Page had a hand on his arm. Judge Ivey nodded to Denni. She continued.

"On the count of first-degree murder of Charles Brinkman Jr., we the jury find the defendant, Damon King, not guilty."

We were three floors up. Still, I could hear a cheer go up from the protestors outside.

Behind me, Gus Ritter swore under his breath. Sam moved in to quiet him. This time, those in the gallery stayed quiet. I stole a look over my shoulder. Stephanie had her head buried in her hands. I wasn't sure she even heard the verdict on the second count.

Denni looked up. She took a breath and kept on reading. I dug my nails into the wooden table in front of me.

"On the count of conspiracy to commit aggravated murder upon the person of Krista Nadler, we the jury in the above-entitled action find the defendant, Damon King, guilty."

She practically shouted the word guilty.

"On the count of conspiracy to commit aggravated murder

on the person of Charles Brinkman, Jr., we the jury in the above-entitled action find the defendant, Damon King, guilty."

Trevor Page dropped his head. Damon King never moved. The judge read the remaining instructions. He polled the jury. They were, of course, unanimous.

I felt a hand on my elbow. Sam was there.

"She needs to understand," I whispered to him. "Can you go be with Stephanie?"

He nodded.

Below us, I heard the wails as someone made the protestors understand. Conspiracy to commit murder. Damon King may have just been spared the death penalty, but he would still face the rest of his life in prison.

When the deputies came to place cuffs back on him again, Damon King saved his eyes for me.

He got close. Close enough that I could feel his breath on my cheek.

"It's coming," he whispered. "I promise."

The deputies paused. Trevor Page was right behind them.

"Damon," he said. "Don't say ..."

"You're fired," Damon said. "Send your final bill to the Servants of Divine Justice."

Trevor turned purple.

"Let's go, King," one of the deputies said.

"It's coming," he said to me again. "All you have to do is wait. Beloved, never avenge yourselves, but leave it to the wrath of God."

He dug his heels in and raised his voice. "For it is written. Vengeance is mine. I will repay, says the Lord!"

The deputies jerked him forward. Damon kept smiling as they led him away.

"Did you just threaten her?" I heard Sam's voice rise behind me.

There was chaos behind me, but I let the stillness settle

over me. It didn't feel like victory. Not yet. It would take some time.

When I finally walked out of the courtroom, everyone else had gone. Kenya waited for me. I kept it together. All this time. But when Kenya opened her arms to me, we both cried on each other's shoulders when we knew no one else was watching.

❧ 47 ❧

One week later, I boarded a train from Toledo to D.C. It left at midnight and I went alone.

No one knew me. No one asked where I was going. No one cared. It felt like heaven.

At noon the next day, Jason met me at Union Station. He, too, was still somewhat anonymous. Small fish. Big pond. Though I knew he wouldn't stay that way for long.

I brought no real luggage, just an oversized purse. I was jostled by the crowd as I stepped off the platform looking for Jason.

He was so tall. I forgot that, sometimes. As he strode toward me, Jason's head towered over everyone else's, making him easy to spot.

I loved him once. I still did. I felt a rush of heat as Jason spotted me and fixed those gray eyes and dazzling smile on me. He turned heads. They knew he was someone. He had to be. And he was headed straight for me.

It's easy to get caught up in the rush of Jason Brent's attention. I knew that's what happened to Abigail Morgan. I wondered then as I often did, how many other Abigails there were he hadn't told me about.

Jason moved to kiss me. I turned my cheek. Not missing a beat, he took my bag and then my hand. For that, I did not turn away.

He had a car waiting. His driver gave me a friendly smile as Jason held the door open for me. The man weaved through D.C. traffic with expert care. Jason couldn't hide his smile. He reminded me so much of Will. Despite everything, I was excited to bring him here in a couple of weeks. Jason had cleared his schedule to set aside an afternoon each day for a week to show him the sights.

"I'm proud of you." Jason and I said it in unison. I took a breath, then laughed.

"I'm proud of you," Jason said again. "Mara, nobody else could have pulled off what you did in the King trial. That thing was dead. The repercussions of Phil Halsey's informant ring are reaching as far as Capitol Hill. You know I can't get into all the details, but you can expect more career detonations from this."

"I just don't want it to fall back on Kenya," I said. "She's the right person for that job now, Jason."

He nodded. "I think so too. She has my support. Please tell her that for me."

"I will," I said. "And thank you."

We arrived at the Old Executive Office building in record time. Jason's driver let us off at the entrance. I'd been here once before. The labyrinth beneath the Capitol still impressed me. On my next visit, I'd walk it again with Will. For now, Jason led me to his new office.

It was small, tucked down a quiet corridor reserved for freshman congressmen. I knew that, too, would be temporary. He was going places. Maybe all the way to the top.

Jason brought me in. His furniture hadn't all arrived. But he had a desk and chairs and American flag in one corner, the flag of Ohio in the other. On the wall behind him, he'd hung one of my favorite family pictures of us. We'd taken it two years ago on a trip to Niagara Falls. Something had made Will laugh as I closed my arms around him. Behind me, Jason had his arms around me. A big, laughing group hug.

My smile faded as I tilted my head to the side. It was just a moment. One frozen second. My shoulders settled as I realized it wasn't really us at all. It was just a projection. It was what other people thought normal was supposed to look like. Like some Instagram life. For a moment, I resented Jason for hanging it. It wasn't us.

My smile came back. I knew my reality was even better. Or would be ...

"I want you to look at a townhouse today," he said. "I have a meeting at four. I mean, if you want to do some sightseeing, that's fine. But I was kind of hoping you'd take a meeting of your own."

"A meeting?"

Jason smiled. "Mara, there's a friend of mine from the D.O.J. who's interested in talking to you. You up for that?"

"Jason," I said. "I'm not staying."

"What? Of course you're staying."

"No," I said. "I'm taking the train back. I reserved a sleeper car."

"Mara," Jason said. "Don't be ridiculous. There's press involved. There's a lifestyle reporter working on a piece involving the freshman class in the House. She wants to talk to you after breakfast tomorrow. I know I should have told you but ..."

"Jason," I said. I wasn't angry anymore. I wasn't even sad. I reached into my purse and pulled out the thick brown envelope I'd brought with me. I handed it to him.

"What is this?" Jason asked. He opened it. His eyes went dark.

"I've made up my mind," I said. "I'm not coming to D.C. I'm staying in Waynetown. I'm keeping my job there. I'm not finished. I want to help Kenya rebuild that office and pick up the pieces Phil left behind."

"Mara, you're being ridiculous. You didn't even want to move to Waynetown nine years ago. I had to drag you there. I made you a promise. I told you if you stuck it out with me, you'd have your reward too. This is it, baby. If you don't want the job at D.O.J., there's another one waiting for you with the U.S. Attorney's office. I mean, I didn't even have to pull any strings. They want you. What you did in the King trial, and Shumway before that ... honey ..."

"Jason," I said. "I know all of that. But Waynetown is home now."

He read the divorce complaint. Blinking rapidly, he took it all in.

"I don't want this," I said.

"I do," I said. "It's best for me. And in the end, it's best for Will. I know you and I can work things out. We're both better parents than we are husband and wife. This will settle things. Will won't have to worry anymore. Neither will we. Jason, Will wants to stay in Waynetown too. You know he does."

"I know. He told me."

"When?" I asked.

"A few days ago." Jason let out a bitter laugh. "Little man told me he thought it would make you happier too."

Love filled me. I wanted nothing more in that moment than to get back to my son.

"But I don't want this," Jason said, his voice breaking. "Mara, if it's about Abby ... Baby, she's gone. I haven't heard from her. She's stopped calling. She's stopped threatening everyone. She's stopped talking to the press."

"No," I said. "It's not about Abby. Not anymore. Jason, I

forgive you. I'm done being angry. I'm done fighting. I want us to be Will's parents together. But that's all."

"This will ruin me," he said.

I raised a brow. "Who are you kidding? They elected you anyway. You've weathered the storm, Jason. So have I. Now I want you to be great at this. I voted for you, remember?"

"Your family ..." he said. "None of them are in Waynetown."

"Yes," I said. I thought of Kenya and how she'd swooped in when Will had trouble at school. I thought of Gus and Sam and how they were there for me while we waited for the King verdict.

"My whole family *is* in Waynetown," I said. "But it's the family who found me. Not the one I was born into. Your sister's still there. Will needs her in his life too. This is for the best. You're hanging on to something just for the sake of ... well ... hanging on to it. I was too. But now, it's time for both of us to let go."

I rose from my chair. I came around the desk. I kissed my husband for the last time.

"Sign the papers, Jason," I said. He sat back. His eyes glistened with tears, but he stopped arguing.

"Do you want me to send a car for you?"

"No," I said. "I kind of want to walk around Lafayette Square on my own. I haven't really had much time to myself in ... well ... years."

I took one last look around his office. There was power in it. I could feel it. "Promise me," I said.

He sighed and found the hint of a smile. "Okay," he said. "I'll be great at this. For you."

"No," I said. "For all of us. But mostly for Will."

I blew Jason a kiss and closed the door behind me. Two junior staffers were waiting in the hall. They rushed in behind me. As I made my way back down the hall, Jason disappeared in the flurry of activity of the office he now held.

❧ 48 ❧

It was early morning before I made it back home. In my sleeper car, I felt like I'd stepped into a bubble, away from the rest of the world. It gave me clarity. As each mile passed, bringing me back toward Waynetown, I knew everything I'd told Jason was true.

This was home. I was staying put.

It felt good. In a day or two, I knew I could expect a frantic call from my mother telling me I was ruining my life again. In the end, it would likely be Jason who talked her down. But that was for later. Now, I just wanted to see my son.

In a few hours, Kat would wake up to take Will to school. She'd stayed over and was sleeping in the guest room. I came home to a quiet house. My house. Where I would watch Will grow up and find his way.

As well as I slept on the train, I was still bone tired when I finally kicked off my shoes. Kat had set the timer on the coffee machine. It had just finished brewing. I had maybe a half-hour before the rest of the house began to wake.

There were flowers on the counter. A huge bouquet of red roses with baby's breath. A tiny card poked up from a plastic holder. Jason, probably. I slipped the card into the back pocket of my jeans. I wondered if he'd sent them before or after he knew about my divorce papers. I'd read it later. Right now, I just wanted to shut my brain off.

I'd just finished stirring in my cream when my doorbell rang. I opened it to find Sam Cruz standing there. I smiled up at him.

"How'd you know I'd be home?" I asked.

"Mara," he said. It was then I noticed he'd come in his unmarked cruiser. This wasn't a social visit.

I still held my coffee in my hand. "Sam?"

Another car pulled up behind him. Gus.

"Sam?" Sam looked back. Gus gave him a knowing nod as he hustled up my walkway.

"Mara," Sam said. "Why don't you step out here. Will's inside, right? I don't want to risk waking him."

I took a beat. Then, I set my coffee on the table in the foyer and followed Sam outside. It was freezing. I should have brought my coat. Without missing a beat, Sam peeled off his suit coat and put it around my shoulders. I walked with him to his car. He kept it running and sat me in the back seat. I sat with my legs outside the door.

Gus moved closer, standing beside Sam. My mind raced through all the things they could be here to tell me. Will was inside. He was safe. Still, I had the urge to race past these two and check on my son.

"Mara," Sam said. "Dan Barclay."

"The farmer?" I said. "Barclay's field?"

"Yeah," Gus answered. "You know we had a big thaw last week. Dan went out on his four-wheeler. Mara, he found some ground disturbed in the northwest section. We found ... Mara, there was another body out there. A fresh one."

I pulled the ends of Sam's coat closer around my shoulders.

"In the pit? Where Lyle buried the murder weapon?"

"No," Gus said. "The opposite side of the field where it

crosses into Lucas County. This isn't even our jurisdiction anymore, but like I said, we needed you to know. You should hear it from us."

"God," I said. "He's got a killing field out there. A copycat, do you think?"

Sam and Gus looked at each other. Then Gus pulled out his phone.

"We've already got a positive ID," Gus said. "But, like I said, I wanted you to hear this from us. Before it hits the news."

"Of course."

Gus turned his phone toward me. It was a video of the crime scene. A wooded area, covered in snow. Crime scene tape crisscrossed through the baren trees. I could see a black body bag lying on the ground, zipped up to the chin of the victim.

I took the phone from Gus for a closer look. My ears buzzed. I couldn't find air. Her lips were colorless. Her skin, blue. But staring up at me with glassy, opal-like eyes was the lifeless face of Abigail Morgan.

"Still getting labs back," Gus said. "But the M.E. thinks she's been dead at least two weeks. It's been so cold. The body was well preserved."

He showed me another picture. There was a note taped to Abigail's body. In red letters, it said "Sinner."

"It was Damon King," Sam said. "We talked to Abby Morgan's roommate. She disappeared almost two weeks ago during the King trial. If that son of a bitch Ivey hadn't let him out on bail ..."

I shook my head. "Lyle was ..."

"No," Sam said. "This was Damon. We're pretty sure he acted alone."

"But how?"

Gus took his phone back. He scrolled to another picture and showed it to me. No. It was a video. My whole body shook as I held out my finger to press play.

The image was grainy at first. Barely more than shadows. Damon was dragging something. As he came closer into view, I saw Abby Morgan. Her hands and feet were bound. She had something in her mouth. Damon pushed her forward, then brought her up to her knees. There was no sound. But Damon stood over her. Her hands were tied in front of her. She brought them up.

"He's ... God. He's forcing her to pray," I said. "Where is this? How did you get this?"

"Barclay's neighbor has a trail camera set up out there. It's motion activated," Sam said. "Damon tripped it. We don't think he knew it was there. It's well camouflaged."

I didn't want to look, but couldn't do anything else. A moment later, Damon King wrapped his hands around Abby Morgan's neck and choked the life out of her.

I heard a sound. A choked scream. A sob. I realized it was coming from me. That girl. That poor girl. I had hated her. I had felt sorry for her. I had wanted to protect my son from her. She didn't deserve this. She didn't deserve any of this. Damon knew who she was because of me. Because of Jason. For a moment, it felt like my hands around her neck. Oh God. I didn't want this. Not this.

"No," I whispered. "No. No. No."

"Mara," Sam said. "He'll be charged with first degree murder in Lucas County before the end of the day."

"Retribution," I said, putting my hand over my mouth.

"What?" Sam said.

Sam put his arms on my shoulders. "He's done, Mara. Do you hear me? Done. He's never getting out of prison again. It doesn't matter if he tries to appeal the Brinkman/Nadler verdict. He'll get the needle for this. It's over. Because of you, it's over."

Because of me. My God. Because of me.

"Sam," I cried. "Oh Sam. I didn't know. I can't..."

I felt untethered. As if my body had lifted off the ground and circled above. It was over. Abby Morgan was dead. And yet, I still wanted to save her. I wanted to stop it. I had to stop it. It was too much. Too real. I couldn't get control.

"Mara!" Sam's voice came to me like a lifeline. He put his hands on my shoulders. I met his dark, steady eyes. He was right there with me. So was Gus. They wouldn't let go.

"Are you okay?" Gus asked.

I nodded. "He did this for me," I said.

Sam and Gus looked at each other. They thought I was losing it again. I wasn't. But with each new breath I took, something else nagged at the corners of my mind.

I don't know what made me do it right then. I don't know how I knew that Damon sent them. Or *how* he sent them. But my mind became sharp. I knew. I *knew*. The Servants of Divine Justice were still serving. With trembling fingers, I pulled the small square card out of my pocket. As Gus and Sam watched, I slowly opened it.

My heart thundering, I read the words I knew would be there. *Leave it to the wrath of God. Retribution is yours. You're welcome.* He knew they would catch him. He wanted it. The sick bastard probably knew exactly where the county line was and crossed it so he wouldn't be mine to prosecute.

I crumpled the card and threw it to the ground. Anger. Rage. Grief. It coiled around me. I wanted to give into it. Then Gus and Sam were there once more. Solid. Strong. Like family. Ready to hold me up if I ever needed them. And in that moment, I knew I'd be there for them too. It didn't matter where I came from. It only mattered that I was home.

No matter what Phil Halsey did to it, or the King brothers, or whoever else came along. Gus. Sam. Kenya. Hojo. Me. This was our town. Our county. And we'd beat back every evil together, no matter how many servants it called upon.

UP NEXT FOR MARA BRENT...

Waynetown, Ohio is about to wake up to a grisly series of murders that will pit neighbor against neighbor as suspicion grows. Someone knows something. The ultimate, shocking truth will test old alliances and reveal new enemies as Mara fights to restore justice to her adopted home town. Don't miss Hand of Justice.

Click here to find out more ==>
https://www.robinjamesbooks.com/hoj/

NEWSLETTER SIGN UP

Sign up to get notified about Robin James's latest book releases, discounts, and author news. You'll also get *Crown of Thorne* an exclusive FREE ebook bonus prologue to the Cass Leary Legal Thriller Series just for joining.

Click to Sign Up

https://www.robinjamesbooks.com/marabrentsignup/

ABOUT THE AUTHOR

Robin James is an attorney and former law professor. She's worked on a wide range of civil, criminal and family law cases in her twenty-year legal career. She also spent over a decade as supervising attorney for a Michigan legal clinic assisting thousands of people who could not otherwise afford access to justice.

Robin now lives on a lake in southern Michigan with her husband, two children, and one lazy dog. Her favorite, pure Michigan writing spot is stretched out on the back of a pontoon watching the faster boats go by.

Sign up for Robin James's Legal Thriller Newsletter to get all the latest updates on her new releases and get a free digital bonus scene from Burden of Truth featuring Cass Leary's last day in Chicago. http://www.robinjamesbooks.com/newsletter/

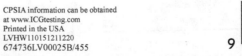